REMF DIARY

A Novel of the Vietnam War Zone

by
David A. Willson

Black Heron Press
Post Office Box 95676
Seattle, Washington 98145

Grateful acknowledgement is made to Doubleday and Company, Inc., for permission to quote material from *North from Malaya* by William O. Douglas, and to the Associated Press and *The New York Times* for permission to quote material copyrighted 1966-67.

ISBN 0-930773-05-5 (hard bound)
ISBN 0-930773-06-3 (soft bound)

Typography by Dataprose, Seattle.

To my father.

REMF Diary

by
David A. Willson

Preface

This work is no *Diary of a Desert Rat,* nor even less *The Diary of Che Guevera,* but I hope to put America straight and Grunts straight, too. This is how it was to be a REMF in Vietnam—the ice cream, the Coca Cola, the air conditioning, the clean starched jungle fatigues, and yes, the parades and the whores. I leave nothing out; it is all in there. The typing and the saluting, too.

These revelations won't make everyone happy. My apologies to Bob Hope, General Westmoreland, and Mr. and Mrs. Nguyen Cao Ky. You were in my life, so I was in yours. You've wondered, dear reader, why we lost the war. I think my book provides the answer!

13 September 1966, Tuesday

I'm writing this at the 90th Replacement Battalion about 21 miles from Saigon. Things are very quiet here, and I'm awaiting orders as to where I'm going.

We landed at Ton Son Nhut Airport outside Saigon at about 2:00 a.m. this morning. It is much like summer in Indiana here.

We loaded into a bus with wire-covered windows and threaded our way out of the maze that Ton Son Nhut Airport seems to be. At one point our bus was stopped (for what reason I'm sure even the U.S. Army doesn't know) and Sergeant Ruttencutter, my seatmate and a man just starting his second 12-month tour of Vietnam and therefore an Old Asian Hand and proud of it, pointed out the window at an ordinary tile-roofed bungalow with a helicopter parked in front and some strategically arranged sandbags and stated, "That's where he lives, Marshall Ky and his bride. I wonder where the fawns and fighting cocks are?"

I caught a glimpse of a purple interior and then a perfect Asian face was framed in the window. Her sloe eyes caught mine and held me thrall.

Ruttencutter asked his question about the fawns and cocks again.

"Probably out back," I replied. There was a cream-colored Mustang parked in front.

Maybe Ruttencutter was pulling my leg. Perhaps the building was the home of the airport manager. That is more likely. I must learn to eschew gullibility. Why is it my reflex to believe everything I'm told?

Our bus then rolled out joining an armed caravan which took us through the countryside to the replacement battalion. I reflected upon the perfect face and those glittering obsidian eyes which had transfixed me. I wondered what adventures Asia had in store for me. She was no Dragon Lady, but she looked like a heartbreaker. Asians had heretofore seemed insubstantial compared to white or negro women, but . . .

The rest of the trip was uneventful except for a blowout which startled everyone. The Vietnamese people and the towns fascinated me. This place will be the perfect antidote for the problems of Italy and will take my mind off my divorce, my previous abject failure. A new leaf for me. I was now a virtual orphan, on my own.

The water buffalo, people urinating in the streets, Vietnamese on motor scooters—a beautiful countryside landscaped into rice paddies.

Water here is scarce—nothing is really cold—the milk is reconstituted. But this is just a 2 or 3 day assignment, I'm told. I expect that things will be better when I'm assigned my permanent post.

14 September 1966, Wednesday, 2:30 p.m.

Still sitting at Long Bien waiting for assignment, doing shit details while waiting. Nothing strenuous, just tedious.

My nervousness is gone now that I'm here, and I'm just waiting to see what will happen.

We're surrounded by all necessary precautions: fences, helicopters. The food is eatable, though not delightful. I'm housed in a cement-floored building, new, with an aluminum roof. I sleep on a cot and mattress which is the best I've ever had in the Army. There are cool spells here. So far the weather is better than in Italy, although the rain materialized unexpectedly.

I've seen a lot of Vietnamese women, mostly out of bus windows, and they are attractive in their own way, but they remind me of the Hawaiians in their squeaky voices and flat bony chests.

The VD rate here is said to run to 90% in some geographical areas. Certainly there is plenty here for my mind to chew on, plenty to take my mind off marital miseries and my Italian disasters. Here with application and a modicum of luck I will be able to get ahead and make something of myself! Up until now I've made Jonah seem like Lucky Jim by comparison.

16 September 1966, Friday

I'm still in hot, uneventful Long Bien. Today I was on a sandbag-filling detail all afternoon. We went about 5 miles from our camp and filled bags with laterite. I was on the wrong end of a shovel. How am I to call myself to the attention of the mighty and the great if I am bogged down here in Long Bien? I must get an assignment and for once a good one, one which puts me in or at least near the catbird seat, where rank and the privileges which accrue will come my way. I know I can make it happen if only fate briefly smiles my way.

Things available here:

    (1) cold canned 7-Up

    (2) Sweden Freezer ice cream

    (3) cold showers.

My motor trip today in the truck allowed me to see the horrendous affects of the USA on the beautiful Vietnam landscape. They're ripping it all to hell, right down to the laterite. With construction work, not combat.

17 September 1966, Saturday, 90th Replacement Battalion

Today I avoided detail in the morning. This afternoon I sorted cards in the post office for a while. I still haven't gotten my assignment.

19 September 1966, Monday, Saigon

I've received my permanent duty station at Tan Son Nhut, back where I started in this country. Typical of the way the Army does things. I'm assigned to the USARV Headquarters, "Pentagon East"—the same place General Westmoreland works.

I'm living in the USARV compound near Tan Son Nhut Airport which is heavily protected and quite safe, I'm told—no trouble from the Viet Cong. The barracks I live in has a concrete floor, metal roof, screens and electric fans. Free movies are available every night.

Today I processed in and got settled in my billets after interviewing with the personnel officer in the section to which I was assigned. The major who interviewed me is also an alumnus of Washington State University. I suspect that was the reason I got the assignment I did.

The work schedule here is from 7:30 a.m. to 6:30 p.m. Monday - Friday, 7:30 a.m. to 2:00 p.m. on Saturday, with Sunday usually off.

The sergeant major of my section gave me until Tuesday afternoon to get settled and straightened away before reporting in. After being at Long Bien most of my clothes are filthy, so I took them to a laundry.

Today (a humorous note) the mama-san who polished my shoes got mine mixed up with somebody else's and the language barrier proved almost insurmountable, but finally I limped off, carrying my lost shoes.

I cut grass with a scythe this afternoon and also assembled a large floor fan which is blowing up a big storm right now.

The barracks I'm in is populated by EMs (Enlisted Men) and NCOs—a lot of sergeants—who are quite peculiar characters. But they're friendly and not mean like in the States or in Italy.

I still don't know much about my job — how much typing and shorthand I'll need to do. I'll know soon enough.

20 September 1966, Tuesday

Today I was promoted to PFC again. I hope I'll be able to hang on to it this time. Apparently my slate has been wiped clean and the blots are gone from my escutcheon. I was told in Italy that if I volunteered for the war zone my sins would be forgotten, or at least they'd not be entered into my records. All that Italian fuss wasn't my fault anyhow, but I learned that the lowest ranked man involved in a mess is the one who ends up with all the blame. My goal therefore is to get as much rank as I can, as fast as possible, so the next time there is a mess, and there always is a next time, I can point to some poor PFC who will have to carry the can. I want to try being a hero for a change, not the goat.

Every silver lining has a cloud around it. I have to scrounge up PFC stripes and have them sewn on.

The currency here is piasters, or dong. Laundry here costs about 1,000 dong per month—about $10.00 I guess.

It's about 200 dong per month to have one's shoes polished and bed made by the mama-san who comes in to perform this service. She doesn't speak any English, I don't think.

Right now in the Saigon area it's the rainy season and it's quite difficult to stay dry. I work about 200 feet from where I live, so it's not much of a walk.

Footlockers aren't provided by the Army so I had to pay 640 dong for a gaudy red and silver affair made out of old beer cans.

I get one and a half hours for lunch and one hour for supper which breaks up an otherwise long day.

The people I'll be working for are colonel, lieutenant colonel, majors—no captains or lieutenants. I work directly under a Sergeant Major Mills, who seems to be a nice man. Everyone says he is. I'll be typing on the second floor on a screened-in porch, which should be quite pleasant.

Off to bed soon. A sergeant just turned on the fan I assembled and it's quite chilly. At night I sleep under an Army blanket. I guess this is the cold season. This sergeant is the one exception so far to my comment of 19 September that the sergeants are friendly and not mean.

21 September 1966, Wednesday

Tomorrow I pick up my first laundry done in Vietnam. Supposedly the soybean starch smells like camel piss. Having been in Italy rather than North Africa with the French Foreign Legion, I couldn't say. Today I had my PFC stripes sewn on, also my USARV shoulder patch. I look like a grizzled veteran (of an office desk).

Tomorrow I'm going on an inspection with a major in our section. He wants me to see some of the country around Saigon. Today I rode with another major in his chauffeured sedan to the Cholon PX where I bought some much needed handkerchiefs and socks.

On the trip to the Cholon PX (Montgomery Ward's, Southeast) we had a long discussion with a middle-aged negro secretary who works in my office about relatives and their idea of Vietnam. She's a civilian GS6 who works here by choice, for the excitement. She's disappointed though, as it's dull as hell, no action at all. I can't believe that a young man who puts his mind to it could fail to find action in a war zone.

People do get killed here, mostly old people who move too slowly to avoid the traffic.

Today I located the library which is about a thirty second walk from my hooch (barracks). It is air conditioned, but sparsely populated. I can hear the Animals singing in the distance—"The House of the Rising Sun."

In the mornings I awake and shower and shave in the

dark without a mirror.

22 September 1966, 10:00 p.m.

Just back from watching "The Hank Williams Story."

My job is easy, though they are still breaking me into the routine. Tomorrow I'm going to be taught the filing system.

Read an article in the local paper about the Saigon Tribunal passing a one-year sentence on Pham Van Doi for selling obscene pictures on Nguyen Hue Street. He was one of numerous colleagues downtown who lure foreigners (guess who?) and "show them a whole paraphernalia on sex, such as sex stimulant, pictures of pornographic scenes, sets of nude girls . . ."

I'll have to be on guard against these apostles of filth when I make my foray downtown. The article almost seemed to be designed to direct foreign troops to this venue. I'm sure this wasn't intended.

23 September 1966, 6:45 a.m.

Just showered and shaved in the dark. Yesterday's planned trip to the field didn't materialize. I also tried to get my laundry back from the gooks and wogs who run the place. I got back a couple of towels that weren't mine, but they kept one of my fatigue shirts which made me quite unhappy. I'm to go back for it. I hope they can dig it up.

I'm still amazed at how cool it gets here at night. The days are quite warm however, and the warm season is yet to come.

24 September 1966, Saturday.

Only a half day today and off tomorrow. I plan to spend the time reading and sleeping.

Yesterday I was told to get a haircut, which I did.

I got my laundry back, except for one fatigue shirt. I tried to get it back yesterday afternoon, but the laundress took out a tape measure and started measuring me for a new shirt. I tried to explain to her that I just wanted my old shirt back, but I was unsuccessful.

Last night I went to the EM Club to get a Coke. I got involved in listening to a drunk sergeant whose wife is nine days overdue with their second child. I couldn't get away from him. Finally they closed the place and I was able to sneak off.

They've got a pass system here that allows only three EMs from each section to be in town at the same time. So it'll be some time before I go into town.

I suppose I should be eager to go into the Paris of Southeast Asia and see how much of Graham Greene's Saigon is left. Time enough for that. Almost a year, although it is rumored that soon we'll be moved to Long Binh. Scuttlebutt is usually wrong, but in this case . . .

Maybe there will be some Asian beauties in Saigon; I've not seen any here in the compound. Of course Oriental girls have never had the appeal for me that white or negro girls have. All these girls have squeaky voices and flat chests.

The perfect Asian face (Madame Ky?) I glimpsed with Sergeant Ruttencutter has much been on my mind. I wonder about her voice, about her chest, about how she'd be to be with. After that fuss in Italy though, I'm on my best behavior. Watching my P's and Q's.

25 September 1966, Sunday

I'm sitting in the ice cold air-conditioned library where I rushed to avoid the soon-to-fall-like-hell rain.

Today at Cholon PX I had a Coke and a cheeseburger but didn't enjoy them very much, although I guess it was (strictly speaking) a cheeseburger.

In the mess hall we eat off steel trays which we wash off in garbage cans filled with hot water.

I'll have to get a camera to shoot color slides of the picturesque sights—to capture the essence of Vietnam. Every curbside space is clogged with someone attempting to sell something. Little stands all along the roads with bottles of red soda pop which sit in even rows sparkling in the sun—surely warm and undrinkable.

Little horses drawing little carts along the streets, motor scooters with two passengers, Shell service stations with all the signs in Vietnamese.

Another thing outstanding about Vietnam is the smell. Can't photograph that!

26 September 1966, Monday, 12:00 noon

Today I've been typing file cards, quite easy and time consuming.

I was reading William O. Douglas' *North from Malaya* last night. "In 1930 one village was wiped out by incendiary bombs because it was supposed to have granted asylum to insurgents" (p. 163).

Counterinsurgency is standard practice here.

Average rainfall in Saigon:

Jan.	Feb.	Mar.	Apr.	May
.7	NIC	.6	1.6	8.4

June	July	Aug.	Sept.	Oct.
13.7	12.3	11.3	14.1	4.4

Nov.	Dec.
	2.5

I'm looking forward to October through April, the dry months.

9:30 p.m.

Just back from "Rio Conchos," the movie, not the place.

Today I was assured that if I kept my nose clean by the time I've been here ten months, I'll be SP5, as I'm filling an SP5 slot.

I'm starting my climb to the top in this man's army, E1 to E5 in ten months—my goal. Like my sergeant major said today, "It's a shitty war, but it's the only one we've got." After Italy, they could have sent me to Korea—no money, but plenty of gooks and kimchi, all you can eat.

My work continues to be easy—no shorthand.

Last night I was reading the *Saigon Post's* "Everything is News" section. I get the impression that anything goes here for GIs; they are really kicking up their heels and taking advantage of a situation. Who can blame them? My recent favorite is "Wanted: American Seducer." The Saigon police are attempting to track down an American doctor captain (or so he claimed) who reportedly seduced a teen-age girl, got her in the family way, and finally when the question of marriage arose, he turned tail and vamoosed. I look forward myself to being a blackguard like that. I doubt if I have it in me, though. When confronted with a similar situation in my own life, what did I do but the *Right Thing.* And where did it get me? I entered the Army because I had no better prospects, narrowly missed the firing squad in Italy, and here I am in Vietnam, divorced and starting over, making the best of a bad deal. The sound you hear is me rubbing my hands together with glee at all the low joys which await me in Saigon.

Got into a minor controversy last night with the sergeant who likes to have the large fan blowing on him (and me). The controversy was about the origins of the English language of all things. He was completely ignorant of the Frisian Islander contribution. No surprise.

He said if I was so damned smart why wasn't I in college. I must have goofed around or I wouldn't be here in Vietnam. He's born to be cannon fodder, but here he languishes in Tan Son Nhut.

27 September 1966, Tuesday, 9:15 p.m.

I had another big argument today with the mama-san at the laundry. It looks as though I'll never get that shirt back.

Today I viewed a sight I wish I could have photographed. An old Vietnamese man was sawing three-inch strips off of a very large plank. He was doing this with a large saw while he sat on the plank which was resting across two saw horses. While doing this he was eating a baloney sandwich.

I spent the day typing file cards and lists. I've got a complicated list to type tomorrow.

28 September 1966, Wednesday, 9:10 p.m.

Tonight the movie was "The Oscar." The Great Critic in the Sky rained it out. He did us a favor.

Went to a Flip floor show at the EM Club tonight. Five girls playing electric guitars. They played Chuck Berry's "Johnny B. Goode." They made quite an impression on all concerned. Brown they were, but their voices weren't squeaky, and they were not flat chested.

I look forward soon to venturing into Saigon.

29 September 1966, Thursday, 8:30 p.m.

Chiggers or mosquitoes are eating me up here. Vietnam will leave its mark on me—the scars of old bug bites!

A little news story in the paper today under the headline "Taxi Ride Costs 500 Dollars." An American living in Truong, Minh-Giang Street, was strolling on Bach-Dang Quay when invited by a beautiful girl to get in her taxi for a chat. After having a delightful ride around the city, he was told to get down. He found a moment later his wallet containing 500 dollars had gone. He reported the case to the police.

A sad old familiar tale. I hope to avoid a similar fate while still managing to venture forth into this land. The headline underneath this story wasn't so sad. "Nude Photo Seller Arrested," red-handed. I can imagine.

Today I met Sergeant Golden Boy who is under house arrest for an alleged currency fiddle he worked while assigned to Finance. He suns himself every day on top of a wall of sandbags and has a suntan to beat all! As I stood admiring him he turned his head toward me and said, "A nation of mouth breathers in conflict with a nation of rice eaters." He then turned back to his avocation. I must have sighed audibly while staring at him, one of my many failings, a failing which when exercised in church never failed to elicit a sharp elbow from my father.

30 September 1966, Friday, 9:30 p.m.

"The Man from Button Willow," a cartoon narrated by Dale Robertson, was the movie tonight. I chose to read instead.

I didn't get paid today; I'll probably get paid on October 3rd.

My job still hasn't turned ugly yet. Everyone is pleasant. It's sort of like working for a bunch of college professors. Almost all of the officers have college degrees. They are, I'm sure, the most pleasant group of officers in the Army for whom to work. It won't all be peaches of course, but mostly the job will be fine and with luck I'll never have to use my nonexistent shorthand.

My laundry is still fouled up. I worked until 7:30 tonight. I get Saturday afternoon and all day Sunday off.

I will sit right here in the compound, I imagine. Maybe I'll
go to the EM Club again. Anthropologically speaking,
there are no women around the compound. Out the
back gate there are plenty, for 200 piasters a crack, of
which I'm having none. I deserve better than a short-
time girl. Really I deserve the best Saigon has to offer. I
just don't yet know what that is. I would like it to be the
woman who belongs to that Perfect Asian Face I glimpsed
at Ton Son Nhut. I find myself thinking of her frequently.
What to do about that? Wait and see. If it's right, fate
may take a hand.

1 October 1966

The little headline which caught my eye today:
"Jealous Husband Beats Wife Working for a Foreigner."
They'll be able to use that headline over and over again
as long as this war lasts.
    After the soup, urinate in the bowl.
    —Old Vietnamese Saying (told to me by Golden Boy)

2 October 1966, Sunday, 9:30 a.m.

Yesterday I was paid $50. My PFC pay rate will go
into effect retroactively next month.
Also yesterday I got a shirt from the laundry to
replace the one they lost. They (the old mama-san)
sewed on all the stripes, patches, etc. free so really I'm
money ahead on the deal except for all the aggravation.
Then on the way to Cholon in the free Army trans-
portation (bus) we went by a muddy swimming hole. A
small brown boy lay on the bank, naked, with his head

resting on a white handkerchief—drowned.

My work is going fine still and I now have begun to take a short nap at noon. "Mad dogs and Englishmen . . ."

Last night I watched some people play the slot machines in the EM Club. Those machines are everywhere. The EM Club has $250,000 in its treasury due to them.

10:35 p.m.

I'm dousing myself in Ammon's powder to get rid of the prickly heat.

I read some Spider Man, Hulk, and Batman comics. The troops here take them pretty seriously.

There was talk today about changing our one-year tours to a for-the-duration situation, but General Westmoreland scotched it. He thinks it would be bad for morale. He's right.

Today or yesterday the mama-san got the shoes mixed up so I got stuck with a left shoe too small for me. Oh well, gooks and wogs.

I skipped the movie, "King Rat," tonight and went over to my section building and sat in the quarters of the SP4 I work with and drank one gin and tonic and listened to Beatles records, namely the "Help" album.

Yesterday at the commissary I bought plum jam and Ritz crackers so I can make little snacks when I want.

Today half the personnel in my building moved into another building, and soon my desk will be moved out onto the screened porch of the second floor. I'll be the steno in the administration part of my section doing the same stuff I'm doing now.

3 October 1966, Monday, 10:15 p.m.

Tonight it rained and put out the lights in our hooch (barracks). The electricity here is very capricious.

I had a lot of typing today. The only way to learn it so it'll be easy is to do it, but I'm not really a born typist. I was meant for better things, Horatio at the Bridge, but for now it is not to be. I'll bide my time and hope I can seize the opportunity when it rears its head, and it will, it will.

Today I bit down on my mashed potatoes and gravy, hit a bone and broke off one cusp of a molar, top left. Nothing painful, yet I think I'll see the dentist tomorrow. Also tomorrow I'm due to pick up my laundry. I wonder what surprises they'll have in store for me?

There's a nasty rumor the Army plans to do away with mama-sans so we'll have to polish our own boots. Today when they polished the shoes, I got still another left shoe. This one appears a little larger.

The Army's installed lights in the shower room, so no more showers in the dark.

I'm scheduled to work late (until 7:30) Friday night again, but I'm also off again on Saturday afternoon and Sunday.

I've just now gotten into another silly argument with the sergeant. Soldiers were making noise nearby, and I said "The animals are restless tonight." He took great exception to this comment and asked for my definition of animals. I said there were plants and then there were animals. That really made him mad. Madder than our origin-of-the-English-language discussion. He started ridiculing my education and my reading. If he starts another argument with me I'll crucify him. Lifers!

4 October 1966, Tuesday, 7:00 a.m.

The radio just yelled, "Good Morning, Vietnam," and then the d.j. played a Patti Page song.

10:00 p.m.

Today I got my tooth fixed. One of the cusps had indeed broken off. The dentist replaced the front cusp with a silver one.

The movie tonight was "The Psychopath," but it was rained out. Soon the rainy season will be over and I'll be able to watch a movie in its entirety.

My laundry was all in place today. Nothing missing. The gooks aren't so dumb.

Lately I've been busier and busier in the office. The work has increased gradually. Everyone is pleasant and not a harsh word has been said yet (to an EM that is). A few of the officers have had words between themselves, but that's that.

I overheard a disgusted voice in the shower this morning say, "If the hair on my ass grew as fast as the hair on my face . . ."

5 October 1966, Wednesday, 10:15 p.m.

I saw "Invitation to a Gunfighter," starring George Segal and Yul Brynner.

I'm getting thirsty for cold whole milk. I guess I'd better forget it. The usual drink with dinner here is a non-sweetened limeade made from real limes. It would cure scurvy posthumously.

My work is still coming along. I'm trying to learn the filing system. It's a little confused.

It's been cool here the last couple of days; no heat rash or anything.

There's a lot of soldier folk lore floating around over here. Like the Viet Cong girl with paper-wrapped razor blades up her cunt. They don't hurt her, but they cut the innocent soldier boy all to hell when he dicks her. Lots of stuff like that. Probably Custer's men said the same stuff about Cheyenne squaws.

The sour old (about 45) sergeant has moved to different billets so he's out of my life for now, but if our paths cross again, I'll not act the doormat as I've done. No self-respect in that!

6 October 1966, Thursday

We've got a new mama-san. Our sergeant got drunk and canned the old one. The guy can't really be too bright. It really hurt the mama-san. That's life I guess.

7 October 1966, Friday, 7:00 a.m.

Usual day. Talked to some guys who'd been to Korea. Glad I got RVN. The Korean tour is 17 months, it's cold, boring, and there's no combat pay. Also very little chance for promotion past PFC. I'm happy in a war zone.

There will be two more stenos in our office by Monday. That should really lighten the work load. The reason we're getting two more stenos is that the two others there now will be leaving in less than 90 days.

Last night's movie was a spy-beach party picture with the Turtles.

8 October 1966, Saturday, 12:45 p.m.

Vietnamese *lingua franca:*

Choi-oi	Holy Cow
Dinky Dau	Crazy, Nuts
Number 1	Good
Number 10	Bad
Number 10 Thou	Unbelievably Bad

The goddamn slopes have the shoes mixed up again, one shoe size ten and the other about ten and a half. I almost think they do it on purpose.

I work a week from Sunday and also the following Monday evening. They are very fair about distributing the duty and there's no room at all to complain.

The Army doesn't issue insect powder. I've seen no snakes or spiders, just lizards, beetles, and mosquitoes.

Life is pleasant over here. Work is pleasant.

9 October 1966, Sunday, 12:00 noon

Lately the only soda pop available here is Dr. Pepper. Wink would be a welcome relief.

9:30 p.m.

My point of view on the war? Nobody ever asks me what it is. Nobody cares. I want to advance myself and have some adventure without any risk to my precious person. True love would be nice, too.

This attitude is a self-serving one. I recognize it, and it is resulting in some terrible stuff. World wide.

Most of the PX purchases end up on the black market. Pussy only costs 200 p., in real money about $2.00. Pretty cheap for the chance to contract a disease previously unknown to modern medicine.

10 October 1966, Monday, 9:35 p.m.

It looks as though when the SP6 in my section leaves I'll be taking over his department, Complaints and Requests For Assistance, a SP6 slot. I don't know whether I want the job or not. It's a lot of work, but it is a golden opportunity for me to Get Ahead!

11 October 1966, Tuesday, 8:45 p.m.

The movie tonight was NFC football games. I skipped it.

I saw Sergeant Golden Boy again today. He's still awaiting trial on his alleged currency fiddle. He is a mellow, droll fellow, a real California surfin' type. Not a care in the world and a great tan!

I watched him sun himself today. He stood up lazily, said "Surf's up," and strode lithely off. One could pick a worse role model—not a care in the world. When I was awaiting my fate in Italy, I felt on the brink of a nervous breakdown every moment and it showed. I've got to learn to say "So what!" when disaster befalls me.

12 October 1966, Wednesday, 8:15 p.m.

The dry monsoon is blowing down hot from wherever it blows. I got my hair cut short today in an attempt at coolness, a vain one, I'm afraid.

I can feel Saigon beckoning on the wind. It offers many recreations — drinking, screwing — people keep referring to it as the Paris of Southeast Asia. Scenery, shops, bookstores, a fine zoo, motion picture theaters. Lots to do.

Well, I've been at Saigon's front door for about a month, but I've yet to visit it. Something is seriously wrong with me. Overcautious! That's what got me into trouble in Italy. I must throw caution to the winds, leave the safety of the USARV compound and immerse myself in stinking Asia. Soon!

14 October 1966, 7 a.m.

The mama-san has been slacking off, so I must now attend to polishing my boots.

9:45 p.m.

I'm sick of living in this hooch. I hope to do better. There are some rooms in the building in which I work where two stenos live.

Today at 6:15 p.m. I was called in by Major Eldman to take some shorthand. I typed a couple of rough drafts which he'll correct in the morning. I got most of it in longhand, so I think I did O.K. He won't reprimand me even if it is a little rough.

I'm so caught up in the trivia of my daily military life

that I don't worry about the VC, but some crackpots or seers expect them to treat Saigon the way the Japs treated Diamond Head. I'll most likely be home by that time.

15 October 1966

Picked up an old copy of the *Saigon Daily News* lying around the hooch. Back page had an interesting article, "Two Foreigners Commit Suicide." An American woman and a French diplomat died of an overdose of sleeping pills in the evening and afternoon of September 23. I'm surprised there are any Frenchmen left in Southeast Asia, and if this keeps up there won't be. My guess is the cause of the suicide is love-related rather than political.

16 October 1966, Sunday, 8:00 a.m.

If I'm lucky I won't have much work today. But if I'm not lucky I'll have plenty to do all day. The duty officer is a good fellow, so that's half the battle.

A Vietnamese Army corporal earns $11.00 per month plus $2.23 if he's married. A gook hooker gets 200 p. for each blow job. In a day she can earn as much as an RVN captain if she keeps busy.

The letters I typed from my shorthand were fine, the major said. Last night our section had a barbecued chicken and steak dinner with plenty of beer; the steak was tenderloin and very fine, indeed.

Weird headline in yesterday's *New York Times.* "Ky Bars Removal of His Police Head." I had visions of the ogre of Southeast Asia performing rites of decapitation and then going home for lunch. I read the article and it was just boring administrative stuff.

Tomorrow we have a 6:00 a.m. formation for the purpose of sorting out just who is here and who isn't. It'll be hell to get up, but I guess I'll survive.

The electricity is off today so the coffee isn't perking, though of course I still don't touch the stuff.

17 October 1966, Monday

The article in the local paper which caught my eye today: "Fertilizer Hoarder in Trouble." The owners of a shop at Ky Son Crossroads here was prosecuted because he had hoarded fertilizer to sell it in the black market. The police searched his store and found a large undeclared stock of fertilizer Tuesday. An official report was written on the scene and sent to the local authorities for disposition. The stock was temporarily frozen.

Directly under this story was one headlined "VC Guerrillas Captured, Caves Uncovered."

If it weren't for the newspapermen's gimlet eye this is a side of the war I'd miss entirely. Thanks to them!

18 October 1966, Tuesday, 7:10 a.m.

I'm listening to "Give Me That Old Time Religion" on the morning devotional program. Every morning a chaplain prattles on about how modern psychiatry supports the findings of the Holy Writ—the Bible.

There have been a couple of bus stop bombings here lately which could make a person who waits for buses a little edgy. The only bus I take loads and unloads within guarded compounds. The people who were hurt were violating the rule against crowds at bus stops. It's their own damn fault really.

The bugs aren't biting me like they were and all the bite welts on my chest have disappeared. I'm also getting a bit of a suntan, although not in a league with Sergeant Golden Boy's.

The popular Army terminology for a person with more than half of his one year served is "short timer." They grow moustaches and exhibit other bizarre behavior.

9:20 a.m.

The last couple of days I lost both of my baseball caps, so I'm wearing a borrowed size 7 cap; it looks ludicrous on my big head. Tomorrow I'll buy a RVN copy of an Army baseball cap. They're funny looking and unmilitary and preferred by everyone. All the Old Asian Hands wear them.

The movie tonight was Martin and Rossi in "The Last of the Secret Agents," a bad movie fraught with all sorts of homosexual implications by Rossi, the fat one with all the hair.

I work this Saturday afternoon, but I'll have all day Sunday off.

I'm afraid that soon my luck will run out and I'll have to stand guard duty. That means I'll have to learn my general orders, polish my brass, and clean a rifle. I don't remember how. I've not had my hands on one in a *long* time.

My work continues to go well. Everybody is amazingly nice. All the people in the office. When I'm given a job to do I work at my own speed. So far I've done everything more or less correctly. I ask a million questions the first few times, but after that it's no sweat. We can sit at our desks and drink pop while listening to the radio, while doing some work.

Oh yes, guard also entails field gear, and a pistol belt. No danger involved because the rifle will be unloaded.

Three name tags I've noticed in the compound: Major Snagg, Privates Pagan and El Toro.

19 October 1966, Wednesday, 7:10 a.m.

I checked the bulletin board this morning—no guard duty for me through the 23rd. If I can make it through the next seven days, I'll be free and clear.

Read an odd article today on a feud in Ky's cabinet. Some nonsense about Northerners and Southerners and favoritism by Ky toward Cabinet members from the North because he's from the North. Why is Ky running South Vietnam if he's from the North? The word "corrupt" is used. I'll bet that explains it.

Sitting in the office writing this. Listening to Radio Hanoi. It comes in real clear. I hope that when the sergeant major returns from his emergency leave I'll move downstairs to begin my apprenticeship so I'll be able to take over as Administrative Assistant of the Complaint Department with a minimum of difficulty in about 85 days when SP6 Dave C. leaves.

Today a bulletin came into the office with a blurb for the Army Suggestion Program: "Columbus Discovered a New Way—So Can You." I'd never heard about that aspect of his character, though I'd always suspected that he and Isabella were up to something no good.

20 October 1966, Thursday, 8:30 p.m.

I'm sitting up in the office under the fan drinking a five-cent Tiger beer, labeled "For H.M. Forces Only Duty Un . . ." obscured by the opened section of the can.

I just saw "Harper" with Paul Newman.

Today was clean sheet day and mine were more than usually stained with red mud. But they'll feel clean enough.

Today they posted the guards for the next week through the end of the week and I wasn't listed. My name must not be on the master list. Somebody fucked up somewhere and I'm glad.

On November 5 our office is having a big blast here in the office backyard. Steak, Chicken, hamburgers, fruit, vegetables, the whole shitarooney. It will be a welcome relief from the diet here which only occasionally includes fresh local bananas, pineapple, etc.

21 October 1966, Friday, 8:00 p.m.

The other night that Flip girl band was going to appear at the EM Club and they were late. The EM provided their own impromptu entertainment that was more amusing. Like intoning "you you you fuck you him him him fuck him . . ." and giving a standing ovation to everyone who entered the back door. A Korean who was given that treatment walked up onto the stage and made faces while clapping for himself. It brought down the house. I'd have died from embarrassment. The Koreans are universally acknowledged to be bright, witty, and fiendish traders. You can never get the best of them. It's thought that they are making fortunes on the black market as they get everything first at the PX.

It's been a dull day at work and I'll be happy as long as it continues that way. I read that Ky has straightened out his cabinet problems and will junket to Manila, presumably with his lovely wife at his side.

Two PFCs in the office got promoted today to SP4. I won't be eligible until January 18, 1967. I suppose that I'll get it then, unless something goes badly wrong.

22 October 1966, Saturday, 10:00 p.m.

I'm writing this by candlelight as there is another partial power failure that has put out the lights in the office.

More rumors that all the sections in the USARV compound at Tan Son Nhut will be moving to Long Binh. No big deal. It'll be as safe there as here, but maybe I'll be forced by the move to make the most of my time here near Saigon, which I've yet to do. Movies, the library, snacks — I could do all that in Korea.

I saw a movie with Chuck Conners in it tonight. During the movie the sound was off about half the time, and the rest of the time the frogs croaked so loudly that it was difficult to hear the dialogue. Everybody threw rocks at them to shut them up, and one drunk got up and rushed them with handsful of rocks, shouting that he was going to cut off their little fucking feet.

This afternoon we had another steak barbecue. I

didn't get very much steak as I had afternoon duty and was busy typing some old shit.

LBJ has visited Saigon recently. No VC terrorism was directed his way.

23 October 1966, Sunday, 9:30 p.m.

Went to downtown Saigon today. Saw a princess whom I love. I'll have to think about this eventuality and all of its unlikely ramifications. Now I know how Danté felt when he espied Beatrice.

The Bom-de-bom stands caught my eye. They will sell you anything: watches, straight razors (Solligen), hats, rubbers, everything.

I went up to one stand and asked the proprietor if he'd sell me a switch-blade knife. He said do you really want one. I said yes, I want to cut someone up. He said do you really want one? I said yes, I want to cut someone up. He said do you *really* want one, or are you just fucking around. I said I really want to cut someone up. I had a certain troublesome sergeant in mind. I'd probably never go through with it, but why not be ready for it? I felt like a fool dealing with the man who ran the bom-de-bom stand and because of that I bought the thing. Who knows? One day it may come in handy. I could be a hero. It could give me an edge, the unexpected advantage which could make all the difference.

The shoeshine boys kept surrounding me. They surround you and stand touching, plucking, almost caressing you as they ask you if you want a shine. It is almost sexual the way they tug and pat with their little hands. And they aren't very happy when you walk away from them. I told them my number ten shoes didn't deserve as good a shine as they would give me.

All this activity made me hungry so I went into a seafood restaurant and had lobster thermador with butter sauce, hot bread and butter, tea, red wine. I would have liked some soup but decided against it. The restaurant was very nice with a bar, and steel grilling across the windows.

I then went to the zoo and walked around and looked at the people looking at the animals. It's a pretty miserable zoo, but it has some tigers and elephants which are indigenous to this part of the world. The stinks at the zoo weren't any worse than the rest of this country.

On Tu Do Street (very different from the Rue Catinat of Graham Greene) I was not pestered by the girls, and the people in the shops were very polite, helpful, English-speaking, and even seemed to be honest. I asked if something was jade, and the woman said no, imitation; I asked if the silk gown was silk and she said no, imitation, and she showed me one that was real.

It was downtown that I saw Her, with a small retinue. She stepped out of a Mustang, the Mustang that I'd seen the first day in country. She was wearing western garb — a blouse, slacks, dark glasses, and a polka-dot scarf. She entered a dress-maker's, and I was stunned by Her who passed only inches from me, leaving a delicate cloud of French scent. As Leland Gardner said in *Vietnam Underside!,* The men look like queers and the women — sex machines! She certainly proved that point.

Before she entered the shop, she stopped, removed her goggle-like sun glasses, and with her perfect almond eyes, looked into mine and captured my soul. She then turned and left my life. Twice now we've locked eyes. When will the third time be?

Only one guy tried to sell me dirty books downtown. I shrugged him off. And at that moment my mind was not yet on higher things. Now I'm truly impervious to low things. Animal gropings.

24 October 1966, Monday, 7:00 a.m.

Awoke with but one thought—to find Marshal Madame Ky's bungalow at Tan Son Nhut, peer through the windows, maybe even knock upon the door and capture her essence, communicate with her. Maybe this week I can borrow SP6 David C.'s bicycle and embark on this odyssey. Fake a dentist's appointment? Or whatever is necessary. One must have one's priorities.

At least go to the library and see what I and the fellow with the cushy, air-conditioned job can dig up to feed or leaven my fevered fantasies.

10:00 p.m.

My ears are all plugged up with mucus (snot) and my head feels like a drum. I'll take a few aspirin, a shower, and it'll soon pass. It's nothing I'm sure.

25 October 1966, Tuesday, 10:00 p.m.

Life goes on. I must absorb myself in the trivialities of the day and bide my time. With the help of the air-conditioned librarian I pursued information on My Darling, but played it cagey and pretended only to be interested in Premier Ky, that dapper little fellow. He has a look in his eye which makes him an unlikely candidate for head-patting. The Head Gook Himself.

I found the *Time* cover story of February 18, 1966. It informed me that Madame Ky was rescued from life as an Air Vietnam stewardess by the Premier. My theory is that the high altitude and the constant possibility of death makes people, whether pilots or stewardesses, sex-obsessed. It's only a theory, but a fond one.

The photo of Madame Ky, leaning eagerly into the camera and calling attention to her lush mouth with her right hand and her knees with her left, supports my theory. After all, what lies midway between those hands but that most precious and sacred of her private territories?

She can't help herself. News photos can't lie. Hitler's didn't. The positioning of his hands gave away his insecurity and helped to do him in.

Madame Ky vivaciously leans forward as if to consume the camera. The chair she sits in looks like U.S. Government Danish modern vinyl upholstered.

I drank a Pepsi today. A welcome relief from Dr. Pepper. The guard roster was posted for next week and I'm still not on it, but someone I'd never heard of was listed. They screwed up and I'll probably end up getting that day. I guess it won't hurt me to clean a rifle and learn my general orders. They sometimes ask chain of command and the rifle serial number and lots of other crap, like the day you qualified on the M14 and what your score was, etc.

It's getting late and I must locate the mailbox key which I've again misplaced.

26 October 1966, Wednesday, 9:30 p.m.

Just took a shower and put on clean underwear in which I'm sitting in the office, doused in St. John's Bay

Rum, scribbling this entry. The ceiling fan is blowing cool air, and all-in-all it's quite a pleasant evening.

My Darling made the front page of yesterday's *New York Times.* She's standing between The Dragon Lady of the Philippines, Mrs. Marcos, and Lady Bird. Mai is lovely and proud-bosomed in a high-necked dress with long sleeves and belted waist. Mrs. Marcos has turned her head away from the camera. Mai and Lady Bird (decked out in a lei) are looking off to their left. Each has a handbag. Mai's hair is pulled back, except for her bangs. Mai looks quite busty in her dress, probably padded. She's the only one of the five women pictured who'd get an invitation to a sex circus. The two pluguglies on the left (Mrs. Kittikachorn and Mrs. Holt) would be lucky to be invited to a dog fight. And they'd be the main event. The article mentions student demonstrators. I'm sure Mai is well insulated from them, but I do feel some fear and trepidation for her and will breathe easier when she's back safe in Saigon.

Talked to SP6 Dave C. and he said I could borrow his bicycle and even have the thing when he leaves Vietnam for his next destination. The question is when will the bicycle's availability coincide with a hole in my schedule?

Today I worked until 7:30 and emptied the trash at the incinerator. I got a ride down there in the colonel's air-conditioned sedan, but the incinerators had almost collapsed internally so that there was a huge line of fellows waiting to burn their trash. The smell of the trash, the inkiness of the carbon paper, the smell of the cigarette butts and orange peels somehow brought back to me those happy months in college when I worked as a janitor and encountered all sorts of stuff in the garbage: chicken embryos, irradiated mollusks, coffee grounds, dog excrement, and live lab mice.

Today I took care of my dog tags by removing the plastic tubes from a couple of hangers and covering the chains of my tags with them so my neck won't have a green ring around it. To look like an old-timer here, I have only a few more steps: jungle boots, jungle fatigues, RVN-made baseball cap, and a short-timer mustache. The jungle stuff I'll inherit from Whit, the steno I've had a couple of gin and tonics with, when he leaves. If I ever find an RVN-made cap that fits me, I'll buy it. Screw the mustache.

27 October 1966, Thursday, 9:00 p.m.

Attended a class on clerical procedures today. It was a bore, but I did learn a few little things. The key word of sarcasm over here is *Outstanding,* said with an accent on the "out" and the standing part sort of dragged out. Every other thing is greeted with "Outstanding," from a minute meal to the electricity going off to the g.i.s to anything that falls short of minimum requirements. Oh yes, today was clean sheet day. No sheets. *Outstanding!*

Old LBJ visited RVN. I have no thoughts on the subject at all.

One heart-quickening journalistic experience with Tuesday's *New York Times* was their story, "Five First Ladies Ride Bus and Dine at Volcanic Lake." The journalist, obviously a com-symp by his cute little turns of phrase — they "traveled in an air-conditioned bus to see poverty-stricken villages . . ." Traveling in a hot bus wouldn't feed any peasants. Although Mrs. Nguyen Cao Ky was there at this picnic chaperoned by five jeeps full of machine-gun-toting soldiers, no quip of hers was immortalized in the pages of the *Times*. I can easily imagine her trading witticisms with Lady Bird about the eruption of the volcano eliminating potential insurgents or some similar light frothy talk.

Mr. and Mrs. Nguyen Cao Ky attended a fluvial parade in Manila. A picture of President Johnson holding hands with Mrs. Imelda Marcos showed up in yesterday's paper—he looks like a hound dog and she, a painted mask. No more info on Mai Ky. She was there and that's all.

My work continues as usual and nothing momentous has yet happened.

28 October 1966, Friday

Tonight the movie was "Women of the Prehistoric Planet." It was very bad, especially as the women in it were bald and in tight pants. Very disturbing. I'm up in the office as usual and in the kitchen. One of the guys, as broke as I am, is drinking a can of quinine water and it is going down quite hard.

Last night I was so hungry that I ate a purple fruit that looked like it was filled with cold cream and sesame seeds and tasted like it, too. The mama-san had it in the freezer so it was hard as a rock.

Today the mama-san tried to figure out who'd eaten her fruit. Of course I said I had and asked her how much it was worth. She claimed it was worth 40 p. Trying to figure out whether I liked it or not she said "Number 10, number one." I said number two and made a face. She thought that was funny and later I gave her a brownie that had come in the mail, and she said that she didn't want money for the fruit. She's a funny woman, but nice too. She's about as different from Madame Ky as a woman could get and still be Vietnamese. My Darling seems a different breed of cat. Not a gook at all.

Today was clean sheet day, and we got clean sheets that were so new that they were still in the plastic bags. I'm really looking forward to slipping between them tonight.

Tomorrow I move to another hooch. Only God knows why. I have all afternoon off and all day Sunday and all day Tuesday. That's a lot of vacation. Monday I get paid. Sometime during that time off I *must* pursue the Asian perfection which smiled my way in downtown Saigon. If I don't, what kind of man am I? Can I avoid troubles of the Italian sort? We'll see, won't we.

29 October 1966, Saturday, 10:00 p.m.

It's been a big day. I've moved to a different hooch at the other end of the compound. In the move I acquired a wall locker which I hadn't had one of before. Also today I went out the back gate and looked around at the scenery. It was difficult to concentrate as little boys kept approaching me with "number one girl" pleas and vainly plucking at my elbows. The area is littered with garbage and quite dirty.

Lots has been happening around Saigon lately, such as the ammo dump at Bien Hoa being blown by sappers. We felt the shock all the way here. That's quite near Long Bien where USARV is rumored to be moving one day. Soon?

SP6 David C. just came into the office with a half pint of Korean apple brandy, 80 proof, made by Samlip Industrial Company in Taegu, Korea. It says it was bottled under Korean government supervision, but from the taste of it I don't believe it. If it was, Korean government is shit. It really is terrible, but cheap. Three sips is all I'm going to have. I've had them and that's it.

David left and just returned with a bottle of Grand Marnier Triple Orange and Fine Old Cognac Brandy. It cost $3.85 over here for one liter. It's got ribbons and bows and sealing wax and all sorts of stuff on it. I'm going to try it now. It tastes lots better than the Korean apple brandy.

30 October 1966, Sunday, 5:00 p.m.

The electricity is just off and the fan quit and it's pretty muggy without the air conditioning.

Today I had dinner at the Golf Club de Saigon: chateaubriand, bom de ba beer (33) and French fries. The meal was on the upper terrace overlooking the golf course and a cool breeze was blowing. It was quite nice.

What made it even nicer was that I caught a glimpse of my Sweet Stewardess Darling as I was leaving. She was just arriving with The Head Gook in tow. She was clad in a lavender diaphanous number, and Premier Ky was wearing a uniform with a scarf at his throat which matched her dress. I don't resent his access to her, but hotshot pilots do seem to have their pick of the young lovelies. More so than U.S. Army stenos anyhow. Life isn't fair! That old complaint. It would take effort well beyond what talent I've displayed up until now to catch her eye in any *real* way. Faint heart never won . . .

Premier Ky was well into his cups and running off at the mouth. "Just because Uncle Ho looks like a hungry Santa Claus who needs dental work, he gets adulation and international sympathy. It's not fair. Americans treat me like a pet. They even pat my head." He and his party moved out of my ear shot. To me, with his Terry and the Pirates packaging and his patent leather hair and that careful moustache, he looked the unlikeliest candidate for head patting I'd ever seen. More readily pat a rattle snake. He probably was exaggerating, the way drunken public figures do.

My Darling didn't even glance my way.

31 October 1966, Monday, 9:30 p.m.

Just returned from "Johnny Tiger." Today I got a haircut, anticipating the laundry I was to get out today. But due to the holidays, no laundry for three days and I'm out of clean clothes. Oh well, I guess I'll get used to the little hairs.

Tonight I was supposed to be on alert, I learned after the movie was over. That was just a bunch of monkey-farting around and nonsense, like tomorrow I'm on barracks orderly duty. That means I sit on my ass in the billets all day, and in the words of Whit, "Make sure the mama-san doesn't walk off with the hooch." Big deal! I've got lots of work to do in the office, but instead . . .

This morning we had an early formation to tell us all about the parade that we weren't allowed to go to. That's the Army.

I got paid today without a hitch, not even a criticism for my buckle, which was polished by a very disgusted Whit last night in an attempt to show me how. I didn't catch on this time, but a few more times and I'll be expected to, I fear.

I'm eating Pik Nik shoestring potatoes and drinking

Rootin Tootin Rasbury. The potatoes have an easy-open lid that leaves tendrils of razor-sharp steel all around the orifice of the can. It's like reaching into a boobytrap to get them.

1 November 1966, Tuesday

I'm sitting in the hooch performing my duties as barracks orderly, namely doing nothing. Other than a runaway monkey, no excitement. I've been listening to all the excitement downtown broadcast on the radio. Quite a bit of trouble. But it's National Day and trouble was expected. It's a lesson that we're really an island in a country controlled by the VC. They had a company or so downtown with several (6) hundred pounds of plastique explosive.

This morning I dug out my field equipment for the first time and discovered I'm missing a helmet liner. Also I polished my belt buckle. I'm sitting here in a T-shirt drinking an RC with the wind blowing on me very comfortably.

Russ Columbo is on the radio now, singing "Madness" — "You call it madness but, oh, I call it love." I don't know what to call it, but She is much on my mind. She of the almond eyes.

Tomorrow and the next day SP6 Dave C. will be gone and I'll be working downstairs with Colonel Coldass. It's not going to be pleasant, but that's life.

2 November 1966, Wednesday, 7:00 p.m.

I've got guard on the 10th of this month. I'll have to start girding my loins and learning the slop and getting my equipment in repair.

Today I rode shotgun out to Long Binh in the jeep for Col. Coldass. Along the way we saw Vietnamese civilian motorcyclists wearing jungle boots that are unavailable for lieutenant colonels in our office. That pissed off old Coldass that gooks could get stuff on the black market that he can't get through supply.

The company has reorganized and added a clothing code, guard, task force, bed check. It's getting like Stateside duty.

I really felt like a trooper today with a loaded .45 on my hip and the dust whipping into my face as we drove past all the slopes on bikes and a million stands selling yellow-green melons. Piled in geometrical pyramids.

Today I transferred my laundry to the mama-san here at work. I still haven't gotten back my stuff from last week and I'm getting pretty crusty.

Currently I'm bit up by bugs; they're a bunch of little bastards.

I'm going to go take a shower and then read a few comic books and then to bed.

3 November 1966, Thursday, 7:30 p.m.

I was late man tonight—washed the cups, closed the windows and burned the trash. Now playing on the radio is "Sunshine Superman" by Donovan.

An interesting saying over here is "That's a rog (raj—rawj)"; meaning that's for sure or you bet your ass.

Last night Whit and Mayer, the colonel's driver, and I went out the back gate and ate chop chop at the Cherry Hill place which is just a restaurant. We had shrimp fried rice and washed it down with Coke. While eating, we

watched the light bulbs fluctuate with the current due
to the lack of a voltage regulator.

Yesterday I saw a huge praying mantis sitting on the
outside of the screen beyond my desk.

Today I picked up my clean clothes. I'm bringing no
more laundry there. Mama-san will do it for 1,000 p. plus
soap.

A swimming pool is being built in the compound. It'll
be ready in a few weeks, I'm told.

The sergeant major has returned from his emergency
leave. Some things in the office will change for the better
around here now, maybe.

Saturday is the Big Party out behind the office. We've
got 80 or so steaks and chicken for everybody and salad
and booze.

4 November 1966, Friday, 9:00 p.m.

I just got back from a movie called "The Hill," with
Sean Connery. Afterward, I had popcorn and Diet Cola
because the only other drink was Swann's Lager in rust-
encrusted cans.

I'm sitting here in the office with the fluorescent
lights shining on the water cooler full of tomato-juice-
colored water. I've got about 9 mosquito bites on my
right elbow but am otherwise in good physical health.
Polka music is playing on the radio.

My mental health, however, leaves something to be
desired and I don't blame the polka music. I hereby
promise myself on the next day I have off I'm going in
search of the Ky bungalow. Now that SP6 David C. is
gone and I inherited his bicycle I've no more excuses
except lily-liveredness.

5 November 1966, Saturday, 3:30 p.m.

Today I went in search (on David C.'s bicycle) of My Darling's bungalow in hopes of a glimpse of her perfect self. I pedaled the bicycle around and around the Tan Son Nhut airfield complex, searching in vain. It was like returning to Brigadoon. Impossible. Asked several times for directions, but no one knew. Maybe it's in an off-limits area. I knew exactly what I was looking for because the *Time* magazine cover story on Premier Ky had a nice photo of the house with the helicopter in front. But no go.

When the Commies win this war she'll wish *she* was running a dress shop in a southern California shopping mall. She could do worse. Look at Marie Antoinette. I could help her avoid all that misery if she'd but let me. If her black-jump-suit arrivals in the peasant back country aren't a modern equivalent of Marie's "Let them eat cake," then I'm still in Italy facing ignominy. Nobody talks straight to people like them. They fool themselves and everyone conspires to help them do so. For their own self-serving ends. Not me though. I'm in a position to see that the handwriting is on the wall and that it's writing about them. I've yet to see pro-Ky pro-US graffiti — and I'll not see any soon. "Yankee Go Home" is about as friendly as it gets. The people who write on walls prevail. We know they will.

People who make public announcements about Hitler's good points, startle peasants with Steve Canyon-Dragon Lady theatrics, and shop for dresses while their country smolders around them are not long for this world. Hubris! Yankee will go home and his lackeys will go too. I don't think they are bad people. Not really.

They are just in a place where they are not wanted and are too elegantly simple to figure it out.

I think one of the reasons I postponed this search was fear of failure. I'm plunged into the pits of depression. But I *will* try again. I must triumph or forever think myself a little ball of shit.

After my failure I went to Tan Son Nhut PX and stood in front of their airlines counter and admired a large aerial photo of the Space Needle. That was further depressing.

Time to go to the Big Feed. Even though I'm not hungry I must put in an appearance. It's expected.

7:00 p.m.

The Big Feed is still in progress downstairs. The gathering itself was interesting from a social viewpoint because the EM and the officers were mixing, mostly as equals. I hear quite a few complaints from enlisted men that the officers are more equal than they. The only officer I encounter this from is Col. Coldass and he doesn't really count. He's not a mean man, just oblivious.

Whit wants me to work for him tomorrow as he'll be all fucked up from drinking all evening, but I think I'll have things of my own to do. Including preparing for guard duty on Thursday, which still worries me.

10:30 p.m.

Against my better judgment, I tried to relieve the sexual congestion I've been feeling as a result of my love for Her. In spite of the fact that I know masturbation to be harmful, I succumbed. I fixated on the newsmagazine photo of her leaning forward. But no go. Things wouldn't come together. And they shouldn't have. Masturbation leads one to look inward for sexual gratification, and the glory and greatness of sexual love is in the overwhelming wish to consume and lick up alive the other person and make her a part of you. Masturbation is worse than a waste of time. It sullies, dilutes, and ultimately negates male-female love. I'll have to think of some other way to cope with the love I feel building up within me. Time will tell.

6 November 1966, Sunday, 7:00 p.m.

Went to a whorehouse out the back gate today and ended up in a room full of beds but with open walls with a sweet Vietnamese girl who smelt horribly of garlic but who had nice plump dark-nippled tits.

Lay down with her on a bare mattress and tried to pretend that she was My Darling, but it didn't work and nothing happened. Beyond her brown shoulder I could see a mixture of fruit rinds and used rubbers littering the grounds surrounding the establishment. She and I were the only people in the whole place, not even a mama-san was in evidence. I kissed the girl, gave her 200 p., and left. Maybe it was the garlic that did me in. Or my lack of imagination. I think the girl, doused in Chanel No. 5, would have sufficed for a short while. But maybe I'm kidding myself.

I'll have to think of another plan.

This Friday is Veteran's Day, vacation for me, and the day after, guard duty.

7 November 1966

Work is going fine. Tomorrow I'm going to get moved out of the hooch and into one of the rooms in the building that recently became vacant.

I have yet to hatch a plan about Her but suspect it will have to involve the one thing I know about Madame Ky, that she patronizes a particular dressmaker. What I'll do with that personally observed datum I don't know.

For now I should concentrate on getting ahead in the US Army. For me that will be a full-time job. That also involves keeping my nose clean. My every inclination is to rush off pell-mell to fling myself at My Darling. I know that approach would be the worst possible thing I could do. To reach my goal I must learn subtlety.

8 November 1966

Tonight I saw "A Thousand Clowns," then a negro fellow sitting next to me muttered at the end of the movie, "What the fuck kind of ending is that?"

I'm still working on being moved into the building so I'll share a room with Whit and be out of the hooch which is getting to be a pain in the ass. This morning we were awakened at 5:00 by the lights being activated by some nut of a sergeant who must have gotten up at 4:00 to so annoy us. And none of us have to be to work until 7:30, with at most a three-minute walk. Lifers have no brains. They're machines and dum-dums.

November 15 I move downstairs in the office to understudy for the job of Coldass' administrative assistant. A real pain in the ass, but necessary to my moving UP and becoming somebody—a SP4. My other preoccupation has caused me to temporarily lose track of my goal to move ahead in the US Army.

Keep your eye upon the donut and not upon the hole. Good advice in this instance.

There will be more money and I'll be one step closer to being a SP5, which does have a few privileges. I can't list any off the top of my head. It's sort of equivalent to buck sergeant but no command obligations.

9 November 1966, Wednesday, 8:00 p.m.

An additional steno has been assigned to our office.

Tomorrow I have guard duty. I don't know my general orders; I never will be able to memorize them. I still haven't a helmet liner.

A contest is now being advertised on AFRTS as I write these words. Write an essay on "Defending Freedom Safeguards America" in 500 words or less and send it to the Freedom Foundation, which sounds like a Commie front organization to me.

I haven't yet finagled a room in the office building but hope to manage it in the weeks to come, somehow. We have meal cards now, PT is planned, also reveille at 5:30 every morning. Christ!

10 November 1966, Thursday, 8:30 p.m.

I'm sitting in the Old Man's (colonel) office writing this. His office has air-conditioning, radio, beautiful new chair, etc.

I didn't get guard duty today. They changed the list at the last minute and deleted my name. I'm so lucky. I'm drinking Minute Maid orange juice and am, for the moment, content.

Tomorrow is a holiday, no work. I work half day Saturday and I'm off all day Sunday. Lots of free time in which to relax from my hectic schedule and to brood about my ultimate fate.

I heard "The Ballad of the Green Berets" today for the first time since arriving in RVN.

Preparing for guard was very traumatic, as was the shock of then not having to do it. I'm not on the list for next week.

The dry season is upon us. It still rains, but there's less water for the shower. I had to walk clear across the compound to find water today for a shower after my "guard" haircut. The haircut is ugly—bald sides, etc. No big deal, I guess, and my head is a lot cooler.

It's raining outside right now. "Casanova 70" was to be the movie tonight, but the bulb in the projector went kaput.

Last night the guy who sleeps in the bunk next to my footlocker got drunk and puked all over my footlocker. I got up all punchy with sleep, went to my foot locker to get out my shaving gear, towel, clean underwear, and a mess of congealed vomit covered the top and oozed stickily down the sides of the locker—not very appetizing. I didn't say anything to the owner of the vomit, but when I returned from my shower, it was all cleaned up. Not a word was said on either side.

Tonight the beer in the EM Club was Olympia. Nostalgically, I bought a can. Was unable to drink more than half of it. It tasted as bitter as alum to me. I'm not doing well at finishing what I start these days. Or any days.

11 November 1966, Veterans Day, Friday, 7:00 p.m.

The swimming pool is just about finished, but all the suits at the PX have 40-inch waists, about 10 inches more than I need.

Somebody said today they heard LBJ announcing victory in RVN soon. Ha Ha.

Our big feed was continued into Sunday, and it was put on by the EM for everyone, including the officers who paid $3.00 each, as did all E-4s and above, while those below paid only $2.00 each.

The most awful music is on; it's driving me crazy. No rock n' roll is available as the AFRTS is giving us some kind of Veterans Day shit.

I take it back. They just put on Bobby Darin singing "Splish Splash." He's a chameleon of musical styles.

12 November 1966, Saturday, 9:30 p.m.

I'm off work tomorrow, I work late Monday night and I have barracks orderly on Tuesday and I work on Sunday next. I feel more secure knowing my immediate destiny. Beyond that I've got nothing figured out, although I brood about it in the wee hours of predawn.

Yesterday dinner time I was eating in the mess hall with Charlie C. and Joe D., both new stenos in my office. Out of the blue this old guy about 50, and only a SP4, started talking about how to butcher a turtle. He went through every little detail while we were trying to eat a big gob of breaded gooey meat, about which we were quite suspicious anyhow. As we got up to leave the table, he sort of clutched at my shirt tail and started to tell me how to cut up alligator tail. We left him sitting there still talking.

Last night Ed C., a clerk typist in this office, walked up to me where I was resting on my bunk and described in great detail an operation on his sternum (mostly for cosmetic reasons) in which his sternum was cut into four sections and convexed. It left him with a nice scar. I couldn't help but think of that turtle I heard about at dinner.

Last night on the radio I heard in rapid succession The Fleetwoods sing "Come Softly to Me," The Coasters "Along Came Jones" and "Poison Ivy," Floyd Price "Stagger Lee," and Elvis Presley sing an "I'm Evil" that made John Lee Hooker sound Nordic by comparison.

Deep thought for the month (year?). I'm not really a Hemingway Hero or an anti-Yossarian. I'm just sort of oblivious and interested at the same time. And the bugs bite silently in the night. Enough introspection. It's worse than masturbation.

13 November 1966

Went into Saigon today. Xmas card sellers on every corner. French ticklers were also for sale everywhere.

Ran into an odd fellow at a little restaurant I was patronizing. He struck up a conversation with me while I was trying to order. He said he was originally an Englishman, but he was now legally living in New York, working for a California firm, and living actually in Saigon. Yes. He did a very funny thing. Without any preamble he took out a 10 p. piece and made it disappear and then he took it out of his mouth and said when you learn to do that you'll have it made. And with that he bade me farewell.

He's got a point, but I doubt I'll ever practice long enough to learn such a stunt. Typing is tough enough for me, even after all the expensive training the US Army has lavished on me.

Tomorrow I move downstairs and take my rightful place as Dave C.'s assistant. Dave C. and I went out the back gate tonight and had some fried rice.

During the preamble to our meal we were listening to a rock n' roll record that I couldn't place so we went around behind the wall to see what they were playing. The Searchers. While we were back there, a negro who a few minutes earlier had argued loudly with the proprietor about the lack of Coke and the Bierley's Orange Drink that they were serving in its place . . . as all I'd drunk lately was Diet Cola or quinine water it tasted good to me . . . anyhow, he sat down hard and said, "I've got the ass!" While we were behind the partition we heard what sounded like .22 pistol shots and breaking glass. We reentered the room a few minutes later and sat down. Large wet spots on the wall showed where he'd thrown the glasses. Also glass on our table and one broken glass.

The girl served us, looked around and said, "Numbah 10 black man." We agreed. Number ten thou.

14 November 1966, 10:30 p.m.

I'm afraid I'm only capable of a brief entry tonight. I just finished moving all my stuff across the compound again. This time into a room in the office building which I'm sharing with Whit. It was a worse Herculean task than cleaning the Augean Stables, and just as dirty. I took an hour's shower afterwards in which to recuperate.

Old Col. Coldass is gone on R & R this week beginning today, so that will be a relief. He's a first class prick.

15 November 1966, Tuesday, 8:00 p.m.

The movie tonight was "Return of the Mothera."

I'm now fully moved into a room in the office building that I share with Whit. It is a small room with a room fan, hot plate, sink, and adjoining bath facilities. I'm happy to be away from the communal living of a hooch. A little more than two months in country and I've dramatically bettered my personal situation. What wonders the next ten months may have in store!

I still haven't gotten guard duty, but I am on Task Force 5 alert for about seven days. This involves no consumption of alcohol and staying in the area and checking out to go to the latrine. Probably I won't have to carry that worthless rifle around. I hope not. It's a waste of time.

16 November 1966, Wednesday, 7:30 p.m.

I like Whit for a bunk mate. He is a cool boy of 19 whom I've never seen read anything more intellectual than Superman comics, but that is intellectual enough today. He's very verbal and tells the story of a movie he has seen better than the movie people did in the novel, and with great wit and funniness. His big brother is an Idaho (Moscow) grad and a second lieutenant in the Army and a little younger than I am. Has my life stood still? Whit is from California.

My understudy job for Coldass' administrative assistant is going. Not well, just going. I've moved into the office downstairs, and I'm being trained for the job and

I'll take over in about a month. No corpses here to climb over. Besides, no one wants a job with Coldass anyhow. He's a prick head.

17 November 1966, Thursday, 9:30 p.m.

I'm sitting here eating Skippy Creamy Peanut Butter out of the 12 oz. jar with a little blue plastic spoon, digging the peanuttiness out of it and wishing for something to smear it on.

Tomorrow I get a chance at a dry run on the job of Col. Coldass' Administrative Assistant. Monday Dave C. leaves on a three-day R & R, and Coldass returns so that will be a real sample of what life will be like under the Cold Ass himself. I guess I'll survive. Maybe I'll thrive because I've a knack for getting along with fussy old ladies who are disliked by everyone.

The main soda pop available here in the compound is Diet Cola with a label which sounds like an inventory of chemicals and preservatives and tastes worse than last year's embalming fluid. Occasionally root beer is available.

Old Whit is getting short and he'll be gone on a three-day R & R starting tomorrow. He's told me the safe combination several times and I've forgotten it just as many. He's tried to teach me how to make coffee and how to fix the Colonels' rooms in the morning; one likes windows open 'til noon, the other likes windows closed, air conditioner on, etc. Which is which? I'll find out soon enough.

Due to the alert I'm still confined to the compound so I didn't accompany my friends to Cherry Hill tonight when they went for fried rice. Oh well ... I'm getting good Army chow anyhow. And it has been good lately, steak and chicken just about every day, fresh bananas, fresh salads, fresh pineapple, peach pie.

There was a parade scheduled for today, but it was rained out. They mustered us up and we stood in the rain just long enough to get wet and the thing was called off.

The peanut butter has made me very thirsty. I think I'll have some quinine water.

Lately my job has consisted mostly of running around getting copies of things made and doing a little typing and logging and suchlike, and in the main trying to prepare for taking over the job from Dave C. Old Dave is an odd duck. A few years short of 30, he is caught in an apathy which he says has characterized his life. It isn't a drab apathy but a good natured lazy cheerful apathy. He apathied through high school and apathied his way through a job in a factory on an assembly line, and then apathied his way into the Army. Soon he'll apathy his way out of the Army into college. Two of his brothers are college graduates and one is a high school dropout. One is an old 30 with a girl friend, and one, 22, has a wife and two kids. A very odd background but his apathy sort of gives a focus to his life and makes him interesting somehow. He's very capable in his job but not flashy, so I think I'll be able to follow him without being over-shadowed, although he's a much better organizer than I. His memory is as bad if not worse, and his typing is just passable, not brilliant. Though mine is just plain shoddy.

18 November 1966, Friday, 9:00 p.m.

R.W. Apple Jr. yesterday reported in the *New York Times* that Nguyen Cao Ky "is eager to counter the idea

that his government tolerates malfeasance . . ." Note
that he doesn't report that Ky is against malfeasance or
wants to stamp out malfeasance. Just that the "idea" of
its toleration should be countered. I wonder if Ky's
English is good enough to understand the difference. I'm
sure his French or Vietnamese is adequate to the fine
distinction but I feel that the reporter is playing word
games. I almost feel sympathy for the Hitler of Southeast
Asia. I certainly sympathize with his bride.

I work tomorrow and Sunday and Monday. Dave C.
will be gone and I'll have Col. Coldass to myself for three
days. I've been trying to prepare myself, but I can't
really. I hate typing, but I will have to get used to it. I'll
be doing lots of typing, but at least in that job I'll be able
to avoid shorthand which would be a disaster if I had to
take some now.

Maj. Eldman, the officer who hired me for this section,
leaves for the states this weekend.

19 November 1966, Saturday, 10:00 p.m.

I spent the evening looking at Dave C.'s slides.

Tomorrow I have to work all day for Lt. Col. Prince
and I'm quite tired tonight, and I also have to get up in
the morning and make coffee, open the safe, get the
office ready for the day. But I think I'll eat breakfast
tomorrow just for the fresh fried eggs and the bananas.

Time for bed if I'm going to arise at 5:00 to eat
breakfast. I'll probably be a reneger in the end.

20 November 1966, Sunday, 7:30 p.m.

I got through Sunday. I checked the new guard list
posted on the board and believe it or not I'm *not* up in

the next bunch that goes through the 28th of November.
I get Thanksgiving Day off and I'll need it as I'm going to
be alone with Col. Coldass from Monday through Thursday. Shit. Good practice though. I'll have to gird my loins
and hurtle onward.

I typed more today than I'd typed in my life, and I
didn't have any real trouble. My typing was fast and
accurate.

Another weasel-word story by R.W. Apple in today's
New York Times about Premier Nguyen Cao Ky. Who
can keep all these Vietnamese names straight? General
Quang was ousted from IV Corps in the Mekong River
Delta. Who's he? Who can believe it will matter? Apple
says in the headline the ouster is "viewed" as a Ky
victory. In other words, Apple doesn't believe it's any
big deal either. Journalist lice on the dog of war. I don't
know who said it, but I agree.

The pith of it, to me, is Quang opposed U.S. troops in
the Delta. So heave ho, because Ky is an American
puppet just as the Commies allege. Proof enough for me.

No more reveille at 5:30 a.m. now that I'm living in
the section office building. I sleep until 6:15 and get up
and make coffee which I do not drink.

It looks as though I'll complete three months without
guard duty and others in my section have had it five or
six times since I've been here.

Tomorrow starts our section's responsibility for
grounds police. Formation is at 6:30.

It's raining like a pisser right now.

21 November 1966, Monday, 8:30 p.m.

This morning I had police, cleaned up pop cans,
trash, etc. Today was also the last day of the alert and

I'm now off it and without having gone out once. A new
list was put up for guard and I'm on it for Sunday. Damn!
Oh well, it's no big deal, I'm told. I'll just have to grit my
teeth an bear up under the brunt. This morning Lt. Col.
Prince told me that I did an excellent job on Sunday,
which made me feel good but reminded me of what I've
sacrificed in personal terms (Her!) to please the US
Army. After praising me, Lt. Col. Prince left for a week's
tour of the Army stockades in Okinawa. Left me with
Col. Coldass. Today was a breeze and if it goes like that
it'll be no strain. However I expect lots of work tomorrow.

My new job is Administrative Assistant to Coldass
and Prince. I type all the letters and organize all the
incoming correspondence and log all the requests and
complaints and file them and keep track of them and
run errands all over the post and make phone calls and
of course open the safe and make coffee, and all sorts of
other stuff.

22 November 1966, Tuesday, 9:30 p.m.

The Mamas and the Papas are singing their latest
right now on the radio; it's great. "I saw her yesterday . . ."
I wish I had.

I survived another day with Col. Coldass. Only one
more in this cycle and Dave C. will be back from R & R
to cushion me from direct contact with the colonel.

I'm suffering a slight cold in the nose and head and
will shower and go to bed now.

23 November 1966, Wednesday, 10:00 p.m.

I made it through three days with Coldass without
being court-martialed. He is a pain, but I guess I can

stand him for three or four months.

His most annoying trait is his daily consumption of a can of pineapple juice. His prissy manner of pouring it out combined with the loathsome odor of the juice itself permeate my brain. The rest of my life I'll think of Col. Coldass when I smell canned pineapple juice. I hope the acid of it eats out his guts!

Tomorrow is Turkey Day and lots of food and work and rest and sleep. We've got to get up early and police up the area, but then back to bed.

The swimming pool has yet to open and I have yet to get a suit.

Time for bed as I plan to eat breakfast tomorrow.

24 November 1966, Thursday, 8:30 p.m.

Well, it's Turkey Day. I celebrated by taking it easy all day and riding over to the Cholon PX with Whit and Torres in the colonel's air-conditioned sedan and having a turkey sandwich. The mess hall here was too crowded for my liking and anyway I didn't like all the ballyhoo and decoration and all the unannounced and unexplained activities that were taking place. Everybody was supposed to be at the mess hall at the same time.

Whit got some chocolates today that were hand-carried to him by a jet pilot from the States. They were fresh and unmelted, and I'm eating a raspberry one (my favorite) right now.

Dave C. is back from R & R, sunburned and tired. Ready for Coldass.

I'm going to start preparing for guard duty, memorizing, etc.

Whit just read the MOS book aloud to me, a description of our MOS 71C20. It gave us a good laugh, as neither of us can do most of the stuff we're supposed to do.

It was fun today, riding in the colonel's sedan, getting saluted, waving at the peasants and in general rejoicing that I'm assigned to a good place, with comforts, and no dangers, and friends.

25 November 1966, Friday, 8:30 p.m.

I've been pulling out a lot of hair lately working for Coldass, but Dave C. is right to insist that I work with him as I need all the practice I can get.

Whit has been writing letters to a bunch of fourth graders who wrote to him as a class project. The teacher is a friend of his. The letters were great; if Art Linkletter got ahold of them he'd have a new best seller. Whit sat down and answered every one of the 40 kids. He's the last of the nice guys.

Col. Coldass does not like me. He doesn't like anybody and nobody likes him. He's a shithead and an old lady and I'm glad I have training tomorrow and won't have to see him.

Another backwards, upside-down *New York Times* story the other day about Ky. Headline—"Ky Says He Favors Brief Holiday Truce." The text states he's against any truce at all because it will give the Viet Cong a chance to get their shit together.

I wonder if he's as indirect in his communication with Madame Ky?

"Dear Premier, would you like to go to Paris for a week?"

"No, Mai, I'd rather go to Vung Tau for a weekend."

When really he doesn't want to go anywhere. He just wants to knock around Saigon with his cowboy/flyboy cronies and see his family on Sunday whether he needs to or not.

26 November 1966, Saturday, 10:00 p.m.

Today I had training in the morning — one well-presented lecture on the evils of fire by the Tan Son Nhut fire chief, a Vietnamese who speaks very good English. This afternoon I worked.

Spent most of the time eating ice cream in the USO and getting a haircut. The haircut was awful but necessary for guard duty tomorrow.

I ate several dozen shrimp today and they have made me feel odd in the stomach.

Time for bed.

27 November 1966, Sunday, 7:15 p.m.

I'm on guard officially. Actually I'm sitting in the hooch where I'm waiting for 8:30 when I go on guard duty. Guard duty for me is from 9 to 12, and 3 to 6. In between I'm free. I'm on a walking post with lots of lights so I won't be able to drift off. Guard mount was nothing. I wasn't asked any questions or anything. I've worried for two and a half months for nothing, as usual. Will I ever learn?

Tonight I'll eat midnight chow, which will be weird, and then when I get off at 6:00 I can eat breakfast and sleep 'til noon, at which time I'll assume my position in the office. I hope old Coldass will whip out the work in the morning instead of waiting 'til 5:00 as usual.

It's now 8:00 so I'm going to have to start girding my loins for the Herculean task ahead of me.

28 November 1966, Monday, 9:30 p.m.

Guard duty went fine. I counted the minutes and the frogs, lizards and night crawlers. I slept in this morning and feel fine. No sore throat, just sore feet from walking. I saw Dick Van Dyke last night in an episode where he'd forgotten to reserve tickets for the PTA to see the Allen Brady Show.

Right now it's raining quite hard. Mike, a driver, and I went up to the USO in his jeep and ate ice cream and Coke and caught a ride back on the bus, getting a little wet in the process. But the Coke is better than the Tom Collins Mix or the apricot nectar which are the sole drinks in the compound right now.

29 November 1966, Tuesday

It's raining like a son of a bitch tonight, blowing and thundering and lightning. The dry season. I worked late tonight and walked up and burned the trash. I wish it were cold here, like about 75° or 80°. That would be nice.

Today it was announced there would be no more guard duty, that there was an early pay formation tomorrow, that SP4 Whit would now be a SP5, and that SP6 Dave C. would go to Fort Ben as a teacher, per orders. He plans to extend over here to avoid that duty. He won't stay in this section, however. He'll go to MACV or somewhere else that's nice. Big day for everybody, I guess. Ordinary for me, but someday my day will come.

The lights went off, and I'm writing this in the dark. I'm going to get a candle. "Puff the Magic Dragon" is on the radio.

I'm back with some candles. I guess a line blew down. No big deal. The lights just came back on.

30 November 1966, Wednesday, 10:00 p.m.

Today was payday and of course the pay got fouled up. I was just paid Pvt. E-2 pay.

We had our fourth early formation this morning. We get up in the dark, march one half mile, miss breakfast, stand in the mist to hear a ten-second ridiculous speech. The first one told us that we'd been broken into two companies. The second told us that RVN National Day was going to be a big celebration, and a parade would be held in its honor, and that although we weren't forbidden to go downtown, we couldn't go downtown. The third told us, "Be nice GIs; don't beat up the natives." The fourth told us that we looked sharp and that we should stay looking sharp and be proud of being sharp. We all groaned at the realization that we got up early to hear that slop.

No beer at the EM Club tonight, just RC. On payday yet.

The bad weather and the snipers have slowed up progress at Long Binh on construction of the USARV compound up there, so it could even be later than midsummer that we'll move there.

If I've not made contact with My Darling (and Premier Ky's Darling, too, although one mustn't assume) by then it'll be too late. I'd better get moving.

I read an article in a newsmagazine tonight in the

ice-cold library that Premier Ky wooed Mai (My Darling) with poetry. As busy as he is these days, what with fending off coups and all, you'd think he'd not have the time he used to have for Mai. Maybe she hungers for poetry. I'm the boy who can give it to her.

I'll crank out a few, pedal over to their modest bungalow and tack them (one per each visit) to the door. Ought to make quite an impression. One at a time for a few weeks and then I'll call her and give her a chance to respond.

I know that I can find that place if I try. I've seen it before, and I've got the picture I tore out of the *Time Magazine* article—the one with the sandbags and heli-copter. Also, if I peer into the interior, the purple will give it away. Slide up, tack up the poem and slide away into the humid Asian night. Should be nothing to it.

The only thing left to remind me of guard duty are the five mosquito bites that I got. One on my ankle is huge. He must have crawled down my sock and sat there sucking up my blood until he had to crawl down my boot and hunker away.

1 December 1966, Thursday, 11:00 p.m.

I did it! I found the bungalow, but it won't be as easy as I'd thought it would be to carry out my plan—nothing ever is.

Tonight Whit, Mike M. and Mike T. and I went down-town and had chateaubriand, cucumber and tomato salad, Coke, and fried onion rings at the Steak House. Cost—465 p. We then went to a bar and had one beer and caught a ride home in an air-conditioned sedan. We later learned that the sixth passenger was a captain. I made him scoot over to get in. He was very nice.

My job with Col. Coldass isn't easy. With a normal person it would be alright, but he makes it more complicated. Nothing I can do though. I will learn discipline; to keep from whanging him over the head requires an iron will. If I disgrace myself again I'll end up in a stockade so I *must* walk the straight and narrow.

I wish he didn't drink that nasty pineapple juice.

2 December 1966, Friday, 9:30 p.m.

Tonight's movie was "Frankenstein Conquers the World." Here in the compound near the incinerators is the fence separating us, the US soldiers, from the little Vietnamese village immediately on the other side. When, after dinner, I walk to the PX with an orange in my left hand, the little kids press against the wire fence and cry something like "Yo Yo Yo" and point to their hearts, wanting of course the orange. I don't give it to them. They aren't skinny children, they look well fed, but even so, it's hard not to give them the orange. But it is "them" and the orange is singular and who should I choose to give it to?

Sunday Dave C. and I are going out to Mama-san's for dinner and I plan to take lots of pictures of her family, husband, home, etc. Also she will serve real RVN food which will be hard to eat probably but which I'll try for the sake of being a guest and all that stuff. And not hurting her feelings because she's very sensitive.

Dinner last night and the few minutes we spent in the bar were a side of Saigon that I hadn't seen before, although everyone says it is there. For dessert I had papaya that was very sweet and good. Looked like a large slab of cantaloupe and tasted best with salt. The cucumber, tomato, something else salad was sort of Korean-like. Very different. The crazy red bright neon signs had the streets lit up with dozens of names: Eden Roc, Queen Bee, Cherry, Bar 25, Kings, Cheap Charlies, Crazy Cat, Venus, Angel, Snow, Airborne, Oceans, Flowers, Royal Rendezvous, Tu Do.

Danny Boy just played on the radio.

Whit and I plan to go to a steam bath and massage place tomorrow, a straight place, no extra services. And then dinner and a few bars, I guess. Those places are very interesting. Bar girls all over the place, they speak good English, too. They wear very strong perfume and are very commercial. Very business-like. No leaving the bars, no short times. Just conversation and lots of Saigon tea for them. In the place we were, there was a little boy about six in a little uniform serving drinks for tips, and a sad little boy he was. Long face and sad eyes. We had Pabst Blue Ribbon and left.

There was a rumor that one of the new stenos, Joe D., will join me downstairs as my partner in defamation of old Coldass. He's a good boy, and a hard worker, besides being Italian Catholic, so we'd get along well and do a fine job, I think.

A new program has been inaugurated by which each of us gets one additional afternoon of PT, or personal time, off per week. That will give us about two days a week off, which isn't supposed to be possible over here, but is something I won't complain about. At all.

A moth just flew into the hot wax of the candle I'm typing by (the electricity is off) and fluttered the wax over himself searching for the light that he then found to be too hot for his pleasure, so he bumbled off, wings burning, into the shadows. I hope such a fate is not in store for me here, in this Asian Gay Paree.

3 December 1966, Saturday, 11:00 p.m.

I have thought of you often
In silk
Admiring yourself
In mirrors
Purple silk.
With burgundy nipples
Peeking out.
Make yourself available to me
Juggle your schedule
Around
Make excuses and lie.
I think sometimes
Of making you mine
Forever
But it wouldn't be right.

I pedaled my ass over to Mai's Bungalow (a good name for some sort of an establishment) and affixed a poem to her front door. It wasn't a herculean task once I found the place. There were a couple of armed guards— ARVN's with carbines, though I'm no weapons expert. They looked menacing but when they started holding hands they weren't as scary.

I spent most of the day downtown, at least from 2:00 on into the evening. I finally found some record stores and bought a record by The Animals for 200 p. and a record by Georges Brassens for 250 p. He sings "Le

Trompettes de la Renommee," "Jeanne," and "L'Assas-sinat." The Animals sing "Bring it on Home To Me," "Halleluyah I Love Her So," "For Miss Caulker," and "Mess Around." It's on the Hongkong label, a bootleg outfit.

Downtown continues to be one different scene after another: a four-legged man begging; a blind guitarist blues type singer with a hat on the pavement.

The shoe shine boys have a chalk-on-the-shoe gambit. If you don't accept a shine they chalk your shoes and then expect you to pay for a shine. They are dummies. The hell with them.

I ate two meals downtown. Lobster, charcoal broiled, with watercress and tomato salad, Coke, and French bread. Rib of beef in wine sauce with onions and mush-rooms, French bread, Coke, hot beef consommé.

I'm very tired and will be going downtown tomorrow for a short while and then out to Mama-san's for dinner with Dave C. So I'll now take a shower and to bed I'll hie myself.

4 December 1966, Sunday, 9:00 p.m.

I spent another big day downtown. Shopping with George Miller. I was afraid that we wouldn't be able to go down due to some mortaring the area got last night. Nothing near us except noise, but some action a few miles away. No gooks were allowed in the compound today.

On the way there, I dropped off another poem at Mai's. The text follows:

I'm all alone
On a Great Plain
Circling above me are ravens,
Their beaks and talons
Dripping blood.
The plain is immense
And offers no place of refuge
I am naked
And the ravens come nearer
Shrieking with blood lust.
I waken thinking
Of you.
Is this dream an augury
Of our love?

Last night I finally got to see more of those whore-houses out the back gate. Whit and I left Mike T. and Mike M. at a house to get blowjobs and we were walking on in through the back gate. The MPs were checking passes so we had to go back and warn Torres to get out his phony pass and have it ready as he wasn't signed out properly. We had to crawl through a few places to find them. Old women and little kids kept catching our sleeves: Number One Girl. We found Mike T. and he got through the gate fine. Those houses were incredible. Dark. Musty. Muddy all around. When we'd go in an old lady would lock the door and trot out the choices. Some of them looked OK but I wasn't having any. One girl was sitting on her bed with her dress pulled up around her twat, said Whit. I didn't see her as I was around the corner and I had a hell of a time dragging him along.

Last night there was a lot of noise and shit flying and I woke up for about five minutes. Everyone else was up for about two hours crawling in the grass and skulking in the bunkers.

Today I rode around in a cyclo, went downtown, shopped through a million shops and found all sorts of stuff.

Earlier today a general ripped through the building, General Seitz, and was displeased at the small staff on duty. We'll probably start working weekends from now on.

I haven't gotten a steam bath and massage yet. Also, due to the alert, I didn't get to go to Mama-san's as she lives way out on the highway and we were cautious about it.

I got the colonel's sedan because his driver is one of my good friends. Mike T. The original dirty mouth and a good guy who excuses all of his shortcomings with a "I'm too short to whatever." I'm still treated fine, I know not why for, but I am.

5 December 1966, Monday, 8:30 p.m.

There's a new schedule from now on due to the shake-up by the general yesterday. Work until 7:30 every other night. Work every other Saturday afternoon and every fourth Sunday. We'll have one afternoon off per week to compensate and take our full two and one-half hours to eat during the day. It'll be about the same. Still plenty of time to ourselves.

Today I left some secret documents lying around and good old Dave C. covered for me. He is a prince among men. Mama-san said today that the VC were number ten to keep us from eating up her boucoup chop chop. Her words.

Tonight José G., one of the clerks, was in my room washing the coffee pot. He held up my shoe brush and asked me what it was. I said that it was my shoe brush and that he should leave it well alone. Later I looked up and he was scrubbing the coffee pot with it. What the fuck are you doing that for, I politely asked. That's my shoe brush. He said, I thought you were kidding. What a dum dum. Tomorrow I'm going to tell his officers that he cleaned up the pot with my brush and they will puke. Like I said: Who wants to brush his shoes with a brush that was used to clean a coffee pot? Who? Not me! José is a dum dum.

I've been riding in cyclos lately when going downtown. They are cycles with a sort of a basket on the front into which can jam two people. Let's hope they are friends because they will sit close together. It's a ride right on the street level with the fumes of the gas hitting one right in the face. Bicycles towering high in the air like draft horses. The cyclo moves fast through all the holes in the street traffic and the driver sits behind and makes lewd noises at all the girls that go past on cycles or bikes and he chews beetle nut or whatever and keeps up a constant monologue about the number one girl that he will procure for the lucky GI.

The rackets flourish in Saigon. The one I've encountered personally is the western-clad sharpie trying to buy MPC or greenbacks. Follow me, Joe, and we'll see, he says as he sneaks off into the crowd. I never went far along behind.

One of the other rackets is the old man with a piece of paper in English or French, depending on the customer. He sidles up and says, you speak French? When he finds out English he hands across a piece of paper about how the French have killed his family and taken his fortune, etc. For the French he has the reverse about the Americans. Others around town I haven't seen yet are: woman with a dead baby, saying it was killed by American bombing; one-armed woman who lost her arm to American bombing; man with no nose, same story; old woman around the corner from the Ambassador Hotel, with no hair, no teeth, calls all the GIs "Handsome"; old mama-sans with children leading them around asking for alms are common sights; one beggar is twisted all out of shape and walks on his hands on which he wears shower shoes. One averts the eyes when confronted with most of these creatures.

There is an alert tonight. We are confined to the hooch. Big Deal. They expect something somewhere will happen. They'll be wrong, of course.

The weather here has been wintry lately, 70-ish at night and only warm in the day. In the morning it's quite chilly. And a blanket is a necessity.

6 December 1966, Tuesday, 9:30 p.m.

Somebody played a Dylan tape today. "John Brown Went Off to War" is a good song, but I think it is an obvious effort of someone who hadn't been to war. Most of war is office work, and I think a song about the pressures to conform to ARMY WAYS and the mental changes brought about because of this pressure is needed. After all, war's effects are mostly mental. Most Army veterans have all their limbs intact. With modern methods hardly any limbs are lost. Casualties are either dead or in salvageable shape.

Finally got to look at the *New York Times* which had not come in several days. I giggled audibly reading

Saturday's paper. US troops will enter the Mekong Delta soon. Of course they will. When Quang got shoved, it was only a matter of time. Corruption? Was that the issue? Ha! I love Ky's statement, "The people say I'm honest." Not "I am honest!" And who were these people anyhow. If he were corrupt and rich, wouldn't he and Mai and their six brats live like pashas? Maybe not, maybe he's too smart and maybe he prefers to be on the Tan Son Nhut base, protected and near his beloved getaway plane, living in his humble bungalow and driving his beloved 1960 Ford Falcon.

B-girls and whores are migrating in droves to the Mekong Delta to gird their loins for the US incursion. My Darling Mai was a stewardess; isn't that only one step from a B-girl and two from a whore?

It isn't raining here anymore. The dry season is here, but it is also cool. Whit gave me two sets of his jungle fatigues and tomorrow I will have them altered to fit and have the stripes and name tags sewn on. A pair of jungle boots and I'll look like a real trooper. The reason for the changes isn't just appearance, but they are much cooler and roomier. The boots are lighter and more comfortable.

Tomorrow I plan to go the the PX at Cholon and look around and buy coffee. Tonight was the first night of the new schedule and it wasn't much different. The officers just sat and waited out the time. And I did much the same.

HAPPY PEARL HARBOR DAY!
7 December 1966, Wednesday, 9:00 p.m.

In an article on Sarah Lawrence a quote from Henry Adams: "The chief wonder of education is that it does not ruin everybody concerned in it. . . ."

Today I took the jungle fatigues in to have them altered and will pick them up in three days. Next I will get a pair of jungle boots, somehow.

> If I had a need to die
> I would wish to drown
> In your dark eyes
>
> I would go down three times
> And more
> Willingly
> To become a part of you,
> Consumed by your darkness,
> Melted into your dark flesh.
>
> Living and wishing to live
> I have found another way to drown
> And another way to melt with
> You.

Still another poem for My Darling.

8 December 1966, Thursday, 9:30 p.m.

I guess the high point of this day was the discovery that tree frogs live in the bushes around the building. I noticed a large yellow one this morning by the light of the porch lamp. It hung by its suckered feet, yellow like a leaf, in the dewy drops of moisture that it drinks. It should never lack for food as the bushes and the air nearby are full of bugs attracted by the porch lamp. This evening I went outside and turned the light on to see if it was there yet. On the brown main stem of the bush was a small white tree frog with black eyes open at me, and a white throat moving in and out, in and out, as small insects crawled near it, undisturbed. Its long, prehensile toes were wrapped about the stem, enabling it to look at me from a near horizontal position. I believe I remember from a *National Geographic* article that some species are quite poisonous. I will leave them alone. Look, not touch. I'd like to photograph them, but don't have the equipment.

Tonight we celebrated Charlie B.'s 20th birthday with vanilla ice cream and by singing happy birthday to him. Outside on the corner a hydrant gushed, broken off by an errant RVN driver.

Today I marched in a parade. We saluted a bunch of times and marched off in the rain. All of my fans (who think I walk funny) were hanging out of the second story windows of the office building to see me march. Everybody was so bad that they couldn't spot me except for my glasses.

9 December 1966, Friday, 8:30 p.m.

The high point of my day, or low point actually, was the discovery that the locals view tree frogs as great delicacies. Or as they put it: make good chop chop. The mama-sans were weeding the garden when I noticed that one of them had three small frogs held up by the feet. Three small brown tree frogs with suction cup feet and squeerk squeerk noises. Tonight when I came back from the library I walked up to the bush and even in the dark I could see the frog, and as I looked he leaped from dry brown branch to leaf. Black eyes gleamed like obsidian

drops enameled on moist brown leather, mouth moving
open-shut, open-shut. And as I left him and went in the
door to the stairs he let out one long squeerk. And I
looked back at him and he sat bobbing on a leaf, recently
landed from a hop.

Lt. Col. Prince in a personal letter I typed for him
described his promotion to lieutenant colonel from
major to a friend: This old blind sow found an acorn.
He's a Georgia boy and quite folksy. A very good guy.

Guess what . . . Old Coldass was put in for a command
so he should be out of the office by the end of December.
His lack of field experience is what's standing in the way
of promotion, and until he gets the field experience he'll
stay what he is. So I hope soon to be rid of him and his
pineapple juice. Yeah, yeah. I found this out today typing
a personal letter for him. I almost cheered. Dave C.
couldn't understand why I was so ebullient so early in
the morning but when I told him he well understood.
What a break for me!

10 December 1966, Saturday, 11:00 p.m.

Brown body scented
With coconut oil
Smooth soft bottom
Soft smooth top
With two small exceptions
Coming to me

Soon?
I keep wanting
To look at your right leg

And test your credibility.
Perhaps I will look
At your left as well.

Don't struggle
And I won't hurt you . . .

This evening Whit and the two Mikes and I went downtown and had dinner at the Lotus (after I ground out and delivered another poem for my obsidian-eyed princess). I had frog legs, French bread, lettuce and tomato salad, and San Miguel beer. A very fine dinner. The frog legs were very tender and sweet and had many tiny bones with sweet meat on them. They were French fried and I enjoyed them. I worked for Coldass today and sat around all day, until 5 o'clock, that is, and then he handed me two letters that I'll have to type early tomorrow.

After we had dinner we went crawling through the bars and I had one 50 p. Coke. One bar was playing the Everly Brothers album with "Kathy's Clown" on it. Very nice sound.

I work with Prince tomorrow and hope that I'll be able to goof off.

Today Dave C. was supposed to work but he was too hung over from last night to do anything except sleep. Last night I drank about one tenth of my drink and threw it out the window and had a sardine sandwich and went to bed.

Tonight the tree frog was sitting in the bush as usual. Every time I see him I notice new things about him. He's quite an unusual piece of flesh. He's like a miniature sculpture in grey-brown jade.

11 December 1966, Sunday, 7:30 p.m.

Today I ate dinner at the Golf Club de Saigon. Didn't catch a glimpse of My Darling. I'd not expected to. It's now closed to GIs, but we walked in the servants entrance and no one stopped us, though the main gates had boucoup guards. Dave C. and I had steak, fries, tomato and lettuce salad, and Coke, with papaya, ripe and with small black seeds burrowed in the orange sweet meat. 220 p. for one meal. Cheap and good.

Today was a big day, and I typed all day, it seemed. I get next Saturday afternoon off, also Sunday, and I plan to start writing a long story that I've got in mind. I don't think I'll have the energy to pursue it far, though.

Whit will be gone next Saturday for home. Soon both Mikes and a bunch of officers will follow and I'm becoming an old timer. Soon, in a month or so, I guess I'll be up for SP4. And I'll have all the status of one million other SP4s.

My tree frog is fine. Yesterday I had to climb in the second story window because Coldass locked us out of the building.

12 December 1966, Monday, 9:30 p.m.

Whit leaves this Saturday for California. He's from LA or thereabouts.

I've been bitter lately about the Army, especially Coldass who, thank God, is supposed to leave this month.

13 December 1966, Tuesday, 8:00 p.m.

They have been installing a new phone system here that is very complicated and full of bugs. One can't call out or be called with any certainty.

I took the time to deliver yet another verse for my polka-dot scarved stew.

> Lean forward
> Into me
> My polka-dot kerchiefed
> Darling
> Dragon Lady
> Of Vietnam.
> I'll woo you
> With Poetry.
> I write 'em
> You read 'em
> Then we'll see what happens.
> How can your heart
> Not swell with love
> For me?
> You're only human.
> The fact that you were
> A stewardess
> Gives me hope.

14 December 1966, Wednesday, 8:30 p.m.

I'm sitting here belching a chocolate sundae I just ate and feeling the ceiling fan blow down on my just-showered body. There is an alert on tonight, but I'm not in it as I don't live in a hooch. Whit took a picture yesterday of a gook drinking out of a faucet on the shower unit next to our office. Whit kept yelling "Charlie, Charlie" at the gook until he looked up and Whit shot the picture of him. He was displeased and will probably

be especially nasty for a while at nights on his VC raids.
(Ha ha.)

My friends don't find their whorehouse experiences
very satisfying, but still I'm tempted to try again because
my chances at My Darling seem nil and I've made no
real move. I've waited for the ravens to feed me and
they've been busy elsewhere. How can I get to her?

I don't mind that he has access to her while I don't.
After all he *is* her husband. Or at least they are billed as
husband and wife. Where is his French wife? At the
bottom of a rice paddy or in a Paris condo? Or maybe in
some odd corner of Saigon. It would be interesting to
ferret her out and ask her a few well-chosen questions.

"Tell me, ex-Madame Ky, what are your thoughts on
Cowboy Ky and his stewardess? They are raising your
children and you are languishing here like a castoff old
boot. What are your feelings?

"Really? You harbor no resentment? That's hard for
me to believe. You're glad to not be in the limelight."

Her upper lip with its incipient moustache trembles
at my Torquemada techniques. I have her on the run
now. Now I get the dirt!

But I haven't found her yet. Where did she go, and
were the proper papers submitted to the proper authorities? Nobody but me has asked? That's hard to believe.

I read in the *New York Times* that Vietnamese women
are frequently in control from behind the scenes. I'm
becoming convinced that Vietnam is being run by an ex-
stewardess. If true, that would explain a lot about the
state of things here.

Nguyen Cao Ky must be her sex slave, something
like that. Flying around the world and catering to foreign
tastes, Mai learned techniques and tricks by which to

enthrall a simple flyboy, to make him her puppet. Ky even alludes to his dependency on her in his press releases. He doesn't mention sex, but who would? This all seems reasonable to me. I'm amazed it hasn't occurred to any of the journalists sitting in the Saigon bars. Or maybe it has and there is a conspiracy of silence. That would explain it. Maybe those acres of censored white space in the Saigon newspapers would have contained a few column inches of speculations on Premier Ky being led around by his short Asian dick by Mai, the Westernized ex-stew! It's all falling into place now. It makes sense to me. I'm not completely stupid.

I don't like the image of them unzipping each other's jump suits and collapsing to the floor to writhe around in a sexual manner. But with a house full of children, that actually must be seldom.

The lack of eagerness and enthusiasm of the RVN whores is much commented upon. Whit says that when he is fucking them they carry on conversations with girl friends, knitting little garments, cooking dinner, etc. They do talk with girl friends he says. He says that when he's home with an American girl and she starts moving and crawling over and around him, it'll shock his morality at first, but he'll rapidly readjust. I explained culture shock and anomie to him and he said he understood and would compensate. He said that the girls (whores) in Bangkok were nice girls who were very eager and played little games and were very much fun. The RVN whores rarely even pretend to grunt and groan and get any pleasure from the fucking. Mostly they just lie there. They don't shower very often and the ones I've seen are very plain girls.

The bar girls are very expensive and cost very much.

Way too much. The whorehouses are tempting and are very unsafe places for me to be, sexually. If one is alone they can be quite dangerous, and I stay with at least one other fellow. Whit will soon be leaving and there is no one else I would trust to go into a place with me and not strand me for a girl, so I've probably made my last trip into a whorehouse. Therefore I *must* seek no more substitutes. I must pursue My Darling. I must develop my alternate plan.

> My sweet entrepreneur
> Efficient and competent
> You dragged yourself
> Out of the muck and mire
> Of circumstance
> And made something
> Of yourself
> You were but an air-bound waitress
> Now you run an empire.
> I like you now
> But I wish I could have seen
> The teenager you were
> Adoring, responsive, passionate.
> Now that I think about it
> You are like that now.

15 December 1966, Thursday, 10:00 p.m.

I went to bed tonight at 7:00 as I was quite tired from a week of going to bed late and getting up very early. Now I feel very rested and clean from the cool shower I just took.

Today Whit, the two Mikes and I went to the PX at

Cholon taking most of the morning off (I managed to fit in a quick trip over to My Darling's to deposit yet another expression of my feelings for her). Very pleasant. Of course we took Col. B.'s sedan. And I did get saluted. Dumb MPs. I had a cheeseburger and a chocolate shake at the snack bar and bought a book, *Drive, He Said*, by Jeremy Larner, which is sort of a combination of *V* and *Cat's Cradle.* It's folky and quotes folk songs and other good songs like "She was going down the hill/at ninety miles an hour/when the chain/on her bicycle broke./ They found her in the grass/With the sprocket up her ass/And her pretty tits punc/tured by a spoke." Also he quotes "Talking Union" and it sounds like modern poetry. *Drive, He Said* is a book about basketball the way *The Natural* is about baseball. As a legend of America. There is a description of the players washing their cocks in the shower afterwards as ritual, purification ceremony, etc., that is very fine.

I bought a Plastic Man comic today that is better than Spider Man. Old Plas'is stretching out on page two to catch a piano that's about to fall on a bunch of little kids from above and he says "This stretch also comes in handy when the butter's at the other end of the table!" and he's all stretched out of shape, arms about 100 feet long, filling the frame. A girl then asks for his signature on her hand; she won't wash it for a year she says. He replies: "I'd rather not encourage unsanitary habits!" Maybe a little corny, but the old ones. . . .

16 December 1966, Friday, 8:00 p.m.

Only tomorrow morning left and I'll have one and one-half days off. This has been a big week and I'm glad to see it almost gone. I've gotten fairly good at the formats of letters, DFs, memos, etc., by now even though my typing is still shaky.

Sunday is the office Christmas party. We've purchased four cases of booze ($125) for 38 people. Quite a bit, I think. 80 steaks, two each. I don't plan to drink anything but ginger ale and Pepsi which we'll have plenty of, too. My stomach is still sensitive from last summer and I don't want to ruin my day off by puking all over my own shirt front.

17 December 1966, Saturday, 11:00 p.m.

Today I was in the sack reading *Now Comes Theodora* by Daniel Ford and the song "The Gold Rush is Over and the Bum's Rush is On" came on the radio and it was sung by Hank Snow. That's not terribly exciting, I guess, but that's not the end of the story (joke). This evening Mike M. asked if I wanted to go see the Hank Snow Show (first I'd heard about it) so we went and it was fine, and Old Hank sang "When the Gold Rush . . ." And lots of other good songs: "Movin' On," some Jimmy Rogers songs, "Orange Blossom Special," and he did some fancy guitar picking. He played only an acoustic guitar. His voice was very old-timey and perfect for the sentimental songs he sang: "Roses for Christmas." His son sang religious songs with his wife, accompanied by an auto-harp which he (Jimmy) played like Mother Maybelle Carter. All in all, it was very entertaining. We sat on the ground very close and could see very well. Old Hank is a little dried up old man with a hair piece and a very sincere folksy personality. Chubby Wise played fiddle and was very weepy and sentimental.

Tomorrow's the big party and I plan to eat as much as possible and hide away a few fifths of liquor for later consumption. Sneaky, but who will notice the loss of so little out of so much.

18 December 1966, Sunday, 6:00 p.m.

The party has come and gone and the steak and French bread (toasted) was good, fine, even. I cut out on the conviviality, except for about 20 minutes when I was trapped by Coldass into a rather one-sided discussion of skiing. I hunted back into my past for any knowledge I had of the subject for intelligent comments to make on his skiing in Europe.

Today I finished *Now Comes Theodora* which, though described as a kook book on the cover, is about people that I came to care about before the end of the book, which was optimistic for a change.

I just found a tiny translucent ant crawling on the lapel of my blue discolored-by-the-mama-san short-sleeved shirt. (Too many adjectives.)

I still see the tree frog almost every day. He's quite a little friend in a way and I turn on the light every morning and look for him among the dewy leaves and dark.

I was just warned that if I don't take off I'll have KP soon, so I'll type a little longer and then take off (*di di*).

19 December 1966, Monday, 10:00 p.m.

Work is as usual. I got tired at 4:00 tonight and quit to prepare dinner of steaks and French bread toasted on the charcoal grill. Good. Took us two cans of lighter fluid to start the fire. We drank about a case of pop, left over from the party yesterday. I've still got a case hidden in my locker which I plan to ignore for a few days.

Old Whit leaves tomorrow, instead of earlier, still in time to be home for Christmas.

20 December 1966, Tuesday, 8:00 p.m.

I had a brief go around with the sergeant major today about promotion to SP4. All of my friends are up for it already. Those who came over here the same time I did. But he won't put me up for it as it isn't strictly legal. But it's done by everyone except him, I guess. He says he doesn't want anybody telling him how to run the office, etc. Screw him. I won't mention it again if I stay a PFC the rest of the time over here. Probably he won't let me go past February or March without a promotion though. I shouldn't have taken it for granted.

I just went downstairs to get some finger nail clippers and I looked for my tree frog and there he sat, white throat pulsing. I walked on and a sudden movement in a bush further along made me look more closely. Another tree frog, identical to the other one, it seemed, sat there and jumped.

Old Whit left this morning, though he should have left last night. He goes out on the plane at three a.m. Wednesday. I'll miss that guy, as he was the best friend that I'd made over here. Mike M. leaves tomorrow night and Dave and I will see him off at the airport, I imagine. Then Dave leaves the first week in January.

21 December 1966, Wednesday, 8:00 p.m.

I just heard the roar of the plane which is taking Mike M. back to the states. I went out to the airport, hitching a ride in the back of a truck, to see him off, pat him on the back, and wish him farewell. The place was crowded with 130 soldiers in khakis, E-2s on up, a quiet group restlessly moving around the large high-ceilinged room. I'd just eaten dinner, but the smells of fried rice made me quite hungry and wish that I had some p. with me so I could eat. When I left it was dark. I'd decided to tack two poems to My Darling's door tonight.

> I would love to knock you up
> To pump you full of seed
> To cause your belly to become
> A swollen brown watermelon.
> But no force of circumstances
> Compels me to merely
> Pump pump pump
> No swollen belly for you
> No hot wet swollen pussy.
> Their delights are yours
> For the asking.
> Lucky you.

As I walked along the road, another truck slowed down and I jumped aboard and in three minutes was back in the compound. It's silent and lonely around here without Mike or Whit, who were in the building most of the time. I can't help but think again and again about my sweet brown princess.

> I would love to fuck my way
> Across America with you.
> In cheap motels.
> You'd see a lot of ceilings
> And floors, too.

Not Motel 6, or Holiday Inn
But those with names
Like
Golden Rule
WIlliam Tell
Lucky Motel
Rain-Bow-Inn
Green Town Auto Court.
Heartland of America
You looking like Claudia Cardinale
In *The Professionals.*
Sweaty, dusty
Hard-used and eternally desirable.

I think soon I'll have to give Her a call and fess up as
the author of all those poems to her ethereal beauty. I
anticipate the moment, but my joy is leavened by some
fear and trepidation.

Billy Graham was here today but I didn't get to go as
I had to hold down the office while Coldass and Dave C.
attended. Coldass continues to be a pain in mine. I hope
he embarks to the north as planned!

Read in the *Saigon Guardian* that Saigon's Mayor
was apprehended with a submachine gun, drunk and
shooting it, down the waterfront. *The Guardian* will be
rewarded, rumor has it, by having its publication rights
suspended. Ah, the joys of defending liberty in this
"bastion of democracy."

22 December 1966, Thursday, 9:30 p.m.

Well, Dave C. and Mike T. and I just got back from
the USO where we had milk shakes and orange juice to
wash it down.

Today the sergeant major said that Charlie B., Joe D., and Ed C. could move into the building, so apparently they don't plan to move us out soon to make offices from the rooms. The sergeant major is a rockhead, but I can't help but like him anyway. He just extended over here until April so I guess I won't be making SP4 for some time. He extended so that he'd get Hawaii as his next assignment. That's his home and the place he will retire this year, 1967, that is.

Today I forgot to get clean sheets so I bullied the mama-san into washing them for me. I started in the morning. Every time I saw her I'd poke her in the shoulder with my long bony finger and say "Washie washie" whilst pointing with the other hand at the sheets. All day she said no washie washie, but by the end of the day she'd washed them. Then she came up to me and brought me into the little room and pointed at the foot locker Whit left behind. She's been trying to talk me out of it for several days. So I said OK and she was very pleased.

With all these guys leaving I've accumulated all sorts of stuff: two alarm clocks, wooden hangers, seven pairs of jungle fatigues, four sheets, an air mattress, an extra duffle bag, this month's *Playboy,* and God knows what else.

Time to go check the tree frog, take a shower and read for 50 seconds before falling asleep.

23 December 1966, Friday, 10:30 p.m.
THE EVE OF THE EVE

I tried to call My Darling, but when I finally got through, all the satisfaction I got was a "Not here, she not here. She never here. No call anymore." I dialed again and got the same response. Poems and telephone calls won't work. I'll have to develop my other plan.

I'm sitting listening to the "Little Drummer Boy," one of the first Christmas songs that I bought on record, a song I really like, even if it is the story of the widow's mite told in children's terms.

I get to sleep in tomorrow, I guess, though someone will most likely wake me up. Coldass will want me to do something for him. Like kiss his dead cold ass. Well he's human too, I guess. Tonight he wanted me to give up my dinner hour to type a DF for him. I slopped through it and walked out of the office and didn't come back until 9:00, I had the key to the office with me. I saw the Gregory Peck/Sophia Loren movie, "Arabesque," which I enjoyed. It was quite frothy and on the same theme as "Ipcress," but not as well done. Peck, though good, is no Caine.

Tomorrow I might go to the Bob Hope show just a little ways from here on the bus. It might be a gas, to quote Sinatra/Davis.

Ed C. is my roommate now that Whit is gone. Ed won't be able to stand the pace of getting up at 5:45 every morning for long though, and he'll probably move out.

24 December 1966, Saturday, 9:00 p.m.

Went to the Bob Hope Christmas show today, primarily in hopes of catching a glimpse of My Darling. Did see her, but with her goggle-like sunglasses, the Air Marshal, their baby and his five little half-breeds, and the 10 million spectators, no real contact was made. No drinking of each other's souls across an ignorant crowd. Only a fool would go to a Bob Hope show with romance in his heart, a fool for love.

The Hope Show, replete with Joey Heatherton, was set up on a large muddy field directly in the sunlight from which I received a mild burn. The show — jokes about coin-op machine guns to help lower defense spending plus the usual propaganda thrown in: ignore those long-haired beatniks at Berkeley, 99.999% of the people are for you, as if the Berkeleyites are against the American soldiers and wish their deaths, when the reverse is true.

Nobody really takes Bob Hope or Westy seriously. Old Westmoreland spoke too. Then "Silent Night" was sung by Anita Bryant, and while it was being sung the APs were chasing off the Vietnamese children trying to see the show. The APs wielded rifles, the kids were barefoot and carried pop bottles they were retrieving. Joey was sexy-looking, but her singing was embarrassingly overdone. Monroe was the last of the blonds who were successful at that sort of thing. Miss World was very articulate and beautiful, her presence here very unpopular at home in India, of course. As if it means she approves of the war.

After the Hope show, I went to see Cardinal Spellman. Very colorful in his robes, a feeble-appearing man, assisted by several priests with his dressing. I could see green jungle boots peeking from under his robes.

I got a lot closer to the Cardinal than I did to Joey Heatherton, or the spoiled brat in her Go-To-Hell jump suit. My Darling. My Stewardess War Baby.

25 December 1966, Sunday

I tried to buy some Coke from the slopes selling it. I
had only a 100-piaster note as my smallest change, so I
gave it to them for two Cokes plus my change. They
wouldn't give me any change, claiming that was the full
price, though we both knew that it was 20 p. each. Later
the slope came around to collect the bottle. I was
standing with one foot on it, apparently absentmindedly.
She tugged on it and I ignored her. She pointed and said
mine, mine. I countered with "What?" Every time she
said anything I said what and pretended to misunder-
stand her. These people are sharp and some people
think they shouldn't be treated as if they are equals, but
coddled and given preferential treatment. Well, I don't.
She cheated me. And I made her try to get the bottle
back throughout the entire show. Caused quite a dis-
turbance, too. She, the poor put-upon native, and me,
the dastardly American bully. We played our roles to
the full.

26 December 1966, Monday, 8:00 p.m.

Tomorrow I have CQ runner (27) from 1730 to 0600
the next morning (5:30-6:00; I finally learned some of the
Army times). It consists mostly of reading and writing
letters. When I get off I get to sleep until noon. And then
up and at 'em.

Ky has been scaring Lodge again with threats of a
U.S. tour for him or his wife. His twenty-four-year-old
wife has hopes of TV appearances, probably dreams of a
TV series. Her English will need some sprucing up. I can
imagine Premier Ky on Johnny Carson talking about his

heroes, Adolf Hitler and M. Kemal. Go over like a turd in a punch bowl. What would Mai do? "Coffee, tea, or . . ."

28 December 1966, Wednesday, 12:30 a.m.

I'm sitting here in the orderly room of Admin. Co. I'm the CQ runner which means I answer the phone from now until 4:30 a.m. when I wake up the CQ.

I slept from 9:00 until now on an Army cot with a flak jacket as my pillow. Tomorrow morning I'll eat breakfast, then sack out.

I'm about half asleep but hope I'll wake up more.

My nose and forehead are peeling from sunburn and pieces of skin are flaking off and falling down to the desk.

I'm listening to the radio. Recorded Merry Christmas and Happy New Year from wives and parents to servicemen in Vietnam. I understand the DJ but all the people enunciate so poorly they all sound alike. KSWO Oklahoma was the station the people were calling. No wonder I couldn't understand them.

We expected an alert tonight, but the brass must have taken pity for it's too late now to have one. All it means is that I'd check out weapons and a bunch of guys would crawl through the grass all night. And I'd then check the weapons back in. The music this time of night is good. Brenda Lee singing "Coming On Strong" is on right now.

Last evening I had a "friendly" argument with some guys here in the orderly room. They're convinced "slopes are lower than animals" and should all be killed. They said they can't be trusted, etc. I said they were ethnocentric, which pissed them off. I tried to explain the elementary, that we're meddlers in their country and all that. They weren't having any.

Sometimes I joke that these goddamn slopes should learn English so I can understand them 'cause we bought this country and paid for it and that's the least they could do. That's just me being irritating, but these creeps really believe it. They use much higher standards to judge the Vietnamese than they do to judge themselves. They're convinced that they could convince me of the people's lowness by showing me pictures of Vietnamese atrocities on Americans. It wouldn't move me. I've got my mind made up. It's their country, we're the inter-lopers, invited or not. We've set up puppets like Ky and here we roost until, like the passenger pigeons, we'll be extinct.

The Mau Mau were brutal but they drove out the British, and the French left here. Colonialism is dead though it dies slow and hard, but these fellows think our being here is a favor (selfless) from which we gain nothing. The American reputation suffers from our being here, but in other ways our country's interests, such as the munitions people, benefit.

Xmas greetings from LA are now on.

Some Americans here are very culture bound, others like the people and country and almost disappear into the ethnos. That's a naive observation but it still amazed me that no matter how wrong-headed an American I parody, a real one, worse, is bound to turn up. I can't change them and they don't affect my point of view, except to reinforce it and piss me off.

10:00 p.m.

I got through CQ runner without any catastrophes or anything. I went to the USO tonight for ice cream. And I listened to the juke box, "Younger Girl on My Mind," etc. for five cents a song. Dave C. played bingo.

Old Coldass leaves here the second of January. Hip hip hooray.

I'm not scheduled to work either day this weekend and plan to take a steam bath, massage and maybe treat Dave C. to the dinners I owe him, if he doesn't disappear into the woodwork.

29 December 1966, Thursday, 9:40 p.m.

This weekend I won't have to work and after I get paid on Saturday morning I plan to go to the PX and buy a swimming suit and a desk calendar. The swimming pool opened last Sunday and has been in constant use since that time. There is no shower water in that end of the compound because of it.

Under the headline (a few days ago in the *New York Times*) "Saigon Assembly Hears Ky Report," Jonathan Randal, in a 16-paragraph story saw fit to lead off paragraph three with "The Premier, wearing a brown silk suit..." So what? Paragraph 14 tells us that the South Vietnamese Army will have a pacification role. But we learn about Ky's brown silk suit in paragraph three. All I wonder is did he buy it off the rack or was it tailored for him. Did Mai pick it out? Does Randal think a brown suit, silk or otherwise, is in bad taste and makes him unfit to rule? If not, why mention it? Lice, lice, lice!

Old Coldass is going, going, soon to be gone. Prince said that I would be writing his easy letters for him, as they bored him. That's fine with me. They'll be short and blunt, for sure.

I got a Christmas card from a little boy.

> I hope you're fighting for me
> get up there in that big fat tree
> pick off enimes one by one
> and jump up and down with lots of fun.

A somewhat macabre poem, don't you think?

Tomorrow I must get a haircut so I'll pass the mustard in the pay line on Saturday morning.

30 December 1966, Friday, 9:55 p.m.

I just took a shower and powdered myself up with some medicated stuff that really feels good. I'm sitting under the whirring ceiling fan and it's quite cool. Every night is cool enough to warrant the use of an Army blanket. Old Fuerstein's views of the Saigon area as being as hot as the surface of a wood burning stove with nothing but cheap gin and rat hair-polluted water to cool it, is his own private view of Saigon.

Everyone has his own view, of course. Lately I've had several very bitter arguments with a nobody who sleeps in the same hooch as most of my section. I see him as a visitor. (Also I saw him when I was CQ runner.) He's a bigot's bigot. Stupid. Ugly. Loud. Biased. Uneducated. It's stupid for me to even talk to him, but I have enough of the masochist in me to keep my mouth going when he's around. He really believes the Vietnamese people to be devoid of culture. (They's like animules.) He judges everything here by how it departs from the

American counterpart, if it has one. The more it differs, the worse it is. Basically his view is that: these people are worthless. If they were worth anything they'd have been born Americans. The irony is that the dullest mama-san possesses more humanity than he does.

Tomorrow I plan to buy a swimming suit, as it's payday and I'll have Saturday afternoon, Sunday, and Monday off and plenty of time to goof around.

31 December 1966, Saturday, 11:16 p.m.

Soon it will be a new year and I have nothing philosophical to say. Eighteen days and I will have completed another year in the Army. Today I am exactly twenty-four and one-half years old.

Downtown today I browsed through all the shops in the Tax Building while my friends bought Saigon tea in a bar in the building.

I had a steam bath today and though I was guaranteed a massage without any fancy stuff, the girl did ask me to go upstairs to make love afterwards. I refused, of course. There was no point with My Darling on my mind. The massage was quite decorous and she observed all the niceties, no blow job or anything. Just beating the hell out of me with her rock hard fists. Also walking up and down my spine. The steam bath was very hot, suffocatingly so. The sign on the door said: please keep clean the room. The room was wooden and damp. We all carried our valuables with us in plastic bags. So nothing was lost except the 500 p. that it cost. About $4.50. Quite reasonable. This was in the nicest steam bath place in town. The girls were decent looking, clean, and the place was also.

We had dinner at an Italian restaurant. I had a Coke and minestrone soup that was very good. Also French bread.

Today I got paid.

I didn't buy a swimming suit today.

Today the sergeant major relieved me of my duties as mail clerk and pickup boy of material at the classified cage. He told me thank you and that I'd done a good job. From now on, I'm Prince's boy. Coldass has departed. Him and his pineapple juice. As he left he quietly said: All of you take care. I said: Yeah, Good Day, Sir. And no one else said a thing. It would hurt if he weren't a complete shithead. Maybe it's arterial sclerotic senility, but I think he's always been that way. Anyhow he's going to work in a unit run by a general (Ploger).

Tonight the clerks in our section had a little party, records and drink. I didn't even drink pop, as it, too, makes me feel sick. Downtown at the USO we had Coke floats and they were very good.

1 January 1967, Sunday, 9:50 p.m.

Tonight the bush outside has two tree frogs in it. One larger, darker one and one smaller, lighter one. They looked very colorful in the green wet bush. While I was watching them a big fat soggy frog jumped on my foot.

Earlier today I bought a new Spidey comic book and was reading it out near the edge of the compound near the golf course. Then I went over and watched a couple of monkeys forage in a large bush, evidence of their presence there given by small leaves floating down.

I don't know who'll be my best friends now that Mike and Whit are gone. Dave C. is too much the loner to be a best friend. He pokes around the city by himself all the time. God knows what he does. Probably has a girl somewhere, or somebody. I've thought of My Darling more since they left, but in a futile sort of way. There's no way I can see her as my best friend.

2 January 1967, Monday, 6:00 p.m.

Today I went downtown. Also today I bought some peanuts from the little kids who sell them on the streets. The peanuts are wrapped in little purple cones of paper. The street vendors today were selling bright orange crabs which looked very tasty and colorful.

Tomorrow I have an early (6:15) formation at which nothing will be done. It's going to be very hard to adjust to work tomorrow after two and a half days off.

4 January 1967, Wednesday, 6:30 a.m.

Last night I had a touch of the flu and dragged myself off to bed as soon as work was over and stayed there until dawn cracked this morning.

7:52 p.m.

Lately it's been very chilly here. If I had two army blankets I'd be using them. Actually down in the 60s. It's the hot dry season and all it's been is cold and rainy.

Old Coldass is gone to the Engineer Command in Bien Hoa. About 30 miles from here. It's hard to believe, but it's true.

This war in Vietnam is a fuss between neighbors. It's been a fuss for a thousand years and will be that way for that much longer. Speaking of that, that guy I've been having that argument with told me today that the next time he saw me in his hooch he'd stamp my face into the concrete floor. I hope he hits me a few times and breaks my glasses or something in front of a few witnesses. I'll have him broken down to E-1 and put in the stockade for a few years. I'd really like to, isn't that immature? Don't worry, it'll never happen. His name is Kozart.

Time to type one more letter for old Lt. Col. Prince before I read my book. Prince is a very nice fellow to work for. A good old Georgia boy, never panics, never sweats anything, always polite and says thank you. For the Army, almost unbelievable. A great contrast to Coldass.

I have to work Saturday afternoon and Sunday this week but that's alright.

5 January 1967, Thursday, 10:00 p.m.

I just got back from the USO where I went with Mike T. for vanilla ice cream. Today I moved my desk so it's in the corner of the room and in very good light. Also I've cleaned out the desk and Dave C. will leave in about two days, so the job is all mine now.

Today was a very easy day. Only about an hour's worth of typing all day, and Prince never harasses when there is no work, so I sat and read Sci Fi and looked out the window. Tomorrow will probably be a bitch to make up for the slack today.

Thoughts on the Army:

About censorship: I don't think the Army worries about it much. The library has all the magazines and newspapers that are critical of the war and they aren't censored in any way.

About prejudice: I dislike the apes like Kozart the most, those who have no concept of peoples' being equal in intelligence or of "foreigners" having any sense. I prefer those who know the right values even if they don't practice them. At least they are a little human.

About promotion: George made SP4 before I did because he's an operator and manipulator in a big office where he can get away with it, and I haven't because I'm in a little office where they know my every move. Now that they have new rules (no time and grade requirement for SP5) he'll probably be SP5 in a couple months. Unless he's watched very closely. I'd do the same if I could get away with it.

I work Saturday afternoon and therefore get out of a dirty company detail. Goody, goody, patio building. I'll be sitting in the office, hopefully woolgathering; like nit-picking, but easier.

6 January 1967, Friday, 8:46 p.m.

Last night I walked up to Dave C. and said "Marcel Proust is a Yenta," and he said, "Well, what does that make you?" And that stopped me. Because I didn't know.

Dave leaves tomorrow for Camp Alpha and 24 hours after for the States. When he returns he goes up to Nha Trang for six months.

Today was another day of sitting around. I went to the USO and had some strawberry ice cream and read a lot of the time.

Prince is still a fine man to work for. I keep waiting for the Jekyll-Hyde metamorphosis, but it won't be forthcoming, I don't believe.

Mama-san is out having her nether regions excised of devils or something, so she hasn't been here to perform her miracles with the clothes, as she was wont to do. And as I want her to. So dirty laundry is building up.

I'm surrendering to the insects, also must shower (me) and polish shoes, as mama-san is gone.

With Coldass gone, my job is the best in the building. No harassment, and even fun at times. I feel good and don't fall asleep on my feet or seat, so know I don't have dengue fever.

8 January 1967, Sunday, 8:00 a.m.

I had the alarm set for 5:30 this morning and slept through it and woke up at 7:25, just in time to scramble into my clothes and open the office. Last night I was reading a book, *Mortal Leap* by MacDonald Harris, that was so exciting I couldn't put it down until 2:00. Also a soldier came by at 12:00, wanting in now, NOW, NOW. I told him to come back at 7:30 and he was parked on the doorstep when I got up.

8:15 p.m.

Yesterday was a very slow day and I spent most of the time BS-ing with Col. Prince about things. I told him I wanted to see this country a little more thoroughly and he said that I could accompany him whenever possible. Yesterday I got back 20 Bob Hope Show slides that were terrible. So bad as to be funny.

Ky is ready to meet with Uncle Ho to discuss peace, according to the *Times*. What great PR men those two are! Ky should tell Ho where he gets his dental care. Ho should instruct Ky in credibility moves. First lesson, don't hang around with stewardesses.

9 January 1967, Monday, 6:10 a.m.

Yesterday I worked all day on the quarterly report so was saved from the sad fate of typing all day on inspection reports which are really terrible and full of numbers and have to be typed perfectly.

Also yesterday morning I didn't wake up until 7:25, as I already wrote, and then I had to deal with that madman who'd come by the night before wanting to go home to feed his horses.

Today is going to be a very hard day, as I have a report to type and many letters and endorsements on correspondence that had been suspended for action for today.

Also I plan to eat breakfast this morning as Charlie B. has moved into the building and is right now doing the necessary stuff upstairs.

I set two alarms for this morning and I heard both of them so I know that I'm not tired, even though I feel a little loggy.

A guy just walked in the door and said: "S-2." And I said what's that mean. And he said "S-2" with a different inflection and I responded as I had. Then he said what section is this and I told him and he said mumble mumble. And I said what and he said never mind and he left.

That's an example of a typical little scene in my life. Usually that's the way it happens, the guy hardly ever says he's going to (like Kozart) mash my face into the floor. I don't know what I said that irritated that S-2 character, but there is something in my attitude that does it, I guess.

It's now 6:30 and about time for me to go over and have a fine breakfast of fried eggs, thick poorly baked bread and good jam, and either warm water or warm fruit juice or ice cold water and ice cold fruit juice.

Then I come back here and dust off the desks and gird my loins for the day.

8:35 p.m.

The goggle-style sunglasses Madame Nguyen Cao Ky wore at the Bob Hope Show explained what I do now. I must bide my time further.

I just went outside and beat hell out of a cricket which was chirping. It stopped but some sergeants playing chess, who witnessed my excesses, thought me nuts. And in a sense they are right. I feel rage welling up from deep within my enraged soul. Man's inhumanity to man is exceeded only by his inhumanity to self. Or I should say woman's . . . etc.

It's being bruited about the office that a full colonel will be taking over as chief of the area in which I work, Complaints, 18 January, and it's pretty certain it's true. We'll have four (4) bird colonels in this office then. Some kind of record.

Also today I started writing letters for Lt. Col. Prince, not from models or dummies, but the whole letter from scratch. He wrote "excellent, print it" on each of them.

Soon I *must* move up in rank. I feel it in my bones.

10 January 1967, Tuesday, 9:00 p.m.

Today fairly smooth, lulls and not much storm. Tonight, fill the water jug, make the coffee, wash the coffee cups, prepare for the new day.

I'm writing upstairs because the bugs downstairs drove me mad. They don't come upstairs.

I've been typing TWXs, messages on a special non-erasable paper. I hate them, but I'm actually learning how to type them without special supervision. It's confirmed that we will be getting a bird colonel as Chief of the Complaints and Requests for Assistance.

Today I reread the *Time* December 23, 1966 article which hit me like a thunder clap yesterday, and it still means the same thing to me. My Darling went to Tokyo and had her eyes "fixed." That she would do such a thing, allow her perfect body to be racially desecrated by a Jap butcher fills me with disgust more palpable than if I were forced to rub dog shit in my hair. That the first lady of Vietnam could succumb to such racism. And she thinks, or so she's quoted, that this atrocity will render her "more charming to her husband." I hope he appreciates her sacrifice.

My love for her perfection has been dealt a blow from which it may well fail to recover. We'll see. I feel like doing something drastic. Something to balance out the desecration. What? Time will tell. Meanwhile, I must hypnotize and anesthetize myself with the monotony of Army life in the war zone.

11 January 1967, Wednesday, 9:30 p.m.

I've just now ceased a discussion of how one wipes one's ass with a corn cob. One reaches back behind where the cobs are kept, picks a red corn cob (the more common variety, field corn) and wipes one's ass with it and drops it down the hole. This is repeated several times and then one wipes one's ass with a white corn cob. If it's clean, place it back for the next person to use. If it's dirty (shitty) throw it away and start over with red

corn cobs. And yes, they are scratchy and tissue paper
is preferable. Edifying.

I offer a partial apology about journalists as lice.
R.W. Apple Jr. has convinced me (for the moment) we'll
never win this war. Quote: "Returned from a visit to
remote Phuquoc Island in the Gulf of Siam, one official
recently sagged into an armchair, took a long drink and
said with exasperation, 'That little place is surrounded
by water, and you'd think we could get it under control.
But no — there are still 150 V.C. there. Our guys chase
them up to one end of the island, but by the time we get
there, they're down at the other end.' "

That "sagged" bugs me, but this probably apocry-
phal tale of an official fits what I've seen and heard. I
think the Kys are smart to stay close to an airport.

Today I got a letter from Whit. He's been enjoying
the booze, women and freedom of California, and I wish
I were there to enjoy my own idea of Stateside existence.

I've been doing the monthly report, and the columns
of figures make my brain numb.

Time for bed. Two guys are asking me right now why
I'm wearing a T-shirt with P.E.A.K.E. written on the front
of it. And I don't know except it was in my locker, so I'm
wearing it.

12 January 1967, Thursday, 10:00 p.m.

I woke up with that same headache that I went to
bed with last night and I had to march in a parade today
and stand in the very hot sun and miss dinner, but still
I'm in a good mood. Not because I've gone mad, either.
Mainly because I'm working for a man who's a decent
human being, who noticed that I hadn't gone to dinner

and wanted to know why not. A man who would rather read *Rogue* or *Playboy* than write stupid business letters, a man who when his clerk sends a message out with a suspense date of September instead of January, doesn't rage, but says Oh well, I signed the damn thing and besides they'll know that we mean January and if they don't, well, so what . . .

I've been in country for four months now, one third of a year gone.

I must go take a shower and gird my loins for another day tomorrow. I have Saturday afternoon off and also all day Sunday, which should be nice. I'll read and wash out some undergarments and hang them on the line. I'll be glad when Mama-san returns from her hysterectomy or whatever and gets things fixed up.

I've been working on the monthly report. It took me about an hour to do, and now I'm going to convince anyone who wants me to work on anything else Saturday morning that I'm still working on it and it has priority.

Not too long and I'll have been here six months.

My schedule is so regular that I can predict from week to week where I'll be. I'm very compulsive. I always thought that was what it would take to rise to the top in the Army, but now I'm not so sure. I've been here four months and in the Army for what seems like forever, and I haven't risen to the top yet. I must be patient.

13 January 1967, Friday, 9:30 p.m.

I just took my malaria pill and already feel funny inside. Tomorrow I was to go fire my weapon, but begged off. Tonight I heard Pattie and the Emblems sing "Mixed Up, Shook Up Girl" and didn't that bring back memories!

No, I'd never heard it before.

Tonight I had ice cream, vanilla, and chocolate syrup which was very good, as always.

The big thing around here with some people right now is the STIF movement, with STIF buttons and all. The price of Saigon tea was too high, so: *Saigon Tea Is Finis.*

I haven't seen the tree frog for a few days now. I think a mama-san ate him for lunch with rice.

I checked out my rifle today to clean it, as that's required. But it looks very clean to me, so I'll turn it back in tomorrow the same as it was.

Today I complained to Lt. Col. Prince about the lack of sense in the Army letters and he said: You'd be surprised how many anti-semantics you'd find in the Army. He followed that one up with a better one that I forgot, but he's a sharp fellow. I wonder why he's in the Army. That's unkind, but it's a funny place for all of these fairly bright, fairly nice fellows to be. I guess it's as good a business as automobile manufacturing. At least the Army men are honest about their business being killing, whereas the car people try and ignore the fact that they kill more people than the VC. The Army people are always trying to fix it so fewer people die, but the car people aren't. All big business is corrupt.

My views on the draft: I don't say make it more equal, or make it a lottery, or make it for social service too, or draft women or any of that other shit. I say abolish it, forget it, the hell with it. Out the window with it. That isn't a liberal position, that's an anarchist's position, and rather unpopular over here, though less so with the officers than with EM like Kozart who are dumb, dumb, dumb! And don't know it.

14 January 1967, Saturday, 11:45 p.m.

My Darling Mai almost became a widow two days ago. "Ky Safe as Mortar Misfires, Spurting Flames Near Him." An Aussie mortar misfired. I wonder was it an assassination attempt? Bodyguards leaped on top of him to shield him with their bodies. What loyalty. What patriotism! How frightened he must have been. He probably was bruised worse by his bodyguards jumping on him. Tomorrow I'm going to the PX and buy some blades and envelopes.

Today the work was very easy. I read the January *Playboy* until 11:30 when a presidential letter came in and I had to type like mad to finish by 12:30, but somehow I did. Old Prince told me I did good and wished me a good weekend. And he even has to work tomorrow. Old Coldass would just have wistfully asked me if I were working Sunday and then hinted that he'd like me to work or Monday would be hell typing the huge amount of work he'd do on Sunday, about three letters and a memo.

Mike T. has sent home his records as he leaves here for home next Wednesday. So tonight I'm listening to all three LPs of mine and the few 45 RPMs I have, all of them good, of course. Charlie B. is the boy from Tennessee who replaced Whit in the upstairs administrative assistant job. A job I'm glad I don't have.

On Kozart: I make him look like an ass, utter and complete. Which is what he is.

This compound is starting to look like Fort Ben, WACs all over the place holding hands with GIs. The best looking ones are, of course, the negroes, as the white ones are the true dregs, the bottom.

Time for bed, and a shower too. As cold as the weather is, one mustn't let oneself go. Must not go native and grow stinky.

15 January 1967, Sunday, 8:00 p.m.

Today I went to Cholon PX and bought 10 bars of soap, 30 razor blades and two root beers. Also packs of tomato juice and orange juice in small cans. Also I walked over all of Saigon that I hadn't seen. The pet shops: pythons, baby bears, and otters pitifully whining in the hot sun, soon to die and protesting it with all of their small bodies, like dry tufted newly born dogs. All kinds of birds and dogs. Also I saw the meat market and fish markets. A million kinds of stuff festering in the sun, collecting flies. I went through one (almost) American-style deli which had everything in the line of deli food at very high prices.

Dinner downtown was stuffed crab and French bread and butter and Coke and fried rice, all of it delicious and costing 315 p. or about $2.85. Which is fairly reasonable. They handed out scented hand towels, hot and wet, before and after the meal.

When I got back at 5:00 I had to assemble a letter for Lt. Col. Prince. After that I washed out my five pairs of socks and seven shorts and seven T-shirts and hung them on the line to dry in the cold breeze that blows.

Four months are gone. Just seven months and days left.

The WACs will provide no female companionship for me. I will avoid them and if any work in our office, I'll pretend I'm queer although according to James Fox that's a sure way to attract modern woman to SAVE the man from himself or something.

Some of the ordinary RVNers are OK in looks, but I think the negro WACs that just entered the compound are much better-looking, and culturally more interesting, and they impress me as being brainless, husbandless dyke types, but I'm not very kind in my judgments of people.

The correspondence I am handling these days is so explosive that if it were leaked to the press much of it could be spread across the pages and blown all out of proportion. Stuff about inadequate weapons and indignities (and worse) done by Americans to so-called civilians.

16 January 1967, Monday, 9:30 p.m.

Things are colder than hell, in the low 60s, to be precise. My fingers are so cold right now that it hurts to bend them to type. Last night it was so cold that I awoke shivering.

A new deal here now is morning formations at 6:00 in front of the orderly room, just like the States. A bunch of bullshit.

The wind is blowing cold and dusty through here, with the screens holding it back not a whit. It blows through my heart.

17 January 1967, Tuesday, 9:50 p.m.

I'm sitting here at my desk (which I moved, as the new colonel arrives tomorrow), eating fruit cake by the handsful and wishing I had some more of the 7-Up floats that I drank earlier today. EAT EAT EAT.

Mike T. left for home today. He left me a set of 25 porno pictures that are pretty good for the type. So I like dirty pictures. The women's eyes are all slanty.

I moved my desk. I'm sitting as far away from the new colonel as I can so it'll be hard for him to catch my attention by shouting, let alone by nodding. I hope he's a good fellow.

That formation this morning was a drag and those all mornings henceforth will be a drag. Getting up at 5:00 and then working all day — doesn't make sense. But that's the Army.

That's only about 30 minutes earlier than I was getting up, but really I wouldn't have had to get up until 6:45 most mornings. Now we can't even sleep in on Sunday morning. The idea is to make it impossible for us to live on the economy. It's part of the crackdown on piaster spending. Dummies, I'm going to continue to spend all I can afford.

At the formation the colonel said "We're going RA, all the way." Dumb shits, they don't realize this is a war zone. Standing around in formation isn't really very smart.

It's so cold here, I believe that I'll confine my shower-taking to every other day instead of daily. I don't sweat these days, just shiver and shake and wish for the good old warmth. I got very cold again last night. Ah well, the hot dry season can't last long.

Today I worked every minute all day except for my one-and-a-half-hour lunch break and my one-hour dinner break. I'll be damned if I'll give them up. If I do I won't get anything for it except tired.

Tomorrow Lt. Col. Prince goes out to Long Binh Stockade to interview the prisoners so I should get a chance to get caught up on my logging and maybe even write a letter on Army time. I bought a swimming suit when I saw one in my size, as I guess that the weather will warm up sometime. Today I typed a letter for General Westmoreland's signature. Big thrill.

18 January 1967, Wednesday, 9:10 p.m.

The new colonel, Col. Ebby, hasn't yet shown up at the office, though he is in country, I guess.

Tonight our team, Team B, of which I'm a member, was supposed to work late typing inspection reports, but I wasn't given a direct order to, so of course didn't. I had my own work to do on my Complaints and Requests for Assistance without going elsewhere to look for work. This may piss some people off, but the hell with them.

Today I read *The Pistol* by James Jones when I could have been working. It is a good story, but not very well written. Several sentences were terrible. I looked for an example to quote, but couldn't find those that I grimaced over while reading the book. The short novel is about a PFC who steals a pistol and the strength it requires for him to keep it. The character that he develops while hanging on to the weapon is fairly well presented and the Army life rings true. I still got the feeling that this was a book to fulfill a contract and that it merely filled the space between *Some Came Running* and *The Thin Red Line.* The early morning formations are quite a drag, but I'll get used to them I guess.

Tomorrow I'm wearing my jungle fatigues for the first time. I've almost completely run out of fatigues due to the mama-san's absence. I'm going to have to make other arrangements soon. I'll probably have one of the drivers drop off the fatigues at BOQ (Bachelors Officers Quarters.)

My hair is getting quite long and until I'm directly

ordered to, I won't have it more than trimmed around the edges.

Premier Ky and his wife are touring Australia. I look forward to pictures of them kissing koalas, petting wallabies, and eating ostrich egg omelets.

I have some fruit cake and think I'll now have some and off to bed. I showered earlier and am all clean and cold.

19 January 1967, Thursday, 9:45 p.m.

Lately the weather has been so very much like that of Seattle that it has been eerie.

The Army is a funny place. A place where they won't let one man stay in bed 15 minutes longer than the others if he feels like it, but the same Army doesn't force a man to fly. If a man has strong feelings against flying, he need never enter an aircraft while in the Army. He'll be sent on ship to Vietnam, allowed time to travel by bus or train in the States, all of this costing the Army time and money, but they do it.

Today was another easy day. I spent the day revamping my file system for the files inspection due next week. Lt. Col. Prince asked me today what the big folder of cases was that sat on my desk. I told him that it was cases in suspense. He said that he thought there was a daily suspense system file in the file cabinet. I said yes, there was, but that there were two interdependent file systems that I used for suspense. The one on my desk consisted of cases that had individual unspecified suspense dates except for impending ones. The file cabinet contained all cases with specified suspense dates, and also unspecified suspense dates that were impending.

Also, I said, any cases with unspecified suspense dates that are brought to his attention, action taken and re-suspended are put in the daily suspense file in the cabinet. He asked why it was done that way. My answer: so that I don't have to look through 50 to 75 suspended cases in a daily suspense file that is arranged non-numerically, but chronologically. Because the file folder on my desk is arranged numerically, so that when he asks for a case by name before its suspense date has arrived I can look up the name in my card index and find the number and look up the case from the folder on my desk unless it's in the daily suspense file, has been filed in completed cases, on purpose or by accident, or is in Prince's desk or has been accidentally stapled to another case and misfiled or a million other things. Prince (said to Major Tief sitting nearby): "Well that's what I get for having a PFC with a college degree working for me." Then he asked does it work. And I said yes. But the catch is that no one else can find anything or even have it explained to them, so I'm indispensable. I'm not so dumb. I don't care what. . . .

"What's New Pussycat" is on tomorrow night in the new theater and it costs 35 cents. "North by Northwest" was on tonight.

What does it all mean? Are the VC gallant fighters for liberty against filthy economic imperialists? Or are the gallant Americans rooting out the black evil of communism and all that rot? It's murder on both sides with both sides wronger than hell. People who wage war for months at a time do lose their humanity and cease to be people, or human beings, whether they be VC or Americans. There was much culture shock to the Marines of WWII coming out of the jungles trained to shoot. To kill.

To knife and cut throats silently. They had some trouble
readjusting. Our American airborne troops come out of
the jungles and they go to the whores and most of them
beat them up and don't pay. Sex is very brutal and
consists mostly of beating the whores very badly. The
VC are guilty of similar stuff. Enough polemic. It would
drive Kozart mad.

I wonder if Madame Ky ever thinks about these
trenchant issues? Of if all she thinks about is how cute
she is in her black go-to-hell jump suit.

20 January 1967, Friday, 9:30 p.m.

Today Colonel Ebby showed up. At the very end of
the day so I didn't really get to know anything about
him. I was assigned to Task Force 5 for the next seven
days. Two formations per day in field gear. Also I work
all day Saturday and all day Sunday. Things aren't really
very leisurely around here now. If I hadn't had task
force today I could have gotten my work done, but I
now have two letters to type first thing in the morning.

I've got flying ant bites all over my arms, and those
little buggers really itch. Another thing: a detail is building
a latrine right under my bedroom window, and I can
already imagine the stench of it in use.

My roommate Ed is a funny fellow, but a dependable
sharer of work he is not. He's very hard to awaken in the
morning.

21 January 1967, Saturday, 3:30 p.m.

This week I'm confined to the post on Task Force 5.
The automobile is ostensibly manufactured for trans-
portation. Murder is a by-product of that industry which

they are taking few and slow steps to prevent. Death is ignored in favor of profits. The automobile is a portable coffin. They are hypocrites of the worst kind.

The Army people are engaged in the straightforward business of murder with few pretenses. But they are also giving the best medical attention casualties have ever gotten. And both sides (ours and theirs) get it; helicopters take them to hospitals with all the medical miracles. Death is the first purpose of our helicopters but when they fail, every effort is made to save lives.

The professional soldier does not view war as necessary for peace someday. He recognizes this as hypocrisy and knows that we'll always have war.

I couldn't restrain myself when I read about Reagan saying that when you've seen one redwood tree you've seen them all. I read it out loud to Prince and he snorted with laughter. That's one of the finest twists on an old cliché that I've heard in a long time.

22 January 1967, Sunday, 3:20 p.m.

I've worked since early this morning, meaning that I've been on duty, not that I've really worked. This morning Colonel Ebby was here, even though he isn't on duty on Sundays. It's too early to tell whether he's a Sunday worker or whether he's just getting oriented. I hope it's the latter.

I had a formation at 7:00 this morning, Task Force 5. A roll call and that was it.

Last night I went over to the library and read magazines. One thing I saw that interested me: An article on love by Peter S. Beagle (author of *I Can Tell By Your Outfit*) in the January 7th *Saturday Evening Post.* The last column is especially good. He is an example of a college educated writer, young and sort of weird who makes a living at writing. Something which I'd like to do. I was told today by Major Tief, of the procurement team, that I should be able to make a fortune at writing. He had me read some very involved legal statements on procurement and rephrase them to him in easy-to-understand English. Which I did without too much difficulty. He said that out of five people he's put that little task to, I'm the only one who has done a satisfactory job. Of course what he has in mind is technical writing, which I don't have much interest in, but which I could do, maybe. I've always campaigned against jargon and governmentese. Delusions of grandeur. I mustn't set my sights too high.

Thursday's *New York Times* had a nice picture of Mrs. Nguyen Cao Ky next to plugugly Mrs. Harold Holt at Canberra Airport. The article mentions Ky's affection for Hitler and quotes some crazy Aussie calling Ky a "little miserable butcher, a gangster quisling." It is interesting to me that Ky's shortness is as bad as being a murderer. Asians tend to be smaller than caucasions, I think due to their inferior diet. That makes the Aussie's accusation racist!

Lt. Col. Prince is having me transferred to his Sunday schedule so that we'll be working the same days. That way we'll be able to get the work done. And still have time for writing letters and reading sci-fi like I've been doing most of today. I've been working entirely too many Sundays which situation I expect to change when José returns from his thirty-day emergency leave. Not that he does anything when he's here.

7:00 p.m.

It's after work now and I've stood Task Force 5 formation and I've showered and I've read most of a book of Robert Sheckley's short stories.

Mama-san is due back tomorrow and I'll not have to polish my own shoes anymore, not that I have been doing much of a job. There's a lizard that lives upstairs by the coffee pot that every morning runs across the wall that I plug the pot in. It's a short stubby lizard with a broken tail and it lives behind the refrigerator.

Gil, one of the drivers, told me a typical trickster tale yesterday:

"There was this guy I know see, he was real fat, about 300 pounds and very tall, and also a sharp dresser. He went to this party that this married broad was having cause her old man was out of town or visiting relatives or at a convention or something. Anyway the fat boy went to the party and he put the make on the broad and she didn't go for it at all. He kept trying and trying and the more he tried the more she fried until she was so mad she told him to get the hell out of the house. He was madder than hell but he wanted to get even with her so he went into the kitchen (which is where he'd been whenever he wasn't trying to put the make on the girl) and dug into the fridge and got a big bowl of chocolate pudding. He took that pudding into the head and he shit into it and stirred it all up and took it and put it back in the fridge.

"The next morning me and another guy was over at the girl's and we was hungry so we asked her if she had anything to eat. She said nothing except some pudding

that my old man eats because his stomach is so bad that
he just eats milk stuff. We said no and she said well it's
real good. My old man got back early this morning and
had some and liked it real well. We felt sick and left. I
mean it's alright to pull some tricks, but that was pretty
low, don't you think?"

Those that are going are gone; it's those that stay
home that are alone. Thought for the day.

"Born Free" isn't on tonight, just some movie called
"Ralphie," or something like that. Well, maybe I'll go
anyway and write later tonight about how it was.

10:45 p.m.

"What's It All About, Alfie": I went to the movie. As
he said at the end, "If you ain't got your piece of mind,
you don't have anything." I thought it a fine movie and
sad—even the talking to the audience I thought very
nice. Every man has some Alfie in him. I sympathized
strongly with him. If all you do is take and don't give,
nothing lasts, you lose your youth and you're gone.
Some moralizing is needed. A fine movie. A big contrast
with "Frankenstein Conquers the Earth," Japanese-made.

The movie made me ponder my own predicament in
life and love—no wife and somewhat obsessed with
another man's. That's the problem with me. The
"somewhat" says it all. Otherwise I'd act. DO SOME-
THING! But what? I wish the Forces would show me a
sign. How to put my plan into action?

23 January 1967, Monday, 2:00 p.m.

I'm sitting here at work sweating in my jungle fatigues,
waiting for the colonels to come back from lunch. The

hot weather has returned and I guess I'll be safe in taking one of the two Army blankets off my bed. It will still be necessary to have one, due to my sleeping with a fan blowing on me.

I just got a phone message for Lt. Col. Bergeron that reads: I have a bitch signed Buck Weaver. Cryptic note.

This morning when I got out of bed I almost stepped on a beetle as big as a mouse, and then going upstairs I almost stepped on a frog (inside the building) and another beetle. Mice usually keep out of sight anyhow.

None of the WACs have made a pass at me. Not very likely. They have so much attention that they will never notice me. Maybe they sense my preoccupation with another. Women have a sixth sense about possible rejection.

Time to do some Army work, I'll write more later.

7:35 p.m. and Very Much Later

I'm on Task Force 5 alert this evening which means I've checked out my weapon and was told that we might go somewhere and crawl through the grass and make like soldiers, all for practice, of course.

I had a busy late afternoon, but all in all I'm able to handle the whole job by myself if I keep hustling, which I hate to do, being a lazy fellow at heart.

10:00 p.m.

I've watched "Combat" on TV and missed the thing to do with the alert. The runner couldn't find where we were living. That's life though. Nothing should come of it because it wasn't our fault.

24 January 1967, Tuesday, 12:30 p.m.

I saw the tree frogs last night in the bushes. I guess Mrs. Cuc was gone for an abortion, at least that is what is indicated. She's a lot slimmer.

I'm a SP4 now. Isn't that nice. I was sent up to the orderly room with Charlie B. and Stone, two other PFC's in the office, and we three were given SP4. I'd heard rumors about it but didn't want to think about it until I had the thing on my arm. Then I could be fairly sure that I'd keep it. I told Lt. Col. Prince about missing that formation last night and he said that if anything came of it, he would straighten it out. I'd like to see him walk into the orderly room with a cross expression on his face. He would bring some piss to those cretins who seem to crawl out of the orderly room walls.

The work schedule just came out and I won't be working next Saturday afternoon or Sunday, so I'll be able to rest up.

That son-of-a-bitch Coldass left here without leaving a post locator card with the mail clerk, although I told him to, so Charlie B. has been using the address on his orders to send his mail. It's wrong and the SOB Coldass filed a complaint through our office on the situation. What a stupid bastard. I can't believe how stupid he is. And on that note I must leave to type the letter to him.

25 January 1967, Wednesday, 7:25 p.m.

I have just 10 minutes and I must be in my Task Force 5 formation. It's been a long hard day, but soon the weekend will be here. Today I badgered Mama-san into washing my clothes and polishing my shoes so I'm in good shape, clothes-wise. I hope to be back here in 30 minutes to finish this. If not, we'll be running through the bushes, practicing being soldiers.

8:45 p.m.

Formation was about 60 seconds long, and we fell out. Since then I've prepared coffee for tomorrow and showered and cleaned up my room. This schedule is catching up with me and I'm extremely tired. I'll last, but this weekend will be very welcome.

26 January 1967, Thursday, 6:45 a.m.

I went to bed early last night in preparation for the last big Task Force 5 formation this morning, the last until next week, that is. This morning I have to mow the lawn and tomorrow I have to fire at the firing range all morning. Afternoon I have off and all day Sunday. Lt. Col. Prince won't see much of his clerk typist so the work will really pile up. The hell with it. It isn't my fault that the Army has added all this bullshit. The only way I could get the work done is to use my own free time (whenever that is) to get the work caught up. And I refuse to do that. It wouldn't be right.

I've got a mosquito bite on my arm that is huge and itchy. The mosquito would have had to sit there a long time and in full view to perform that little task.

My section cracked down on the pit latrines that were being used here and they all are being replaced by septic-type operations that will never work due to the lack of water. The shit will sit in the toilets and ferment and get really cruddy. If that's what they want though. . . .

José G. is due back from his emergency leave so the clerks will get more time off, hopefully, after he returns, if he returns.

It's been hard to get used to answering the phone as Specialist but that's the kind of problem I like. I hope that I make SP5 while I'm over here as I might as well get as much as I can out of the bastards.

Carver from Nha Trang is supposed to be coming down here when Dave C. returns from his leave. Carver and José should remove the pressure. What I'd like to see here is a detail man to take care of all the lawn trimming, clipping, errand running, etc. We had a trustee from the stockade at first, but that didn't last. Things never do.

Oh well, all this picayune quibbling about time and who does what is kind of niggling small, but the Army makes a man think that way. Even me.

27 January 1967, Friday, 1:15 p.m.

I'm scheduled to spend Sunday firing. Everyone else in the office got to fire on office time, namely Saturday morning, but I have to use my day off. That pisses me off, but then the Army isn't supposed to be fun. Somehow I don't think it's fair.

I didn't have to mow the lawn today as a detail was assigned the task and they got to use power mowers, so I don't feel sorry for them.

Lt. Col. Prince told me about a place, the International Restaurant, downtown, which has the finest Chinese food he's ever eaten, and he's quite a connoisseur. We had a detailed discussion of the finer points of egg rolls and he realized I knew of what I was speaking. That is their specialty, I guess.

The weather is fairly warm again so my hair is going

to get shorter. It's not comfortable to wear long hair when it's very hot.

I had another go-round with the laundry mama-sans today. Not the office mama-san but the one in the laundry that sews on patches and stripes. All I had was 45 p. for a 50 p. job that should have cost only 42 p. First they couldn't find the shirts, just some belonging to another guy with a similar last name. They weren't mine but they had a hell of a time figuring it out. My shirts were hanging on the wall in plain sight. The dummies. They're as dumb as the laundry people in the States.

My optimism will survive all of the Army bullshit. But I wish I didn't have to put up with it. I'll probably be back on task force again next week. The orderly room takes two men each week from our USOM building which sleeps four men, and one man per week from the hooch which sleeps 20 men. It isn't fair but that's the way they get even with the guys who live in USOM buildings instead of the hooches.

7:10 p.m.

I've burned the garbage and run errands all over the place. I just came back and Lt. Col. Prince had a great huge thing sitting in his OUT basket for me to type. I picked it up and he said no don't type that tonight, wait 'til tomorrow. The one thing the Army has done all day that had any kindness in it. I'm going to take a shower at 7:30 and spend the evening sitting in the library reading and soaking up the air conditioning. I told the sergeant major that the firing Sunday was cutting into my only morning to sleep in since the 15th and he said: "Outstanding!" Very kind of the SOB. That means that I'll probably go from the 15th until sometime in February before I get a day to sleep in. I'm compensating by taking it very slow during the day, and stretching my lunch and dinner hours beyond all previous limits.

Typical little snippets from the local daily papers usually contain gossip involving rape and suicide. The language of these columns always interests me. Wicked foreigner is a nice way of saying American. I think it has charm. The US information (military) that I've read is true. Downtown one can buy the local peanuts wrapped in a FOUO publication (For Official Use Only).

For weeks now I've been reading these local papers hoping to find something about My Darling or her husband, the Premier. But the Saigon English dailies rarely print anything interesting about the Kys, except mysterious white space. I have to read the *New York Times* or newsmagazines to get even a hint of gossip or dirt. It's like there's a news blackout in the Saigon papers.

28 January 1967, Saturday, 8:45 p.m.

I just ate a can of applesauce spooned out onto some tortillas. Funny taste, but I was hungry. Also I'm watching Phil Silvers play the clarinet, which is very edifying, musically.

There's a brutal blues shouter on TV right now, a certain Wayne Cochrane who is singing: "I'm going back to Mama, going back to my girl," repeat, etc. He's wearing a huge blonde wig and a white suit. Terrific.

If mama-san (Mrs. Cuc) joined the VC, she's back with us doing spy work. I don't think a veteran of this war of freedom that I'm now so valiantly engaged in at such great risk of life and limb would be welcome.

Hell, I could choke on a banana or die of shock stepping on a beetle when I step barefooted out of bed onto the beetle-covered floor. Cheaper than rugs, and they don't ever need shaking.

Old Bing is on right now singing: "You make those old Magnolias blossom . . ." He's folk, no shit, he really is folk. He's too bad a singer to be square, but he's got charm and folksiness.

Tomorrow up at 5:00 to go fire on the range. The trip's interesting and I guess I can sleep in the afternoon.

29 January 1967, Sunday, 8:10 p.m.

Well, the day is drawing to a close and it hasn't been an unpleasant day. This morning I got up at five o'clock and loaded in the back of a truck, and out to Long Bien we were trucked. Dick Van Dyke just came on. The great show about the stick-up artist that held up Dick and Laura in the elevator. His umbrella kept opening, etc. Great bit. Then the elevator got stuck. What happened, Mel says, and Buddy answers nothing, they are still in the elevator and the kid was born there and they named him Otis.

I just had a dinner of canned prunes and cold barbecue beans. Very good.

In the library this evening after sleeping several hours and having a dinner of steak and hot beans and potato salad.

Dick is on the top of the elevator now reading graffiti on the walls. "Fred is a f . . . . never mind. Danger High Voltage," etc.

I read several articles that I liked very much. The January 14 *New Republic* has an article called "You Tell

'em, Buddy" by Bernard B. Fall on Vietnam and the
quote is continued as "war is shit." He quotes the graffiti:
On the wall of a shack in a particularly crummy part of
Vietnam— "I can't relate to this environment." Oh yes,
this morning I fired nine rounds and the target was hit
nine times.

I read an article about a Vietnam vet. It was interesting and I differ with him quite a bit. He calls the US
military system an intrusion into civilian life. Sure, but
one must be careful not to get involved with much else
that is equally destructive. The US school system, Boeing,
etc. Lt. Col. Prince is a better boss than I ever had in
civilian life and he does an important job with a minimum
of fuss. Sure his job wouldn't be necessary if the Army
didn't create the problem in the first place. But this
selective condemnation of the military is senseless. It's
merely an extension of modern life that is in most of its
aspects instrumental in killing creativity, individuality,
the person. It's all wrong and the modern age, as it is
thus represented, is evil and results in death. This is
what causes all the shit that we see around us, this
disregard of anything but the profit motive. Some American soldiers are cynical about our being here. Others,
and many they are, have been convinced by the lie that
"if we don't stop the Commies here, we'll be fighting
them in Dubuque" or some such. Idiots. But they are
many, so I don't think that we have an army of cynics
over here. Most of the officers aren't hawks, but among
the men there is a refusal to admit to the difference
between a dove and an active Communist agent. Like
Kozart, who carries yet onward with his battle against
me, the active Red agent.

I don't think Duncan goes far enough in his article.

The military system is dead wrong of course, but the problem can't be so simply attributed to the military. Duncan himself admits this in his statement on the CIA's and the United Fruit Co.'s bringing about the collapse of the Guatemalan government. Private business is guilty again and again of this sort of thing. I agree with his statements on the corruptness of the Vietnam government, the censorship, the Vietnamese people's dislike of the Americans being here, the complete failure of the Happy Hamlet program, the lack of interest in negotiation. I don't know why he says American prestige would be higher if we withdrew. Who gives a fuck if it is so. Prestige be damned. Withdraw. And his horseshit: "The military's sole purpose is to teach people to kill." The purpose of war is death, I agree, but I don't agree with his statement. If it's true, they are doing a bad job. This philosophy does not reach very far. I don't know how to kill and will never learn. They just want me to use my typewriter. That will allow others to kill. I share the guilt, but they didn't teach me to kill and I'm no more guilty than those who allow the system to continue or talk of ridiculous measures such as draft by lottery. That's very machine-like and inhuman. The old method at least allowed the bright ones to dodge around a bit.

Another addition to our schedule, soon, it's rumored, is Saturday morning drill and ceremonies.

30 January 1967, Monday, 8:15 p.m.

Today was a very busy day. I typed 22 letters, which is about three times as much as my usual day. I have much work to do to produce those letters besides typing. I write most of them. Get copies made (make them myself), log them, etc. A lot of work really.

I found out that Kozart has two purple hearts and a bronze star and a metal plate in his skull, so "I guess he must be a right guy after all, huh?"

The TV set is OK and my opinions on war are more uncompromising than ever. If I were sent to the place where the battle is, don't think for a moment that I wouldn't try for one of them bronze things, though. It would look damn good on my record. I don't want any purple hearts, though. Kozart can have them.

"Combat" is on and it's one that I haven't seen. More behind the lines stuff.

I'm going to take a shower and then hit the old sack.

31 January 1967, Tuesday, 8:00 p.m.

Today Lt. Col. Prince took a picture of me with his new Polaroid camera and told me to send it to my "Dearly Beloved." He took it in natural light, no flash. Lt. Col. Prince is a very cool guy. He's a very youthful-looking fellow with a baby face and a bald head which, when covered with a hat, doesn't make him look younger than his 40 years. If I send the picture to my Dearly Beloved would she wonder, would she know? I doubt it. She's too busy running Vietnam by proxy. Maybe I was wrong about that.

Today I went to the PX after I got paid, the Cholon PX, and bought beef stew, a case of pop, soap, shoe polish, 10 bottles of apple juice. So I'm ready for the month.

Prince and Major Kolosky were talking about our four colonels tonight and apparently all colonels aren't like the four we have, all gentlemen, intelligent and friendly. All four are on speaking terms with each other and are really good bosses. Major Kolosky said that in one section there are 11 colonels and only two of them are on speaking terms. So the Army isn't as reasonable as the officers in this section make it seem. Major Kolosky said that many of them are inhuman bastards to work for, very unreasonable and eccentric. Thank God that Colonel Ebby, the new colonel I work for, is a fine fellow. Gracious, considerate, all that. Always thanks me if I bring him a cup of coffee, asks me if I'd like to go the PX with him, stuff like that. Makes it easier for me to put My Dearly Beloved, My Asian Darling, out of my mind and to concentrate on getting ahead in the US Army.

Today was payday.

Mrs. Cuc is back, doing her job. I can't imagine who would screw Mrs. Cuc. She is a very unappetizing woman and not very nice in appearance. Her older sister, though. She's very attractive and dimply and she has twice as many kids, too. I can't understand it. But that's the way it is. Lt. Col. Prince is married and has, I think, six children. I've seen pictures of his family and the girls are giants. Very large attractive girls, as is his wife. He writes them every day and is very irritated when he doesn't receive mail from them. Prince has until June in RVN. He is a very nice man and a fine boss.

1 February 1967, Wednesday, 8:45 p.m.

Today was an easy day.

For dinner I just had a can of beef barley soup, undiluted, Dr. Pepper and apple juice as dessert.

Today I went over to the medical dispensary and got my shots up to date: cholera, small pox and plague.

Nothing really serious about catching any of those of
course, but no point in taking chances even about
piddling items. Better to be safe than sorry.

2 February 1967, Thursday, 7:32 a.m.

People (the sergeant major) have been dropping
hints that my hair is getting a little long for the Army
career which I have chosen. I think I'll con old Charlie or
Joe into taking some pics of me in my jungle fatigues
and long hair and SP4 stripes.

I just went upstairs and got Col. Ebby his morning
cup of coffee. When he first came to the section Prince
had a little talk with me about courtesies due a full
colonel and one of them, he said, was a morning cup of
coffee brought to his desk. I asked him whether he
wanted a cup brought to him too, and he said that he'd
get his own as he hadn't made it yet. So I bring down a
cup for Col. Ebby and Lt. Col. Prince walks up and gets
his own. That's an example of the daily drama of life in
the USARV compound.

9:00 p.m.

Today I got a haircut. Just a trim. Also today a friend
of mine in the Information Office interviewed me and
will send a news release on my promotion to the Seattle
papers, Yakima papers, and Kennewick papers. Isn't that
a kick. Sort of a campy thing of me to do. I think it's
funny. Won't they be surprised I'm in a war zone! I guess
this will be the extent of press coverage of my war
heroism.

I went out to Cherry Hill tonight and had some fried

rice and Coke. Quite good and a change from food in the compound.

Tomorrow Lt. Col. Prince said I could accompany him to Long Binh Stockade unless something came up. That should be a good way to get through the day.

Nothing much has happened since yesterday. Things are dull. Even though I have this Sunday off, it looks as though I'll be on Task Force 5 again so I won't be able to sleep past 5:15 a.m. I haven't slept past that time since 15 January. Oh it's a hard life. The quiet evening here is punctuated with firecracker explosions in celebration of the lunar new year, Tet. Could be pistol fire, I guess, but I doubt it.

I feel all hairy and dirty so I think I'll go shower and hit the hay. I've got seven clean pairs of fatigues in my locker, four regular and three jungle.

3 February 1967, Friday, 8:30 p.m.

My trip to Long Binh went fine. We only got one complaint from the prisoners that we could handle, three of them wanted to "denounce" their US citizenships, and three wanted to contest their courts-martial. We can't touch those cases as they are the responsibility of the legal officer. RVN would be foolish to accept those fellows, as they are just a liability.

My smallpox vaccination has been itching like a mosquito bite for the last two days. It took, I guess.

I work all day tomorrow and because I'm on Task Force 5 again starting today, I'll not be able to sleep in tomorrow or Sunday or any other day of the week. And next week I'll work Sunday so that means I'll go one month without sleeping past 5:15. Also I hear on the vine that soon we're going to have weekly rifle inspections, and also PT should start pretty soon.

I took my malaria pill today and I've eaten cookies, raisins, salted pecans, drunk pop, etc., and feel queasy as hell.

4 February 1967, Saturday, 3:45 p.m.

I got another letter from Whit today. He was given the job of company clerk and he hates it. He wishes that he had extended over here. He types morning reports and does all sorts of crummy little jobs. Stands inspection and all that other horse shit too.

Not only didn't I get last Sunday off, but it looks as though I might not get much time off this Sunday either. I'm working this afternoon of course, and I have 6:30 formation tomorrow morning so I won't get much sleep tonight, but maybe I can go back to sleep tomorrow after formation. And maybe not. Guns are becoming more a part of my life these days. I don't approve of guns generally, but then lots of people do and I shouldn't be narrow-minded. Charlie B. was assigned an M-60 machine gun last week on Task Force and he'd never seen one before and he complained to Lt. Col. Prince and Prince spoke to some people and now Charlie B. no longer has the machine gun.

I gripe plenty about the Army. My section treats me fine, but the bullshit that the company put me through drives me batty. All the details, formations, parades, rifle practice, cleaning, Task Force, etc., is from the company. You'd think we weren't in a war zone. This chicken shit stuff keeps my mind off my real concerns, though. Can I go a month without feeling driven to make a journal entry concerning Her?

The beetles on the floor are big and black, like big shiny soup plates with legs, and boy, can they run.

10:10 p.m.

Well, had Task Force formation. New policy: no falling out on day off. Firecrackers are blowing like mad around here — Tet. Orientals (devious) love firecrackers and so do Americans.

The office will be short one clerk tomorrow and Prince works, so they'll probably want me to work. I surely don't want to.

5 February 1967, Sunday, 6:55 p.m.

I'm on Operation Parallel right now and due for another formation at 7:45. I spent the day very pleasantly, slept in and read most of the day except when running a few small errands for the sergeant major. I read the new *Hit Parader* which has some good stuff in it.

Lt. Col. Prince and Col. Ebby spent the day out at Long Binh conducting an investigation as to why the ammo dump got blown up again.

10:05 p.m.

Tom Wicker this time has a report on Ky's attire (*New York Times,* 4 Feb.) — "nattily dressed in black overalls and a baseball cap with military braid on the peak . . ." Wicker has carefully chosen the words to paint as bizarre a word picture as possible while still technically not lying. Ky looks sharp in that outfit, although from Wicker's description you'd never know it. Mrs. Ky looks even better dressed that way.

I watched "Bonanza" and now am going to bed. Looks like nothing is going to happen tonight.

6 February 1967, Monday, 1:30 p.m.

Lt. Col. Prince and Col. Ebby are spending the day out at Long Binh continuing their investigation on why the place gets blown up every week. They'll be out there most of the week. Today I've been trying to call some units to get information. First I call Saigon long distance and ask for Can Tho. When and if I get them I ask for Me Tho or maybe Soc Trang or maybe something else and when I'm finally connected, the circuit is so weak I can't hear a word they say. We shout for a few minutes and then give it up.

Today I wrote a letter to Whit.

Last night while waiting for the alert to begin, I drank some beer and ate some corn chips (ugh) and was affected by neither. Even the corn chips seem alright. I guess I'm finally over my psychically-induced teetotalledness.

I have only eight more Task Force formations and I'll be done with them for this week. Joy, oh Joy.

Four more days and I can say that I've got just six months and days left. That's the optimistic view. Although they are death on extension over here. There's an absolute rule against it. One can leave a few days early or a few days late, but only a few days, not weeks or months.

4:00 p.m.

Sat in the frigid confines of our fine library and read *The Military Review,* January 1967. No evidence anyone else had looked at it. Fresh as a daisy. Lieutenant Colonel John R.D. Cleland in his article "Chinese Rimland Strategy" agrees with my theories. He too thinks that North Vietnam is out of the control of Red China. Uncle Ho marches to no beat but the beat of a unified Vietnam. Holding the same view and verbalizing it to old Kozart is what started off this feud that is now in progress and this view is the same in many ways as that in an official Army publication. Funny how far the views of the leaders differ from the men fighting the war. The colonel says don't fire any of the houses for any reason. The major says don't fire any of the houses unless you're absolutely sure there are VC in there. The lieutenant says don't fire the houses unless you think there could be VC in them. The sergeant says fire all of the houses because they're probably filled with VC. So a few hundred more VC (women and children civilians) die. It strikes me as peculiar that the medal winners (EMs) see things in such clear blacks and whites and expect others to see the same way. What would Kozart say if he heard the colonel espouse the above views in front of the troops. Kozart would of course never read the *Review* himself and he wouldn't understand a speech either, I guess. He hasn't finished high school, one of the few that I know of around here.

6:30 p.m.

Well, Lt. Col. Prince came back from the investigation and so did Col. Ebby. They were tired but not in bad moods at all. They were supposed to have late duty, but they left me in charge and Col. Ebby said that I'm acting chief of Complaints and Investigations. That means I do nothing except sit here and type two little teeny letters that they left. Prince spent ten minutes going through the list for today and took action on it all. Col. Ebby reviewed it in another ten minutes and it'll take me ten minutes to type it. Col. Coldass would have been on it for two days.

I hope that Task Force doesn't amount to anything tonight as I'd like to go to a movie. Or even read a book.

Folk Saying: Roses that are red are ready for the plucking. A girl that's 16 is ready for college...

7 February 1967, Tuesday, 7:15 p.m.

I have just a little time before I go to Task Force formation. This has been a bitch of a day. That report on Long Binh is in a stage of preparation and what a lot of typing. Also the usual emergencies keep arising.

8:48 p.m.

That's a short formation. Only two more evening formations and I'll be done for this week. Tomorrow I have to march in a parade in full field gear and rifle. UGH!

Nancy Sinatra is in the compound tonight giving a show. Bosh on her and her boots. Lt. Col. Prince is now letting me sign things with his signature. Oh, this new found freedom. Also Col. Ebby is writing letters now and he allows me to rewrite them for clarity without his permission. He's a very fine fellow.

If I could get ahold of my steno teacher now, I'd have a few things to tell him about the facts of being a steno in RVN. If one accepts the Army as a necessary evil (necessary to be undergone, not necessary to anything else) one can survive with no strain. Also one must be lucky enough to have a good boss. I'm set up for the rest of my time here with a good boss, as Col. Ebby will be here longer than I. And Lt. Col. Prince will be here until June.

I'm now drinking a Dr. Pepper and I just finished reading the February 6 *Newsweek* which had lots of interesting things in it. Tomorrow both my bosses will be out at Long Binh again so I'll have a chance to get caught up in my work.

My hair is getting quite long and I'm wearing a pair of skuzzy old jungle fatigues so I really look the part of an old Saigon hand. Or foot, even.

Time for me to hit the hay in preparation for another day which will soon be under way even before the sun ray breaks through to play upon the bed in which I seldom lay. Today I got a case in which the wife of a serviceman was going crazy because and solely because of the morbid, crummy letters from her husband. Crumb that he must be. We admonished him severely to lighten the tone of his letters to the wife "if you care about her."

8 February 1967, Wednesday, 9:20 p.m.

I just got off ammo guard, which consists of sitting in the back of a truck for two hours. With the cold wind blowing on my cold and sore throat. Tomorrow is a holiday, but everybody in our section has to work. Of course. Today was a very heavy day with only a few minutes for lunch and about 15 for dinner. The movie "Texas Across the River" with Dean Martin is on tomorrow night, but I doubt if I'll get a chance to attend.

It's really wild around here, with firecrackers exploding every other minute. Old Dead Head Ed, my room mate, just threw one at me a few minutes ago and I just about went for him with my rifle (unloaded, of course.)

Tonight I must take a shower, no matter how much it hurts.

This morning was very foggy and so of course we marched in a parade anyhow. The parade field was flooded especially for the the occasion, I'm convinced, because it hasn't rained here for weeks.

We are reminded to send valentines to our loved ones because Jody can hand carry his. (There ain't no use in going home/Jody's got your girl and gone.)

Roger Miller is on TV right now.

9 February 1967, Thursday, 6:30 p.m. — TET

I just fell out in soft cap and no field equipment for Task Force and old Kozart turned me in for not having on proper gear and I was excused and exonerated because I pulled ammo guard last night and didn't know any better.

I've got a monthly report due this Saturday which I should do tonight as I'll have boucoup typing to do tomorrow, but instead I'm going to the movie "Texas Across the River."

February 1967, Friday, 6:00 a.m.

Today I've been here five months. Now I really do have six months and days left. The movie last night was quite funny. Could have used John Wayne, of course.

I was going to work on my monthly report at least a little last night, but of course I didn't. It's going to be a big day today.

6:35 p.m.

That report that I had to do, well, it was no sweat and I knocked it off in about 45-50 minutes. I typed like a fool today all day long.

We got a form from the orderly room today requesting that my section submit me for punishment for missing a formation on the 8th. It was a muster formation and I was very much there, and in fact later that morning the sergeant major chewed me out for munging up my boots so badly. Well, the sergeant major was madder than hell at the orderly room and wrote up an answer that burned the paper, so I don't guess it's likely that we'll hear any more about it. The sergeant major said that if they attempted to carry it further they would wish they hadn't. And I'm sure he's right. I'm not on Task Force this week, praise be.

I get Saturday afternoon off, but I must work on Sunday. I'll be glad when we have our full quota of clerks. John and José are on an inspection. When Dave C. gets back from his leave we'll have one of the clerks from Nha Trang Field Office down here. Back on old easy street again. Tonight I plan to spend most of reading in the sack until the electricity goes off as it does every

night now that Tet is on and the gooks are using lots of
electricity for their electric barbecues and all.

11 February 1967, Saturday, 6:30 a.m.

I just ate breakfast after 6:00 formation. Now I must
dust off the desks and get ready for a big half day.

10:00 p.m.

I got the day (afternoon) off and I work tomorrow,
but Lt. Col. Prince didn't leave me any typing to do, so it
should be a light day.

This morning at 5:55, walking up to the formation, I
heard the opening chords of "I'm going to Louisiana, get
me a Mojo hand . . ." with the harmonica droning along
behind the guitar, whaa, whaa: "Behind the sun . . ."
Muddy Waters on the Army radio station. I really about
fell over. They probably play that kind of stuff every
morning when I have no way to listen to it.

I've still got a bald spot on the back of my head,
though I pluck it less with old Prince and Ebby at the
helm than with Coldass.

This evening we (the clerks) went to the USO for a
steak dinner. We're confined to the compound but we
don't mind extralegal methods.

Old Dead Head Ed is calling radio signals on the
intercom: Ragaspeck this is Zero Niner Four . . . Ragaspeck.
Now he said Nnnnnn, Nnnnnn, Na, Nnnnn, Nnnnn.

More characters want to denounce their American
citizenship. All Lt. Col. Prince does is set up appoint-
ments for them with a legal officer so they are legally
advised how to go about it if it's legal. We make no value

judgments on them, except that they are scum and not too bright. Which they are. They have to be dummies to think RVN would want losers like they are.

I went to the doctor today and got pills to relieve my cold symptoms: nasal congestion and nagging cough.

12 February 1967, Sunday, 6:30 p.m.

My writing isn't too steady today as my left little finger has a nasty cut on it from a razor blade. This morning I was putting a blade in my razor and a rat ran into the bathroom and scared the shit out of me. I jumped and oh, how the blood did flow. I typed so much on it today that it became numb, but now it hurts again.

Another Tom Wicker article a few days ago, which reveals Tom's latent obsession with the finer points of haberdashery. The first five lines of his story are name and clothes—

"Air Vice Marshal Nguyen Cao Ky, wearing his black Air Force jumpsuit, his long-billed, silver-braided baseball cap and his purple silk scarf . . ."

The black overalls of 4 Feb. have been transmogrified into an Air Force jumpsuit and the baseball cap with military braid on the peak has become "long-billed, silver-braided."

Wicker then does most of paragraph five on Ky's mustache and paragraph nine calls him "dapper." He doesn't mention Ky's night-clubbing and penchant for cockfighting until paragraph twelve.

Not mentioned are Ky's French wife (divorced?) nor Mai, his stewardess second wife. Maybe Wicker is much married himself.

Dave C. came back today. He had a good leave and

has no regrets about extending over here. If I were a colonel I'd stay over here and get rich, but I'm not yet a colonel. More's the pity. It's not a bad racket. Just like it wouldn't be bad to be a top Boeing executive, it's getting there that's shitty. Walk a few miles in their moccasins, though, and maybe I'd recant my envy.

14 February 1967, Tuesday, 6:10 a.m.

Yesterday I felt very flu-like all day, with diarrhea, nausea, bones aching, and all the other things. My cold seems to have gone away, however. And this morning I feel as if I'm recuperating from the flu, too. Except for the diarrhea, which is still afflicting my nether regions.

Yesterday was a bitch, as I typed constantly from first thing in the morning til 6:00 p.m. Typed a couple of rough drafts on the Long Binh thing, plus all the regular letters and endorsements. While upstairs two clerk-typists sat doing nothing. Makes me kind of mad, but they seem to think that typing requires no real effort, thinking of me as a machine that just punches out the words. Old Prince started bringing some things upstairs to be typed toward the end of the day, and even began running some of his own errands to buildings some distance away. He continues to be reasonable. But Major Resnig, who's helping him, though he's a nice fellow, isn't very reasonable about the whole thing.

They just blew the whistle at HHC for them to wake up. And it's 6:25. It must be nice to sleep in an hour and 15 minutes longer than the company I'm in.

I got a haircut yesterday and took a shower last night to get rid of the little hairs and it was cold. I wish it would warm up here. If I could take a shower mid-day it would be very warm, but late at night or early morning it still is cold.

I guess I'll have an orange and a ginger ale for breakfast.

If times don't get better boys,
it's down the road I'm goin'.

10:00 p.m.

I just watched "12 O'Clock High" and "Rawhide," two of the best, I'm convinced. Today was a better day and my health is fine.

I'm still typing those goddamn rough drafts but tomorrow should be the last day of that, and then the final and that's all. A quiet spell for a while, I hope.

There's some kind of a weird program on with Ricky Nelson, about a has-been rock & roll singer.

Korean males hold hands, etc., as do Vietnamese males, and it is homosexual, though not in the sense as in the States.

It's 11:00 and time for a shower and then bed.

16 February 1967, Thursday, 5:45 a.m.

I have a command formation this morning that I forgot about. The damn things.

We're finally getting that Long Binh report finished, though I thought I'd never see the day.

Well, I guess I'll continue this at about 7:15 when I've opened up the office after the command performance (stumbling sleepily around on a field of mud to an off-tune band playing "Colonel Bogey's March" over and over again and to listen to a colonel who will probably say: "No comment." And for that we muddy our boots and brains with this early morning stuff.)

7:15 p.m.

I'm just returned from the bullshit. The colonel told us not to miss formation and that this is a wonderful opportunity to muster all of our troops and all the rest of that Army stuff. At least the field wasn't muddy for a change, which was so pleasant.

The officers are filing in and all . . .

17 February 1967, Friday, 6:30 a.m.

Last night I sat at my desk trying to get caught up in my work typing letters, and everybody got called out on a practice yellow alert or something, and we sat in the bushes and got mosquito-bit until 11:00 and then it was too late for anything except shower and bed.

Old Lt. Col. Prince and I had a small difference of opinion yesterday. He gave me a 20-page report (Long Binh) to type in the late afternoon, he left for the PX and when he got back I'd typed about two pages. He had seriously expected it to be finished. He was wrong. Today he's going to give the thing to someone (clerk-typist) upstairs to type it. Goddamn it, I don't have time for that stuff and filing and logging and writing all those goddamn letters too, I told him. When I'm a civilian again that's the way I'm going to talk to my bosses, and see how long I last. Well, he expected me to type on the thing all evening. And I was on alert and out playing their silly games. And yesterday I spent more than an hour painting the latrine and also taking the garbage to be burned. If they must have all those menial tasks

performed too, they are going to have to make adjust-
ments. Lt. Col. Prince and I are still on good terms, but
I'll be damned if I feel it necessary to convince him I'm a
superman. The more work one does, the more they
expect. It's like a snowball (in that old cliché). And the
slaves aren't the ones that get promotions either, but
guys like old Dead Head Ed, my "roomy." This morning
at breakfast he told me one of his favorite stories of the
guy at Fort Hood who left for Vietnam and told an NCO
that when he got out of the Army he was coming back to
kill him, and he did come back and he beat the guy's
head in with an ax or a table leg or something and then
shit on the fellow, laid bare of the protective bone and
skin and hair, and I was sitting there eating toast covered
with strawberry jam. He's unbelievable.

I march in bullshit parades at which they give medals
and stuff at the end of them and we salute about a
million times and they blow horns and things and it's all
quite stupid.

7:45 p.m.

Ky is talking about peace because it's fashionable
these days, and I'm reassured he was "dressed in a white
dinner jacket, holding a glass of scotch in one hand and
a cigarette in the other . . ." I'm glad he wasn't swilling
beer out of a can, chewing a stogie and wearing Levi's.
That would be tacky. A tacky ally, what a thought.

It looks as though the Long Binh thing is through
and Lt. Col. Prince will be gone tomorrow so maybe I'll
get a chance to get my files and cards and letters in
good shape and even have time to answer the huge
backlog of letters that have built up.

A WAC was assigned to our office and she's a nice looking girl, though a bit on the dull side as most of them seem to be. One of the clerks in the office has already begun monopolizing her time and is chasing her madly to the amusement of all concerned except him and the WAC. He's married, he always claimed in the past, but nary a mention of it now. A red ant just flew into my typewriter at the very instant that one of the keys went down and he was horribly mutilated and fell into the inner regions of the machine, writhing in mute agony. Poor dear.

I'm drinking a Dr. Pepper right now and it doesn't taste as good as Pepsi has begun to taste to me, and Coke I can't stand. Pepsi seems to have a soft, soothing taste and a can of it is gone in no time. Coke and ginger ale sit and I drink about half. Wink, oh if I just had Wink, I'd really drink the stuff down. Their new ads show it as a vodka mix which I think would be good.

18 February 1967, Saturday, 4:10 p.m.

Leisure time at last. This morning I got all caught up on my work, logged all the cases, filed, typed letters and have things in generally good shape after what has been the most hectic week I've had since I got here. If it had been this hectic before I knew what I was doing, I think I would have collapsed.

I look forward very much to having all day tomorrow off, to browse in the library and sleep in and nap in the afternoon, etc. Prince is on an investigation and Col. Ebby is on a flight somewhere up or down country.

Col. Ebby just came in, so I guess I'll continue this

later. Probably he'll have plenty of work to keep me busy the rest of the day (45 minutes).

5:00 p.m.

It appears that Col. Ebby, good old guy that he is, has nothing for me to do that can't wait a couple days, as he just said.

All the people who were rattling around the place just left. I have yet to get the garbage together for its nightly burning and will do so now. Just gathered up about two ounces of garbage on this floor. Now for upstairs.

10:05 p.m.

I just watched "The Man from Istanbúl" with Horst Buchholz. I think it was him anyhow.

Lt. Col. Prince got back late from Bien Hoa and Dave C. was very exhausted from accompanying him and taking shorthand. He spent the evening transcribing tapes of testimony while I was at the library and the movie. Prince didn't ask me to work on the stuff and I don't want to and won't unless directly ordered to. Tomorrow Lt. Col. Prince goes out there again and I plan on avoiding that, too. I'll hide or do anything. Officers can work all they want, but I ain't in this Army to work all the goddamn time. Not by a damn sight. I'm going to heat up a can of beans for a snack and eat some crackers and drink ginger ale and then shower, and then to bed I'm bound to go. I think I'll get up at seven o'clock and duck out for the outdoor theater until I'm sure that

Prince has left the compound for Bien Hoa. Sneaky, you damn bet.

20 February 1967, Monday, 6:10 a.m.

Yesterday I went downtown with Charlie B., somebody I halfway knew at Fort Ben. He's married, from Tennessee, and has taken over Whit's job upstairs. Twenty years old, besides. He took pictures, we had steam baths and massages and dealt with the natives in our usual boyish, charming ways. A guy tried to sell him dirty pictures: girls with dogs, Coke bottles, all sorts of things. Big pictures, too. The gook wanted thirteen hundred piasters for them. Charlie said no, and off we went around the block on some fool's errand or another and when we came back we went by the dirty-picture guy without even slowing down and he sort of loudly whispered, "Seven hundred p?" And we kept going.

An old lady with child came up to do the usual con bit with the baby (live this time). She carried a note saying, "All of my children have been foully murdered by the commies, except for this one dear babe in my arms." We kept on going.

If I knew why Long Binh gets blown up every week, I'd be very happy. I know why it's blown up. Because unknown persons plant high explosives in there that are detonated by cheap wristwatches as timers. The newspapers say that much.

That's where USARV is moving late next summer or fall, probably fall, but where I'd be would be some distance from the ammo dump, so I guess there's no reason to worry. Long Binh is a big place. A big place far away from realizing my diseased and damaged dreams.

But who even thinks about THAT anymore. I just go through the motions of being a desk-bound soldier like a soulless automaton. No more thoughts of things above my lowly station. Who am I kidding? Don't lie to yourself even though you lie to everyone else.

That corn chip-beer thing was short lived. I haven't had any of either since.

This is the worst war in history for civilian fatalities. All the magazines deplore the fact. *Nation* or *Reporter* had a long poem entitled "On a Child Hit by Napalm" that described the effects very well. One million children have been killed over here. Nice war. And our government won't let the Friends send money to help the NVN civilian wounded. The civilian wounded just must suffer. *Redbook* has a good article on the civilian hospital situation in Saigon by a doctor (American) who served over here with some foundation. The Vietnamese doctors aren't aware of bloodtyping, so transfusions are usually fatal. Nice? The North Vietnamese don't cow into submission; we should have learned that much by now.

Last night I went to the movie "American Dream." Like Anita Ekberg, it was a complete bust. Not like the book, and Steve Rojack was played by Stuart Whitman who played him as a real weakling which he isn't in the book. The movie both begins and ends differently from the book. Number ten thou. And I paid 35 cents. Yesterday morning I got up and sneaked out to avoid any details, like accompanying Prince to Long Binh.

The Army has been giving me lots of days off lately, now that our clerks are back from inspection and things have settled back to normal. Somewhat. I shaved last night instead of this morning and my face feels hairy and stickery.

Kozart wouldn't turn in most people, but he thinks I'm different and should be punished for being different. He's just a dumb harmless southern boy, like Wallace or those southern assassins that spring up in Texas and learn to fire a high-powered rifle in the US military. But nothing else.

Old Dave C. left this morning for Nha Trang, where he's to work, and at least one clerk from up there will be coming down here to further relieve the pressure. Things should be getting nice. Dave C. went with Lt. Col. Prince yesterday and recorded several hours of testimony which I'll probably have to transcribe today. UGH.

Scribbled in an Army latrine: The job isn't complete until you finish the paper work.

8:35 p.m.

"Combat" is on. The one where the French girl says she has a baby buried in the rubble and the Americans and Germans get together to dig it out and then they discover that she's nuts. I might get Wednesday off, because it's old what's-his-name's birthday. But if I do that means I work on Sunday next and I don't want to do that. At the end of the day a whole bunch of work came in, but I'll have all morning to do that, as Lt. Col. Prince won't be in. So I'll get all caught up, though I'm still not very far behind this week. Give me a little time though.

Old Joe D. is ridiculing old Dead Head Ed because he doesn't know who Ralph Story is. Joe is the kind of guy who knows who Ralph Story is but doesn't know that Humphrey Bogart is dead.

21 February 1967, Tuesday, 9:15 p.m.

Radio Announcement. Bernard Fall was killed today on the Street Without Joy.

Another easy day for me. Lots of work, but just typing little letters, nothing of any scope.

I work this Wednesday, all day, and then have Saturday afternoon off and all day Sunday off, too.

I'm drinking apple juice and ice out of a gold-rimmed Canadian Club whisky glass. Life for me goes on.

22 February 1967, Wednesday, 6:45 p.m.

I had a dream last night. Uncle Ho appeared to me — skinny and snaggle-toothed but somehow Uncle Remus-like. He said to me:

"Vietnam has been the West's Tarbaby. The French did get thrown back into their briar patch, but you Americans . . . You are hard to convince. We want you to leave, but you won't go. Because I look like a goat and Marshall Ky looks like a Hollywood cowboy—more than for ideological reasons—you have hitched your wagon to a turd. Appearance and reality. Like Bernard Fall said, North Vietnam has their George Washington, but the Americans are stuck with a platoon of Benedict Arnolds. That's the essence of it, anyhow. Ky is a palatably packaged turd, I admit. You Americans haven't learned from Uncle Remus, nor have you learned from Bo Diddley. 'You can't judge a book by looking at its cover.' You ignore all your seers. You ignore Fats Waller, too. A man with whom I spent a few golden Harlem hours. 'Your feets too big.' So true of you well-meaning Americans."

And then he faded.

Ky has again been threatening a US tour. Imagine the luggage! The black jumpsuits, the brown silk suits, the mustache wax. The mind boggles. And if Mai goes, too . . .

There was a game today (softball), the sergeant majors versus the WACs—ridiculous.

Today was one of those days. Work, work, work. I'm looking forward very much to having Saturday afternoon and all day Sunday off. I woke up this morning with flies in my eyes and then I realized it was still dark outside.

My flu is all gone, and I feel at my peak, considering that starvation is setting in. Last night Joe D. cooked spaghetti and it was good.

Ricky Nelson is something of a has-been, but a has-been with considerable residuals, both in records and in TV shows. He can well afford to be a has-been, though he's still played on radio quite a bit, at least over here. Better than being a never-was.

23 February 1967, Thursday, 6:15 a.m.

Today is the big parade in which I'll get to march. Last night I went to "Penelope" and of course it wasn't very good. Another movie about one of those non-conformist broads like Holly Golightly in that Capote concoction of sugar and rain drops. This one has a long scene in a coffee house and the coffee house looks like a set for a musical with Howard Keel and Co. Very uncoffeehouse-ish. Sometime, one of those writers ought to visit one, just for the hell of it.

Overheard in the line waiting for the movie to start: Do you know what 77 is? 69 with 8 guys watching.

10:10 p.m.

I had another one of those damned investigations to type and worked on it until after 9:30 tonight, which is too long and too much, but that's life. The investigation was interesting. The villain of the thing is named Allgood. Shades of Natty Hawthorne!!

24 February 1967, Friday, 2:30 p.m.

Only the rest of today and a half day tomorrow and I'll have one and a half days off!! Lt. Col. Prince and I are sitting here praying that no emergency comes barreling in as it has every Friday for three weeks now. He's worked every weekend this month and when he works I work, if not at the same time, harder later.

The Task Force 5 list was posted for next week and I'm not on it, so that's nice, too. Now if I can just sit here the rest of the day and doze and woolgather, I'll be happy. I spent the morning making final changes in the Report of Investigation and it's done and gone, unless unforeseen difficulties ensue, and they often do.

Lt. Col. Prince is in the back of the room throwing darts at the dart board and whistling his tuneless whistle that he whistles whenever he's throwing darts or building models of planes, cars, etc.

Lt. Col. Prince tells a story he's fond of about the fellow who, while traveling on an airline, found a cockroach in his tea. He complained bitterly to the stewardess and later wrote a letter to the airline that threatened them with the loss of his business, his friend's business, his company's business and sale of all stock in the company, etc. Almost immediately he received a letter from the airline telling him that the entire staff of that airplane had been fired, the plane had been destroyed by fire and that all airplanes flying for the company had been fumigated and the interiors replaced. This satisfied the fellow until he noticed a little note appended to the letter that was obviously for the typist only and had been enclosed only in stupid error. "Send the SOB the cockroach letter."

The whole point of the story is that every business has its cockroach letter and I have a bundle of them for several contingencies. Nothing is done because nothing can be done, because that's the way things are, but a letter must be written and it is written, but both sides know that things haven't really changed.

I just played a game of baseball darts with Prince and he won 50-32. Not bad, eh. I guess I'll do some typing now.

6:30 p.m.

I work until 7:30 tonight, but there is nothing to do for a change as everything is caught up. Lt. Col. Prince isn't to be seen around here so he must have left early. If luck will hold out until 12:00 tomorrow, it'll be a good weekend.

There are lots of hungry women who would be happy to make a mess out of me. The funny thing is that when the girls approach me and say something, I always am abstracted and in a daze and turn to them with a very annoying "Huh" which seems to drive the people over nuts, especially the women. It makes them madder than hell. And they answer "Huh" right back and it turns into a huh-ing match. They don't get far with me, I'm too supremely annoying. I have annoyance down to an exact science. I'm saving myself. For what?

Old Dead Head Ed just told me that our room fan is broken and it does indeed seem to be.

Old Ed isn't really a bad fellow. Old Stone is the guy who is hard to take. He's the one with the story of wiping his ass with a corncob. Nice table talk. Swinging Sixties just came on the radio. "At the Hop, Hop, Hop" is the first song. Let's go to the hop.

"Born too late." We were all born too late. I was also born the wrong color and in the wrong country. A very good old song. Next they'll probably play "Sitting in the Sand, Oom badada" by the Chordettes. I think. The Pony Tails. "Born Too Late", that is. "Personality. . . . a great big heart." These songs really make me nostalgic. The old days. Lloyd Price. When I was but a youth, an infant, but not of Prague. The Beach Boys said they were going to devote the year to making good-time music and nothing else. They are very capable of doing it. "Good Vibrations" is fine. What's malaria? We get the worst commercials.

Especially Ebullient Jones. Sounds like the name of a negro child in a book of Booth Tarkington's. "Peter Gunn" by Duane Eddy just now. Or that negro in the . . . The Teddy Bears. "To Know Him is to Love Him", by Phil Spector, I believe. This one brings tears to my eyes. I'm just an old softy. Tom Whatever and the Electronic Underpants. Phil Spector was one of the first of the millionaires made by rock & roll. Dee Clark: "Just Keep it Up." Never heard that one before. One of the lieutenant colonels just said let's take and go home. "Babytalk" is on now. I remember that one. Christ, I was but in junior high school, I think, when these were hits. Jan and Dean in 1958. "A Theme From a Summer Place" by Percy Faith.

"Let the little girl dance." I wish I could. I'd love to see her dance. Great old rock and roll. The music in it sounds like the Coasters. "They called it puppy love." Paul Anka. Brenda Lee. "Dreamin', I'm always dreaming." Johnny Somebody-or-Other. Perrantus? "It's Finger Poppin' Time." Sure it is. My fingers itch to pop.

A fire engine just went by and I can hear old Dead Head Ed upstairs popping his fingers through a hole in the floor. Hank Ballard and the Midnighters. The Drifters. "Save the Last Dance." Yes, I'd love to dance. With Her. My Princess. "Don't want your love anymore," by the Everly Brothers. Great. "Cathy's Clown." Fine song.

I just used a can of chili to pound in some nails to hold my light cord out of the reach of the typewriter carriage. Bounty Chili. The goddamn hammer is gone again. I don't know where it went, but wherever it is, I hope it's happy. The All American Star with Bill Parsons. I remember it well but don't remember the names.

I'm going over to the library to read the latest *New York Times* book review section.

25 February 1967, Saturday, 8:25 a.m.

Only four more hours and I'll have the weekend off, except for the painting that I have to do in the colonels' latrine upstairs. That should only take an hour or two at the most. That room fan of ours worked most of the night and then conked out in the morning early sometime, and I was quite bit up upon awakening. While I shave every morning, the little mosquitoes sit on my bare feet and nibble away so I always have itchy feet, and of course the Army wool socks don't help a great deal, or even a little deal, whatever that means.

Last time I went downtown with Charlie B. We were poking around a courtyard off Tudo Street. We were walking along and saw a family eating dinner back in the corner of a courtyard between some tumbled-down buildings. We got fairly far in there, Charlie with his camera, and a police dog about the size of an elephant started for me, barking like all the claxons of imminent death. I am so afraid of dogs anyhow. I took off running and that damn dog chased me about two blocks. Nobody I know has these problems. When I go into the Tax Building downtown to browse through the shops, I'm wearing those crummy old green-with-mold desert boots. The little shoe shine boys always come up to me and attempt to shine the damn things. When I try to walk away they embrace my leg, the one with the shoe on the end of it that they are trying to shine, and I have to drag them almost out into the street to get shed of them. I must have the look of a real sucker.

I'm mighty hungry. I eat breakfast most mornings, yet hunger is still a constant companion. I wonder if it's psychological hunger? If I could have My Darling in my arms, would my hunger be quelled? Or only fully awakened.

5:55 p.m.

Well, I've had my afternoon off and spent it in the library reading. I read an article by Bernard Fall, on the RVN situation in that review magazine that used to be *Review of Literature*—he's dead now four days. *National Geographic* has an interesting bunch of pictures of Hue, which I hope to get up to see one of these months.

Big surprise! Ky has postponed his triumphant U.S.

tour. I wonder what inducements he was given?

Discussed LSD with Col. Ebby and Lt. Col. Prince and decided I was hasty in my condemnation of it. After all, as Prince said, one can't criticize something he hasn't tried, even for himself, and if he tries it and finds it bad, it is only bad for himself, not everyone. Relativism. But that's Prince all the way, a liberal relativist from Tifton, Georgia. Really. Ebby said that as long as the LSD trips were supervised by people (medical) who knew what they were doing, he could see nothing different about it, just another drug to be used for prescribed or appropriate situations. But as James Terrill says in a footnote—The writer has found that warnings against self-experimentation are ineffective: it is like telling children not to put beans up their noses.

I'm itchy from the haircut that I got this afternoon, but a shower will remedy that. Charlie and Joe just rode in on bicycles that they bought today, 2500 p. each, about 20 dollars. I suppose I'll have to buy one. That will add some spice to my life. Also get me in better shape, something I never have worried about and still don't though I ache from the dart game I played yesterday.

Our WAC may be OK-looking but she's doggy nonetheless. Dumb dumb dumb. But not dumb enough to make her interesting. Just the golden mean of simplicity, in the boring sense.

An orchestration of "Wildwood Flower" just came on the radio. Now it's "On Top of Old Smokey."

26 February 1967, Sunday, 7:35 p.m.

It's another Sunday night and the weekend is shot. I spent most of the time sleeping and some time reading and also painted part of the latrine upstairs. Now we're trying to prepare the building for a pre-AGI, which means Adjutant General Inspection, and I don't know what they'd inspect here as the whole building is a mess. Replacement is the only thing that could alleviate the shitty condition, dust and mold that permeate all buildings in the tropics. Soon I'm going to sneak off and get some Dr. Pepper at the club.

Last week Major Kolosky, our XO, went on a big game hunting trip to Thailand or some such place. He shot three owls, two monkeys, and a porcupine. He said the owls were the tastiest of the three animals. I'm not really in much of a writing mood due to my dislike for physical labor of any kind, especially futile work that accomplishes nothing, and is done just to humor some idiot and his rules.

1 March 1967, Wednesday, 9:15 p.m.

One day I lost down the toilet in a diarrheic flood that is now stopped by what Buffy Saint Marie calls codein'. That's what I'm taking and I feel fine. The doctor said it would stop the diarrhea and stop it it did. Plus any other moves my bowels may have planned making. The codein took away the aching in my belly and the shaking in my head, but it did make my ears ring and make me see little faces on the latrine floor (guess whose faces?).

Dead Head Ed is going to be put up for SP5 next month. He made SP4 about 4 months ago, so that means I have quite a wait before I'm even put in for it, most likely.

That "Where Has All My Money Gone" thing is plastered all over the Army landscape in an attempt to keep us from spending piasters. We spend them anyhow. But it's a nice little poster.

The codein has made my ears very sensitive to the clicks of the machine and I feel like it's hitting on my eardrums. Not quite, but it is a little loud.

2 March 1967, Thursday, 5:50 a.m.

This will be a short entry as I have a 6:15 command formation at which we will march to a band and then be told that there is nothing that our colonel wants to tell us and then we will march across the compound again. I just took my codein' pill and I feel dizzy already, but I have to march so march I will. No exceptions. I have a doctor's checkup this morning to see if I'm fully recovered. I feel good, but my bowel movements aren't normal. They seem to have stopped. Which is better than diarrhea anyhow.

Last night I went to bed very early and slept well, like a rock. I must now tape my glasses so they won't fall off when we march.

3 March 1967, Friday, 7:00 a.m.

I work all day today and all day tomorrow. I hope that the schedule isn't too crowded. Mama-san just came in. Lately we've had a real falling out with her. The quality of work that she does is low and getting lower. Also she's been pestering me terrifically to pay her for last month and I haven't had any time to get any piasters. She takes her sweet time to do anything for us, but she expects gifts on holidays, and all the trimmings. Right now we are working on getting a mama-san who will be better and more dependable. Mama-san pay is pretty good by RVN standards, but most of the young strong comely girls make their living on their backs. The only mama-sans we can get are the old toothless monkeys with no ambition or drive.

I still feel well and it's great not to have diarrhea every 30 minutes.

Lt. Col. Blue just came in. He's a reincarnation of Coldass. Not at all bright and a real grind. I'm glad he has no authority over me. As far as work load goes. He could tell me to do something and I'd have to do it or pretend that I was anyhow.

4 March 1967, Saturday, 9:10 p.m.

I just saw "The Rare Breed" with James Stewart and Maureen O'Hara. It was a good film, though for the whole family. The Stewart film I'm waiting to see is "Flight of the Phoenix," and after that "Shenandoah." He's a fine actor and it's a shame that all these years I've held his Air Force affiliation against him. I understand these old fly boys better now after working in an office filled with aviators. They love those damn planes and flying and the whole concept. Some days around here it sounds like a tape of "The High and the Mighty" with all the flying tales. "I remember back in '42 and old One Eye Kite . . ." one of them will begin, and another will join in, "He's over in whatever now flying the whatever. Me and him flew over . . ." On they go with the stories and most of them are damn interesting and I listen too. I might get a chance to use some of them.

"Premier Ky has made elaborate preparations for the race." Ky is running for president. So says yesterday's

New York Times. R.W. Apple also calls Ky "nominally a Buddhist." Can he see into Ky's heart? What does he know of Buddhism?

I worked steadily all afternoon today trying to get caught up after being sick last week. All morning I was at the PX making purchases. Coke, dried fruit, deodorant, apple juice, razor blades. And many other sundry items. I only have $34.00.

5 March 1967, Sunday, 5:00 p.m.

Today has been an easy day. I worked all morning, but have goofed around all afternoon playing trivia with Lt. Col. Prince. He's got as many useless facts in his head as I have. He started the thing off by commenting out of the blue, "I wonder when they are going to have a Bruce Cabot Film Revival?" I said who and he said Bruce Cabot. There's going to be a movie in which he stars this afternoon on TV. Then we started off. He mentioned Wayne Morris. I remember him in that film about the Seattle lumberjack. And Tom Brown. And Una Merkel and Patsy Kelly. I asked him who had the male lead in "This Gun For Hire" and he said Alan Ladd. He then countered by asking me who the female lead was and I couldn't say. He stated Veronica Lake.

Pretty ridiculous. Think of the lieutenant colonels I could be working for. Like Lt. Col. Blue. He asked me a bunch of questions today and kept poking fun at me as if I'm a mental cripple or something. It started off with my saying that I wouldn't put in a request to be a door gunner in a helicopter. And he wanted to know why. And I said that the Army had made me a typist and they must know best and I'd stay one, and then he asked me what school I'd asked for when I'd joined the Army and I laughed in his face. And he said a draftee working in section.

Lt. Col. Prince says he was putting me on. But I don't know. I told him that I went to steno school and he said then you take shorthand and I said no and he said then you flunked the school and I said no I didn't but I can't take steno. He said what are you going to do when you get out of the Army and I said get a masters in folklore anthropology and he said too bad I didn't know steno, then when the fad for folklore faded I'd have something to fall back on. He pisses me off. Next time I get him in a discussion I'll try to get him on the defensive, if possible.

6 March 1967, Monday, 12:45 p.m.

Lt. Col. Blue is standing by me right now giving me the old evil eye, probably for looking at the keys while I'm typing. He's bad, but not one millionth as stupid as Coldass.

7 March 1967, Tuesday, 6:10 a.m.

Last night I went to the USO and gorged myself on ice cream and washed it down with a chocolate milk shake and a Coke. I could barely move when I finished. When I got back it was about 8:30, I showered and went to bed and was asleep by 9:00 p.m. I woke up of my own accord this morning at 5:00.

10:30 a.m.

Tonight is "Up to His Ears" with Jean Paul Belmondo and Ursula Andress and I'm looking forward to seeing the thing. Today so far has been very light workwise and promises to continue thusly. I hope. All of the big things are finis.

8:30 p.m.

On a whim after dinner Charlie and I went to the early movie of "Up to His Ears." It was a very Oriental movie in setting, but the usual frantic jump-and-run Belmondo that I've seen so many times. "Wild Mountain Thyme" is playing right now on my record player.

8 March 1967, Wednesday, 12:45 p.m.

Today I must go over to the orderly room at 6:30 and sit for 12 hours.

Irrelevancy: Dead Head Ed's dog tags say "Blood— no preference, Religion—type A." Amusing?

9 March 1967, Thursday, 2:10 p.m.

Well, I lived through CQ runner again. Slept most of the night.

I haven't gotten too far behind, sleeping 'til noon today, but I do have some little work today, besides the huge pile of unlogged and unfiled material which I'm not counting as I don't feel like doing that stuff.

7:40 p.m.

I marched in the parade today, this afternoon. It was no sweat. I'm afraid that I will be on Task Force 5 this coming week and won't be able to get downtown this weekend either. It's been a long time since I've eaten dinner there. I'm hungry for that lobster and French bread. Yummy.

I have a couple of letters to type for my old Army job, so that everyone will be pleased with me, and then I must get things ready for tomorrow, make coffee and such. One must go in front of the board now to get SP5 so I no longer want that promotion. I'm happy to stay a SP4. The terror of facing a board of examiners would finish me off.

10 March 1967, Friday, 9:00 a.m.

I have only five months and days left now. I'm getting short. I don't feel too short timewise, but I feel plenty short in other ways: stamina, physical comfort and all that kind of stuff.

I've got a huge folder of cases that I must log, and I guess there is no reason for putting it off, other than sloth and mental torpor. Both of which I have in great abundance.

12:55 p.m.

I'm not on Task Force this next week (which would have started this eve) so I'll be going to "The Wrong Box" this evening, which I'm looking forward to very much. Also the office has instituted a plan by which each clerk gets an extra day off each week. That means that not only do I get next Saturday afternoon off (the 11th) and all day Sunday (the 12th) but also I get Tuesday, the day I picked, off and next Sunday too (the 19th). That will make the week go by more quickly. It won't last long but it's a good idea anyhow.

I just got the *Stars and Stripes* so shall read it and try not to gag up my recently consumed lunch of tuna salad, macaroni and cheese, and iced tea, bitter as bile and darker.

12 March 1967, Sunday, 10:30 p.m.

I've spent the day very lazily, slept 'til 6:00 a.m., got up and made my bed with clean sheets, ate a breakfast of salami, cheese and apple juice and then showered, shaved and read until about 10:00. I then slept until about 2:00 and upon waking went to the PX, got a haircut, ear trim, and returned to another shower and the reading.

I'm already looking forward to my day off on Tuesday and today isn't gone yet. Oh woe, what a worthless work hater am I. Tomorrow will be one of those days, I can see it coming.

13 March 1967, Monday, 4:25 p.m.

Today has been very slow and I've done very little. Nothing of great moment has happened. Colonel Mc-Cartney went to the command briefing wearing my baseball cap instead of his cap with the big wings on the front of it. That's somewhat ludicrous but it didn't bother him one bit. I didn't dare wear his hat, though.

Later today I went with Col. McCartney and Col. Ebby to Tan Son Nhut PX where I helped Col. Ebby with his liquor purchases: two bottles of Old Granddad for $3.10 per each, and a bottle of something else for $2.85. I wish I drank the stuff as it is so cheap. That $3.00 was for an imperial quart, not a fifth.

10:00 p.m.

I've spent the evening watching TV. "Combat," "Third Man," "Bewitched," and reading *The Masters* which I've almost finished. I work this next Sunday, which displeases me, but it can't be helped. The laundry here lost my laundry. They'd best find it. I'll know tomorrow.

14 March 1967, Tuesday, 6:50 p.m.

I spent the day (my day off) in the library reading, magazines mostly. I learned that Trumbull Stickney died of a brain tumor in 1902, and a sad death for a promising poet it was, too.

There is a new plan instituted here for training. I'm to train one of the clerks in my job. My absence when sick and today has made them sadly aware that without me they're in deep and dark water. Same with Charlie, though he gets to train our second new WAC to come soon in his job. I'm glad he got the WAC. She's not said to be very fine and I'm sure it's true. "See that girl with the diamond ring/She knows how to shake that thing. . . ." The radio is playing oldies but goldies.

I wish that "I Spy" was on here. They do have some good ones here. "12 O'Clock High" and "Combat" can't be beat, as hour-long dramas, but some comic relief would be nice. I watch all the old Dick Van Dyke shows, and there are many I've not previously seen.

"Rawhide" just came on, one of the best, of course.

8:55 p.m.

"Rawhide" was fair, but not up to its usual standard. Guest stars were James Coburn as an Indian killer colonel and Debra Paget as his Indian (unsuspected) wife. Very hokey and unrealistic.

15 March 1967, Wednesday, 5:10 p.m.

Last night, we had the unfortunate thrill of being awakened at 12:00 to go on a practice alert. The thing lasted until 3:00 so I'm tired today, along with everyone else. No allowance is made for the sleep lost, of course. We just have to make it up on our own time and I have by semi-dozing at my desk all day.

Nothing much has been given me to be typed today, although when I first took over this job it would have been two days' work.

I get so hungry for sweets, candy I mean, that it drives me to distraction. The food here is so bland, no extremes of spiciness or sweetness are offered. And I never seem to get time to go downtown for dinner anymore. When I don't have to work, none of my friends are free. They are working or on Task Force or some other Army b.s. This week Task Force is being increased from 25 persons per week to 100 so that I'll be on the thing almost every week, maybe only as seldom as every other week. And when one is on the thing one can't go downtown and spend piasters. The weeks that one isn't on Task Force one will have to work Saturday and Sunday. So farewell, downtown. They have it planned so we'll be confined in the compound most of the time. And they're charging for both the indoor and outdoor movies (35 to 50 cents) so even that won't be a free release. Ah, if the times don't get better, boy, it's down the road I'm goin'. To quote an old philosopher, this time a negro blues singer.

Played trivia again with Lt. Col. Prince. The officers I work with are unusually considerate of me and the other clerks. They are gentlemen. Really. I never thought to find them in the Army. But there they are. And most of them are southern. Lt. Col. Prince and Col. Ebby are both from the south. I think it has something to do with their consideration and even-tempered ways. Coldass was from New England, and a more puritanical Angry God with the sinner (clerks) one could never imagine. All of the southerners are quiet, calm, and never panic. Of course I've encountered others that stink.

Lt. Col. Prince is right now setting up a volleyball net so he can play a game of volleyball with the clerks. Also his face is all scratched up this week from diving into the officers' swimming pool in his clothes and in a somewhat inebriated condition. Of course no one is perfect. And although I tend to hero-worship my two leaders a little, there is good reason. The contrast between them and Coldass is the thing that initially caused my appreciation of their finer qualities. They are human, is what I'm trying to say, and the Army has it's full quota of monsters and tyrants as does any large concern.

How can you tell if you passed an elephant?
The toilet seat won't close.

I've checked out Graham Green's book *The Quiet American* and am reading it in this atmosphere which is most appropriate. It is very Vietnamese in atmosphere, and real. I've just reread the first few pages but I can see that it's going to go very fast.

Old Ed (Dead Head) was dropping some more aphorisms tonight. His latest: Your mother's got a bent bung, so she comes around corners. He's got a million of

them. Last night he went to bed drunk and shouted for
about an hour, one after another, aphorisms of that
type. He's very verbally talented in an unusual way. His
theme is always about the kid who wears a beanie and
runs into the wind following his boner to THE BIG GAME
and the dance. And from there on he gets less coherent.

Tonight I washed off the ceiling fans: covered with
lizard shit, red laterite dust, and black grease. They
sparkle now, except for the rust spots.

Off to bed and read about 32 seconds until I'm over-
come with sleep and off I go into dreamland where all is
golden and king crab sandwiches grow on trees.

16 March 1967, Thursday, 10:15 a.m.

I heard a song this morning sung in the oldest hill
style called "You're Gonna Change or I'm Gonna Leave."
The dissonance is remarkable. The line "You're gonna
change" is dragged out in a semi-whine yodel that is
beautiful. That song was on the 5:00 to 6:00 country &
western show in the morning.

There is a rumor afoot that although the Task Force
5 is being increased from 25 or so to 100, the formations
will be almost eliminated. I hope that is true.

Today I finally got back the laundry that was reported
lost by the laundry mama-san. Somebody else got it by
mistake.

I'm about half done with *The Quiet American* and a
good book for Saigon atmosphere it is too. I hardly
remember it from the first reading. Things have changed
little here in the fifteen or so years since the book was
written. The political groups are all switched around
and the Americans rather than the French hold the

streets, but it's mostly the same: the spirit, the cyclos, the markets, the people in their black silk PJs. The whorehouses with the girls clinging and fighting. This clinging characteristic is a strange one to me who has been exposed to it only on the street and from shoe shine boys, but the people are so grasping after the foreign dollar. It's a good book, though I haven't seen any Americans like the Quiet One. Most Americans are of the We-bought-and-paid-for-this-stinking-hole-and-should-be-treated-like-gods variety. Or the type who really don't think about it much and are just marking time with no commitment for or against the people. I'm sort of semi-committed against them. Especially the French-created elite who are fighting this war. I don't know anybody who came over primed full of book knowledge and ideals they couldn't wait to apply to the people. The Quiet American is so morally immoral. For instance in the fully moral way in which he takes the girl away from the old Asian hand and feels justified in doing so because his intentions are honorable, i.e., he can marry her whereas the old Asian hand loves her but can't marry her as he's married already. I can see that it might happen more logically among the diplomatic corps. The Army people don't carry many ideals which they try to apply to peoples and beliefs. They are here for different reasons. And men like the Quiet American with their ideals often kill more of the indigenous peoples than the soldiers who are here for that purpose. Green mentions right at the beginning that the Quiet American was responsible for the loss of approximately 50 lives so that we will judge his actions in the light of this fact.

Tomorrow is St. Pat's Day and I won't have to dig deep into the wardrobe to find something green to wear.

I've been typing like mad today and have a respite for a few minutes now only because Col. Ebby is so busy writing up work for me to do that he doesn't have time to initial all the stuff in his IN basket and transfer it to his OUT basket so I can grab it and type it up.

7:00 p.m.

I'm still working and have at least an hour more work to do before I quit. Tonight I burn the garbage too. Oh woe.

I guess I'll go burn the garbage now and then return and work for a while. I'm about two thirds done with *The Quiet American.* Old Dead Head Ed just came in and said "Naah Naah Na Na Naaaaa," he doesn't have to work tomorrow. He's lucky.

Ky is going to Guam to meet with President Johnson. We are told by the nameless *New York Times* reporter that "Premier Ky disclosed his plans while sipping a paper cup of iced tea . . ." So what? Does the fact that he was engaged in this activity negate his statesmanship? Human interest? Or just bad journalism?

17 March 1967, Friday, 9:00 p.m.

I just got off Task Force and they've added more bullshit than ever. It's going to be a long week coming up. I work all day tomorrow and all day Sunday and I already have a desk full of work for tomorrow that I didn't have time to do today. Most of the clerks have sat around all week doing nothing, but not old me. I work all the time, it seems.

I'm drinking Pepsi Grenadine and in a minute I'm

going to make coffee for tomorrow as I have to open up in the morning.

I didn't have time for dinner tonight so I'm going to eat a can of chicken which should not hurt my tummy in any way.

I've almost finished *The Quiet American,* a fine Saigon-ish book which sets the mood and style of the place just the way it seems to me.

I plan to read *The Quiet American* tonight until I finish it and it's such a short novel that there is no reason to drag it out. For some reason it reminds me of *The Outsider* by Camus.

18 March 1967, Saturday, 10:40 p.m.

Charlie B.'s grandfather died so I've spent most of the evening with Charlie getting him ready to leave tonight (he's left) for 30-days leave in Moshiem, Tennessee. With his wife. For Charlie this is quite a blow as he was very close to his grandfather who I think was almost a father to him. So he'll be gone for 30 days and the burden grows. He was to work with me tomorrow, but now (heavy is the load, oh my Lord, and the flesh is weak and the person a born sniveler) I must carry on alone. Well, that's that. To quote an old philosopher.

More about Ky meeting Johnson on Guam. One official (unnamed of course) characterized this meeting as a pre-election "kiss of approval" from President Johnson. What a thought. His holding hands with Imelda Marcos was disgusting enough, but kissing Premier Ky?

I'm hungrier than anything so I'll go eat a can of fruit, and then to bed.

19 March 1967, Sunday, 6:00 a.m.

Today I have to make 180 copies of some financial documents which won't be much fun but it's better than typing. They just played reveille which is a record and blares out of loudspeakers right behind this building, sounding like all the hounds of hell. About three days ago they played the thing and left the loudspeaker on a few seconds after the bugle call. Some wise guy belched into the microphone—one big BLECH!! that was heard far and wide and was appreciated by everyone as more appropriate than the bugle call.

Soon I plan to go eat breakfast, which won't be worth the trouble, but I'll do it anyhow.

Things will probably be too rushed today. If only the WACs worked on Sundays, it would help a lot, but those WACs don't pull their full load. They don't take out trash, or do any typing on complaints (the language is too "frank"). I'm prettier than the WACs. And much smarter. They aren't as sharp as they could be, but then no woman who joins the Army can really be too bright.

Time to go eat breakfast.

12:10 p.m.

No electricity since 6:30 this morning. I'd already shaved before we were plunged into darkness. Upstairs in the freezer there are several dozen steaks that won't be frozen much longer, won't keep until the party next weekend and I'll be eating broiled steak all week or until they rot.

There is a game the officers in the Army play. It's called "Why didn't Bill get promoted?" or "I wonder how the Army made the decision to promote that slob when he doesn't have a college degree, was removed from a command, has a wife who lays all the NCOs and four children who've been in the Army, three of whom received dishonorable discharges and the fourth is up for one?" Around promotion-list time all the old scuttlebutt is dragged out and their chances are weighed and reweighed.

One of the guys here, Joe D., is driven bats by my constant complaining which to me is just matter-of-fact commenting on the situation in what I think is a good humored manner. He said yesterday that complaining just made everything twice as bad. And when I replied: "Why not three or four or two point five times as bad? What makes it exactly two times as bad?" he got very pissed off. I don't know why. I have really been in a good mood (considering the circumstances) most of the time since I've been over here, convinced that the time would go faster if I were. He should see me when I really am complaining.

I'm going to go to lunch now and will be back shortly and write some more if I'm not doing some Army shit.

1:00 p.m.

I'm not doing any Army shit yet. Lt. Col. Prince is here today but he's not in the mood for work. As the electricity is off, the fans and air conditioners are off and it's hot. Not the humid-suffocating-wish-you'd-just-die-and-get-it-over-with heat of Indy, but more the heat of Yakima with the heat burning down from the clear blue sky and baking you, not unpleasantly, but still too hot to do anything.

I spent the morning in Reproduction, not fucking, as

one might guess from the name, but copying 200 financial tote sheets, and then arranging them. The machine broke only about 40 times. I'm getting rather good at running business machines, the simpler ones anyhow, and am glad I'll never have much of a chance to fall back on that particular training.

Edwards, one of the drivers, just put a large dab of Bryll Cream on his hand and was pretending by gestures, facial movements, grunts and groans that it was jism that he had there. Humor!

So I asked him if he'd eat the Bryll Cream off his hand for a dollar and he asked me if I was crazy. I then upped it to two dollars and he repeated his remark. I jumped it to ten dollars and then he moved his hand up to his face and sniffed the stuff and said well there isn't anything really wrong with it, it's just hair cream and said yes. But it seemed quite funny or weird or something. Maybe not.

All afternoon I've been shooting the shit with Lt. Col.s Prince and Blue about the Army and suchlike. Blue isn't such a bad guy. He tends to understate the wit of his jokes to the point of extinction, but he's okay. Nothing malicious about him.

Time to burn the garbage.

9:45 p.m.

Tonight at our 8:00 Task Force formation, roll call was drowned out by a group of blue grass musicians practicing about ten feet away. Southern boys singing "Mountain Dew." And they were beered up and sounded great. Who can't get enough of that wonderful stuff? Nobody!

20 March 1967, Monday, 10:35 a.m.

The work is stacking up on Lt. Col. Prince's desk and he isn't moving it on as he is busy with an investigation so the work will swamp me later today when he gets time to review it and throw it on Col. Ebby's desk and then it moves to his OUT basket and I'm responsible for it. Lucky me.

With Charlie B. gone I am the only man in a section of gigantic proportions who can open the safe, make classified pickups, etc. So Charlie's absence affects me directly and I'll be mighty busy for the month. Maj. Kolosky knows the combination but doesn't know how to open the safe. He lacks that feather light touch. Isn't that a laugh. I actually know how to operate a machine. If I were to be taken ill or be afflicted with amnesia they would have to call in a locksmith and have the thing opened and the combination changed.

This morning I spent my time calling units and harassing majors and colonels to get their work done faster on things we've sent them for action by their units. I've got two things to call Lt. Col. Coldass about but haven't the courage yet, maybe later today. He's as slow and stupid as ever. He sends us things all the time, using us as a clearing house to forward work he should have sent directly if he only was bright enough to know how. What a dum dum.

It's now 10:55 and I'm on my way to do the mailman bit.

7:15 p.m.

I've got about two more hours of work to do tonight which Col. Ebby told me to forget as he's not pushing

me and in fact he and Lt. Col. Prince rarely push me. But
Maj. Tief, a guy working for them now on an investigation,
is pushing me so I suppose I'll type some stuff unless I
go on an alert tonight and in that case I plan to forget it.
Maj. Tief isn't the only officer in the US Army with a yen
for terpin hydrate (G.I. gin), but he's the only officer I've
seen with a cane. Tonight was Gonzales' night to burn
the garbage but since he worked Friday and Saturday
and Sunday his sergeant gave him the night off. Of course
I worked the same schedule, but . . . It will even out, I
guess. (Never in a million years.)

In *The Quiet American* the old Asian hand smoked
opium every night and it gave him great release. He
smoked just the way all of the RVN workers in the
compound do on their lunch breaks. Maybe I should try
it.

I have a Task Force formation tonight and I hope to
God that we don't have to go out and run through the
bushes for practice.

9:00 p.m.

I went to formation and heard "Penny Lane" on the
radio while in formation.

When I returned I watched "Combat" on TV, Charles
Bronson was the guest star and the show was good.
About an artistic demolitions expert who didn't want to
blow up a grotto which would kill a bunch of Germans
controlling a valley that the Allies had to cross the next
morning, because the grotto was filled with art treasures
that were hidden by museum people. Just a straightforward narrative with no folderol.

"Bewitched" is on but I'm not going to watch it. I

think I'll do a little typing for old Major Tief. I'm stupid to do it, but I guess I will.

21 March 1967, Tuesday, 11:50 a.m.

I'm caught up for the present on my work, not counting the quarterly report that is soon due, the filing I'm behind on, the unlogged cases, etc., but I've done typed the letters that I had to type, anyhow.

I've been eating jelly beans and other little candies and have developed a mouth sore. I would rather have a mouth sore than a continual craving for candy which seems to be the alternative.

I ran into a new word this morning typing some garbage for Maj. Tief: Definitized. Or, in English: Made definite. Isn't that a killer. Old Tief kills me. I hope I have very little to do with him.

R.W. Apple reporting. The kiss was conferred on Minitz Hill, Guam from Johnson to Ky. Ky went out on a limb and declared that "the major Viet Cong and North Vietnamese units were now 'on the run,' and no longer capable of mounting sustained attacks." That may well be true. They'll keep running for the next thousand years and mount unsustained attacks. A picture shows Johnson and Ky in a Mutt-and-Jeff pose, always intrinsically funny, I think.

Oh yes, I wrote the other day that some blue grassers were singing "Mountain Dew." The refrain was "And them that refuse it are few..." which I don't think I'd heard before. I don't have to work this next Saturday afternoon or Sunday the way things are set up right now. One never knows what will develop though, do one.

Lt. Col. Prince will be leaving soon. In June, that is. His replacement will arrive by May 1st, so I'll have another man to train. But no matter if I like him or not I'll still have Col. Ebby to protect me from any insanities on his part if they by some chance get ahold of a dud. They screen them very closely so I doubt if it will happen.

I learned that José G., that clerk here who cleaned out the coffee pot with my shoe brush, was the third highest in his graduating class in high school. What an indictment of the public school system.

22 March 1967, Wednesday, 5:40 a.m.

This morning we have a command formation and we'll be told by our colonel that he has no comments and then we'll march back to the orderly room for a roll call and then dismissal.

I've got head count on April 6, which means I sit and count heads as they enter the mess hall.

Last night I went to the library and read a bunch of interesting stuff.

R.W. Apple, Jr. reports (trivializes) the end of the Guam talks. "The confident, almost jaunty South Vietnamese delegates left Guam this morning . . ." Mrs. Nguyen Cao Ky must have stayed home with the brats this trip.

This morning I have to open up, but I've already made the coffee so there is nothing much for me to do. Last night I was up until 12:00 reading *The Zebra Striped Hearse* by Ross MacDonald, the author of the Lew Archer book from which the movie "Harper" was taken. The same character was in the book I read last night. Divorced, trouble with his wife in the past, 45-ish. A good book but

I shouldn't have stayed up that late as I already am feeling tired and the day has hardly begun.

4:30 p.m.

Today has been very hectic and the food here has lately made me feel bloated, as if stuffed with old burlap and moldy raisins. I don't feel ill, but I sit and belch in an attempt to relieve the pressure on my innards.

I was going to go to the PX this afternoon and buy some French rolls, salami and cheddar cheese, but that fell through as Prince and Ebby were in a big conference upstairs with Col. P. and therefore no one was going anywhere. Also the results of the conference will probably be thrown at me in a few minutes to be typed by tomorrow. Oh well, I work until 7:30 tonight and have nothing better to do except read another Ross Macdonald book that I started today that is even better than the first one. Also the library is cool and filled with magazines that I haven't completely perused.

Tomorrow is the parade for the week and I hope I am exempt because of my fine performance last week.

Any minute I feel I will be given a huge insurmountable typing job to do, but that's the way I always feel and it hasn't happened lately. That reminds me of one job that I farmed out to the first WAC that was assigned to this section. A big investigation that used very folksy language. I gave the thing to Joe and he gave part of it to the WAC. After about a half hour she came up to him and asked him to explain what one word was. It was affect or effect or something. Right above it was the phrase "You worthless motherfucking nigger." They didn't discuss that, however.

I did have some discussion just now with Col. Ebby and Col. Mc. on boiled peanuts, which are a big delicacy in Enterprise, Alabama. They said lines form in front of the store just to buy the things. They bought and weren't impressed.

That (I just learned) investigation I feared to have to type has to be done over from the top so I get a reprieve. Yea. I think I'll doddle over to the mail room now. Oh yes, got another complaint from Lt. Col. Coldass on his mail and called the dumb bugger today on it.

7:03 p.m.

Today Lt. Col. Prince looked up from his desk and said would you believe a Bruce Bennett film festival?

I'm not near as tired tonight as I thought I'd be. This morning that colonel demanded our presence on his field so he could tell us he had no comments. But I don't mind. Right after he said that, someone out there turned up their portable radio very loud as some sort of a futile protest.

23 March 1967, Thursday, 6:35 a.m.

I just came back from Task Force. Only two more formations and I'm off the thing until next time. Only one more chance (tonight) to go out and sit in the weeds at the golf course and I hope it doesn't happen. I'm going to eat breakfast now.

10:35 a.m.

The office got a letter today that Major Eldman, the ex-XO, has made the promotion list for Lieutenant

Colonel, No. 818, and has successfully climbed over the corpses of his friends to some degree of power. Actually he's one of the nicer fellows I've met so far in the Army. The present XO is a little frantic although he's nice enough.

Old Dead Head Ed came up with a new one this morning: The tight, bright, ever-so-white wool horse, to ride. Guess what it is?

I just made a trip (about 30 minutes ago) over to the PX truck and had a drink of Lemon Limon with the usual ice covered with dirt and detritus so that the bottom of the cup looked like the moraine of a minute glacier. I complained about it bitterly, of course.

Sgt. Rhett Ruttencutter just came in and withdrew a complaint. It was nice to see him again. But seeing him awakened in me passions for Madame Ky which I'd thought dead, but were only dormant. I'm a worthless soul, acted upon but never acting, a piece of jetsam on the sea of life. Why don't I take charge of myself and become the architect of my future? Because I lack a single shred of gumption, that's why. I'm just a doormat. Now and forever, Amen. Capable of recording laundry lists of detail, but don't expect me to *do* anything. You'll be disappointed.

8:10 p.m.

Task Force has been and done and only one more formation left this week.

I haven't yet gone swimming. They've moved the pool across the compound and are still erecting it.

Ed (Dead Head) is a very puzzling character. His father is a college professor in California and has a masters in English lit. and has doctoral credits from Berkeley. Ed is very bright, two years of college, but his only experience was working in a Columbia record-packing factory with a bunch of grass-smoking Mexicans. Ed thought the people were great but the work was lousy—although he got away with some records.

24 March 1967, Friday, 3:45 p.m.

It seems as though this week is lasting forever, but that must only be an illusion. I've been typing rough drafts all day and I hate the things almost as much as I hate finals. Major Tief gave me a little job to do and said for me to take my time and give it last priority. He's plagued me about it all day. "I'm not needling you," he'd say, "but have you finished those things yet?" "Why no, Sir. I guess I haven't." He then drinks some terpin hydrate, for his cough! I hope I get tomorrow afternoon off and Sunday as scheduled, but there could be an investigation come up and in that event I work. I had my last Task Force formation this morning, for now anyway.

The phone repairman came in and fixed my phone today; it hadn't been ringing and now it rings very shrill and piercing. I'd rather it didn't ring at all, as it did before. It won't stay working long, most likely.

There is a company party scheduled for tomorrow, steaks, chicken and potatoes and all that kind of stuff. Last time I went to a company party old Kozart harassed me, but he's gone back to the States now so it's a free choice and I think I'll go. All of the WACs will be there, of course, so we'll all have fun, watching them make fools of themselves, get drunk, make passes at the more innocent soldiers, etc. Should be entertaining. There will be dancing even.

I'm very hungry right now, but also full of feeling as if I'd been stuffed full of cotton wool, and belching doesn't do a thing to relieve that vaguely unpleasant feeling. Maybe it's self-loathing. Maybe only indigestion.

Both Lt. Col. Prince and Col. Ebby are at this very moment writing interminable drafts that I'll have to type sometime, I imagine. I hate the damn things.

I don't think I've commented on the weather lately. It's been warm and no rain for months. About two months and we'll be in the rainy season again. It's still cool at night and when I take a shower at 9:00 or 10:00 or 11:00 I am quite cold upon stepping out of the water, and in fact quite cold whilst under the thing. I'm going to have Charlie put in a work order when he gets back to have our hot water heater in this building hooked up. Charlie has the charm to get it done. If I asked, they'd come around and we wouldn't even have any cold water left.

Col. Ebby just handed me a huge draft so it's work time.

25 March 1967, Saturday, 6:20 a.m.

I've got a huge pile of drafts to do today, but I hope to get off at noon.

10:15 p.m.

I saw the movie "What's Up Tiger Lily" today. The background music was all Lovin' Spoonful and very good. Little bits and pieces of guitar music all through and good harmonica music. Also two or three shots of them singing good songs, something about caught with his finger up his nose. The Woody Allen jokes were good. He worked all the Oriental folklore clichés in, even the one about Oriental girls being made differently, having it going in the other direction. Once again I find myself thinking of My Asian Darling and her awful burdens.

I'm eating some malted milk balls, something I've never cared for but now eat with fond nostalgia of choking on them as a child when gulled into popping them mouthbound.

26 March 1967, Sunday, 9:00 p.m.—EASTER

I went to town early today with Larry C., and first we had a steam bath and massage, which was very good, as I had an older woman who seemed to be something of a sadist and she walked all over my back and cracked my joints and all that, and then we were hungry so went to the Steak House and I had grilled lobster and Cantonese rice and French bread and two Coca Colas and papaya with lime for desert, very good. That was 1,000 p. so far. About $8.50. Then we went to a big RVN movie theater, and as the only Americans in the place watched "Fistful of Dollars" with Clint Eastwood in French with Chinese, English, and RVN subtitles. If the Chinese and RVN subtitles were as bad as the English, nobody knew what was going on, as the plot was as complicated as that of the "Maltese Falcon." We did know what they were saying in that, at least. The English subtitles were out of this world. I can't imitate them and I can't remember them, they were that indescribable. If the movie comes here in English we'll go to see it just to find out who wins. One thing I know: there were more men killed than ever before. In one scene Clint hangs some steel plate around his neck and allows himself to be shot at by a rifleman at short range. The plate is covered by his serape. The rifleman keeps hitting him and knocking him down and he keeps rising again and walking in closer. Finally Clint gets right in close, flings aside the serape and the steel, and goes at it with his revolver, killing four of them and leaving the fifth without a rifle. He allows him to pick up the rifle and then he kills him. The theme music is very good and loud and the credits are backgrounded with red and black cartoons of a man on a horse and are very good. The audience was appreciative.

The news reels consisted of three million shots of Nguyen Cao Ky and his wife dressed in husband and wife matching black jumpsuits, seeing the American troops out in the front whatever. They looked very cute. No patriotism was observed, no shouting, cheering or other nonsense. Madame Ky, My Darling, gave my heart a jolt when she appeared on screen. God how I'd love to unzip her from that black go-to-hell jumpsuit, peel her like a banana and eat her like one. At the same time watching her in front of the peasants reminded me of Marie Antoinette and the cake she suggested her peasants eat. That thought fails to dilute my passion for the woman. A woman I don't even really know, truth to be told, although on a deep atavistic level I feel I know everything there is to know about her. I *want* her and will have her. I know that. What is my plan? I have only the merest inkling of one.

Today I also went to the Cholon PX and commissary and bought twelve rolls and some canned turkey and plan to sup therefrom for a few days. Also cheddar cheese as they had no salami.

This was an expensive day comparatively but a decent Easter Sunday. I wasn't born again but the good food and the relaxing massage allowed me to produce a shit worthy of Pantagruel after I arrived at my roost.

At the USO today they had free food and free Coke, but it wasn't one tenth as good as the food at the Steak House. Carver had two filet mignons that were, he said, delicious and they looked so to me. April First we're having our big steak feed for the office and I'm one of the cooks, and they expect me to cook steaks. It was either that or mix drinks and I thought I'd make less of a fool of myself at cooking, though maybe I'm wrong. I'll find out.

One of the drivers is sitting here whistling "Stewball Was a Racehorse" and it brought me back to the times of old "And Screwball Was a Racist," the thing that Steve Lawler used to sing in his folk days.

We got a note from Charlie today saying that he was having a ball and would we please get his laundry out of hock for him and he'd see us in three weeks.

27 March 1967, Monday, 9:00 p.m.

It was another one of those Mondays, all work and no play.

I watched "Combat" tonight. I'd seen it before. Twice.

Old Col. P. was in a bad mood today, but when he walked by he punched me in the breadbasket and said "Losing weight," and I stammered something sharp like yeah, I guess I am, kinda . . . sir! I'm so very quick on the uptake with my betters. He'll soon be leaving and he'll be missed as he's one to stick up for his men.

29 March 1967, Wednesday, 8:30 p.m.

Ky's orders have allowed 3,000 Buddhist monks to march into Saigon. So said Sunday's *Times*. Maybe he isn't only nominally a Buddhist.

30 March 1967, Thursday, 7:15 p.m.

I just screwed up a letter for a general's signature. I'll have to try again later.

Dead Head Ed just told me a story about the sheep that fell down the outhouse and got all covered with shit. Why was the sheep in the outhouse?

Tomorrow I have the afternoon off and then I have until noon Sunday off, but I work most of Saturday, though the party starts about 4:00 so that won't be a full day either. Col. Ebby said that I'll get tomorrow afternoon off if he has to type the stuff himself, which of course would never happen, but it looks as though I'm assured of an afternoon off unless for some reason I decide I don't want it. That could happen. Tain't likely.

Greene has many books that appear to have been written by a man who is alienated from his country. *The Burnt Out Case, Our Man from Havana,* to name at least two offhand. But this book, *The Quiet American,* contained details that were just what it is here, not traveling stuff, but tiny details, details that make the difference.

Old Lt. Col. Prince came in last evening after a long day in the field with a sour expression on his face and Col. Ebby asked him what the trouble was. He said that he'd gotten up that morning and reached for his gargle and got ahold of Aqua Velva and he'd tasted the stuff all day. That bit about getting shaving lotion instead of gargle is a cliché of course, but that's typical of Prince.

He lends truth to the cliché.

I've taught the safe combination to Stone so I'm not essential anymore. Today Col. Ebby told me that I was indispensable and that an afternoon off would indeed be felt by them, but that I'd get it anyhow. I said that I shouldn't be that indispensable for what if I were sick for a week unexpectedly, and he said that would be bad indeed. We're going to train someone, I don't know who, so that it won't be a big deal for me to take time off.

I'll never be sent to the bush. It could never happen in this section. Roberts, who was a huge fuckup and a criminal besides, requested a transfer to MACV which is downtown Saigon and they did everything they could for him so he'd get it, and they all hated him. If any of us joke about wanting to go north to get combat infantry-men's badges the sergeant major frowns mightily and says that they'd never approve it, and he means it. It will never happen as long as I have Col. Ebby as my man. Lt. Col. Prince says that I'll get a chance to go on a few chopper trips around the country if I want, but that's *safe* and only at my request. These people are good to me and like me. They make things as nice for me as they can. I told Prince and Ebby that I don't like shorthand and never learned it so whenever they need someone to take shorthand, they call on Joe D. who enlisted for shorthand and wants to keep in practice. I'll never have to take shorthand, because they are nice enough to allow me not to.

Tomorrow is payday. At command formation this morning Col. Shitbird had a long speech on the delights of alert practices and how they don't cut into our day at all but give it a pleasant punctuation, a break, a needed difference that brightens the boredom and lifts our lowered psyches. We all groaned and cursed him for a fool.

31 March 1967, Friday, 9:50 p.m.

I had the afternoon off and it was pleasant, though I did nothing except read, get a haircut and fight with the laundry people for the second week. They again gave my laundry to another person with the same name. I chewed their asses, but that still leaves me without clothes. I'm really down to nothing and will have to wear a pair of Dead Head Ed's pants tomorrow. Those worthless people. They have such an attitude of carelessness. Well, you'll get them back. Come in tomorrow. That doesn't help today.

One thing about the afternoon off, they just saved up my work and I'll do it tomorrow instead of today. One can't have everything.

I got paid today and have the money stashed away.

I got my hair cut quite short as it's hot enough that the long hair was bothering me and hung in a damp wad on my head.

I discovered another place to get free paperback books. The A&R lounge. I picked up three this afternoon and plan to get away with a couple each day. The assortment is wide: from Loren Eisley to Agatha Christy. Also a Nick Carter detective novel entitled *Saigon* which should be a laugh. Another *Quiet American.* Tomorrow is the big party. It's not really very exciting to me, but they'll have lots of steaks for me to cook and I'm sure that I'll get some to eat, although I don't care for steaks too much. Unless accompanied by a baked potato and all the trimmings. They'll have chicken too, which I prefer.

I'll arrive late enough so I won't have much cooking to do, as I work all day tomorrow and have to burn the garbage.

I went up to the club tonight to buy some corn chips and a Coke and things were flying, with a Flip band and a bunch of WACs dancing with those who chose to step into the floor show. Everyone sat and gawked at the dancers. I did, too, while I was in there.

Dead Head Ed and Joe just came in and are making fun of my haircut as RA and strak and all that nonsense just because it's short and not hanging down in my eyes as it was.

1 April 1967, Saturday, 6:40 a.m. — Fools Day

This morning I have a class on security which I hope doesn't take up much time but will surely. I looked at the work that piled up while I was off yesterday afternoon and it looked as if there are only two little letters.

In about five minutes I'll be leaving for breakfast if I'm lucky enough to have somebody come to relieve me. Breakfast isn't great but it's better than the starvation that I feel by 9:00 if I don't eat. Some mornings they have apples even.

11:15 p.m.

I'm sitting here listening to the Spoonful and listening also to Joe D. play his favorite game of reading the men's magazines and looking at the pictures illustrating lurid articles and identifying the movies that they were stolen from. For instance: *Action for Men*, Mar. 67 — "Weekend Only" Sin Sprees of Vacationland Call Girls, photo stolen without credit from "What's New Pussycat";

Men, Jan. — "I Crashed the Nation's Seven Wildest Easy Love Parties," picture from "Tenth Victim" of Ursula and Marcello with their eyes marked out with little black squares; from *Men* also—"Bigamy Epidemic" with picture stolen from "American Dream" with Stuart Whitman and whatshername. The first two were easy but the last was harder and the more skilled you get the better you are and you spot them everywhere. One of the pre-requisites is a thorough knowledge of current sex movies coupled with the ability to waste vast amounts of time.

Today was the party. It was okay. I talked to Col. Ebby most of the time that I talked to anyone. He talked about how extroverts have an easier time getting places, speaking of Lt. Col. Prince who was dancing the watusi or somesuch with Kathy, the first WAC we got. Prince has it, whatever it is, and women go for him. Without offending anyone or hurting feelings he dominates things whereas old quiet Col. Ebby just was there and talked to his clerk quietly and literately. Prince is a good man to work for, but Col. Ebby is the greatest.

I'll never be able to write the *Catch 22* of this war. I was fortunate to get with men that I respect mostly. Our section has its *Catch 22* characters, but I mainly see them lurking around the compound in other sections. Like old Major Rocca who spent much (most) of his time trying to catch people going into the mess hall late or walking on the grass. Col. Ebby has 1200 pounds of books that he moved last time he moved and he said he hoped he wouldn't move again. He says he gets a feeling of pride from possessing the book as a book itself, not to read necessarily. Not a new idea, of course, as I feel that way sometimes, but for an Army officer . . . They are human too. Why these valuable bright kind men are in

the Army is beyond me, but here they are. Col. Ebby
narrated a couple of long stories to me, one about a
sidewalk conversation with a Japanese whore that was
illustrative of his philosophic turn of mind. He's a steady
stable churchgoer, moderate, gruff. A character that in
fiction I could only treat kindly as I respect him. I've
always found it easier to write of people for whom I
could feel some detached scorn, which is a limitation of
mine, and Agee and Thomas wouldn't be able to compre-
hend it as humane writing.

Today those of us living in the USOM were told that
we have room and locker inspection from now on.
Everything arranged geometrically, large books on the
right fading down to tiniest on the far left, can you
imagine. One of Major Kolosky's bright ideas. Like having
toilet seats salute or fancy marching or that horseshit.
Also he said he wanted to see nothing but fit literature.
How about that.

I worked all day today until the party and was going
to work for a while this evening to finish a thing that is
deadlined tomorrow and another thing that is deadlined
for Tuesday as I won't be working tomorrow or Monday
morning.

The water here finally gave up and we must shower
in a dribble that a two-year-old child could better with
his own little tool.

Today Major Kolosky told me to get my steno pad
and take some shorthand and I told him to forget it as I
don't take shorthand. I told him not to be deceived by
my MOS. He dropped it with the comment that I'd missed
the chance to make a few points and I said don't I
always. A nice exchange. But I'll be damned if I'll take
shorthand. Screw the Army. They wanted me and they

took me and they're going to have to put up with my idiosyncrasies. Put up and shut up both.

On one of my little errands last week I dealt with a negro captain who is a nice fellow and capable, but after all I'm the extension of a bird colonel and I didn't get done just what Col. Ebby wanted and when he asked why I said that I didn't feel I had the authority to argue with a captain. He said you sure do, a measly captain, and besides what the hell are you talking about, you argue with me all of the time. And it's true, but that's my job, to make sure he does things right. This Army is so much different than Fuerstein's view of it. The RA lifers don't know what they can get away with. Whenever I asked Fuerstein about what it was like to work as the assistant to a full colonel, he described only the menial servile humble aspects of it, of which there are few or even none. Would I dare to take dictation on my colonel's desk. Hell yes. He said it could never be done. What a dum dum. And stand at attention when being given directions. I slump down with both elbows on his desk and sometimes, I guess most of the time, squat on the floor by his desk, hunkered on my heels looking up at him. I was afraid of the protocol, the picayune details, the little everyday aspects mainly because no one told me the way it was. Why don't they ever tell it the way it is, what it's really like, why can't they make it come alive and delineate a situation and give the extremes of behavior one can get away with. The sociometry of it was always so stiffly described, so impossible for me to believe, so impossible to have ever existed, anywhere at any time in any dimension, as people are all human, even colonels, not special creatures. No wonder I was afraid. Reality, if it were as described in school, would out-Kafka Kafka at his most Kafkaesque. It's not Burgess' *Wanting Seed* with planned murder of troops to keep down the population. It's a chaotic mess resulting from a democratic republic that lacks the totalitarian thoroughness and power to accomplish anything so mean and inhumane, no Nazi extermination here. The locals aren't being mercilessly massacred as were some American Indians, especially the civilized tribes. No, the people here are a match or better for the might and power of the US, and one can't take that point of view, things just aren't as simple as they used to seem. One thing I know, though, is that it's all wrong. To me it matters not whether we kill our own men with our own artillery or whether they are killed in the Saigon streets with blowguns quietly, poof, or whether we napalm the civilians or just the VC or just the North Vietnamese. It doesn't matter how who is killed. Just the fact of the death of any of them is wrong and should be stopped. Why the liberal can carp that we are killing civilians needlessly, and thereby imply that somehow it's alright to kill soldiers. The people are all the same in that any of them could be shooting us. How select, how choose, who decide. Just as with capital punishment, it gets awfully sticky who deserves killing.

Just the same to me is this carping and caterwauling about the draft and how men are selected. To me it doesn't matter. It won't be pure, good, equal any way one does it. Men are still being tapped to kill other men. And damn the details of the selection. It's still unreasonable to decide who is least inconvenienced by the job or who does it best.

2 April 1967, Sunday, 8:20 p.m.

I've been in this damn orderly room a lifetime, it seems. I'm very thirsty and in a couple of minutes will go get some soda and put in the refrigerator for later drinking.

This morning I typed a letter for General Cole's signature though it was my morning off and I did this in my t-shirt and old Lt. Col. Bergeron came by and rebuked me for working indecently clad. Some people are such pukes. And some people are good and thoughtful — meaning Sergeant McKee who just brought me a barbecued steak and which I'm eating with one hand whilst writing this with the other.

Read *Saigon,* the Nick Carter Killmaster novel. It held my interest, probably not to my credit, but my experience here in Vietnam is totally different than the Killmaster's.

I haven't seen a woman with large breasts since I arrived here (though I have no complaints on the size of My Darling's attributes). They lurk around every corner for Nick.

One thing amused me. A GI on page 95 holds forth on the war and the VC: "All they left us is a little open space in the middle so we can go around in circles in it. Jeeze, some crazy war, this is." I agree with him, circles is what we're going in militarily, but as long as we go straight ahead in promotions, it's the best war we've got.

I've read about 80 pages of *Time of Hope* and like it and plan to finish it off tonight unless I fatigue more quickly than I think I shall.

3 April 1967, Monday, 7:12 p.m.

I slept most of the morning and also read. Therefore I have work stacked up to the ceiling as nobody did any of it for me. Whimper whimper. But they don't push me; it's mostly my old compulsiveness about having things done that bothers me. So tonight I'm not going to do the slop, just take it easy and do it tomorrow and see if there are any repercussions, which with Col. Ebby there won't be and Lt. Col. Prince won't say much either. I drive myself mostly, outside force isn't necessary as I'm driven by some success motive. Next month I can be put in for SP5, and I don't want it as I refuse to go in front of the board, but still I want to be put in for it. The board asks questions like who is Westy and what do you think of those commies rioting at Berkeley campus, and I'd give them both barrels on that one. I have nothing to gain as a SP5 except a few dollars. And some command responsibilities that I don't want.

Old José G. who cleaned the coffee pot with my shoebrush and made SP4 one month before I did was put in today for SP5. Life isn't fair.

Today the rainy season started and it rained very hard for 20 minutes and then quit. It'll be like that for two or three months. Before it begins raining in earnest.

Next Saturday I have head count. It's absolutely deviously unintelligible how the company unerringly picks me and everybody else for company details on our days off. They are so good at that and such failures at everything else. The rock and roll just went off and crud will be on. I guess I'll take another shower now and read for a while and write some more in the morning.

4 April 1967, Tuesday, 6:15 a.m.

It's 6:15 a.m. The little radio I'm listening to is making funny little noises like Howdy Doody's clown and his horn. I'll change the station to the My Lan show which is a program of US rock and roll dj'd by a sickening little Vietnamese girl with a wretched little voice, a "how I love you GIs," "so wonderful to be fighting in Vietnam for freedom for the whole free world, take pride in what you are doing" voice. She just said that. Really.

Last night I felt something dry and papery crawling on my face and I jumped out of bed and looked around on the bed and sure enough a great brown cockroach was on my blanket. I whanged it a good one and it landed behind the water heater in the corner. Inoperative. My Lan is now telling a story of the first American to visit RVN. Nauseating. She's so terrible and her English is atrocious. Most bar girls speak better and some little girls about 11 or 12 who sell cloths, silks, etc., in the Tax Building speak English almost perfectly with an American accent. Of course My Lan learned her English in a French school whereas the bar girls learned their English from GIs. It's the French-educated who hold down all of the secretarial jobs, the ex-factotums of the French ruling class. They make me sick. It won't be long, yeah, yeah. Is that by the Beatles? It just was played. The owner of the radio just told me that the batteries came all the way from the States, which he meant as a hint that I shouldn't be listening to it. I told him that we came from the States too and what did that prove.

It's time to start getting my desk set up for the big day. Yesterday Maj. Tief came in all pale and liquorish, or terpin hydrated, and asked me if I'd be done with all of my typing soon. Implying that he had something for me to type. I said no, not soon, or probably ever for that matter, and that's the truth. I've got stuff that has sat on my desk for weeks now that should have been sorted and filed. My files are in terrible shape. All cluttered and jammed and ugly. Tomorrow Maj. Kolosky inspects the room and we haven't begun to clean the walls or anything else.

Now that Sergeant Major Mills has been replaced, as he's going home, I appreciate his rock-hard unyielding attitude on things. He's been replaced by a couple of wishy-washy yes-men who don't do anything except support Maj. Kolosky no matter how stupid his idea might be. Sergeant Major Mills ran the office, but now the EM are unprotected by a sergeant major and the thing is in the hands of the officers. Old Mills pissed me off lots of the time, but he was a good man and one knew where he stood. Oh well, I have Col. Ebby to protect me from any special insanities from upstairs.

8:20 p.m.

Today late in the day, desk heaped with work, ears ringing from ten hours of continual typing, I went upstairs for some more paper and two clerks were doing cross-words, one was painting her nails, and one reading a letter from his wife. I stomped down the stairs in a rage, stomped over to Col. Ebby's desk, pounded emphasis on his desk with my fist and said: Goddamn it, I need help down here, why don't you get me an assistant before I go nuts. He smiled and laughed and said that's a good idea.

Twenty minutes later he told me that tomorrow I

have a permanent assistant, that WAC who was the first one in our office. And I start training her to do the typing of all the slop so I can devote more of my time to filing and calling and making copies and the legwork that is so important. I think that will improve my spirits immensely because, as some have noticed lately, I've become quite resentful and simpery about the long hours that I've been putting in. This should be a cure.

She's not a complete idiot so she should be able to take much of the detail and copy and rough-draft work off of my back and leave for me the more difficult and administrative-specialist type of work, which I enjoy more anyhow. She'll be doing all of those investigations that I hate so. Col. Ebby asked me which of us had the most time in grade, i.e., which of us had rank on the other, and of course the WAC outranks me. Col. Ebby said well that doesn't matter, you'll be the boss and in charge of the job. The WAC, Kathy is her name, will probably soon be a SP5 so I'll have an NCO as an assistant.

I have to open up tomorrow, which is not a big deal. I have two beers in the freezer upstairs which should soon be cold.

5 April 1967, Wednesday, 7:35 p.m.

Well, I'm getting things in better shape, have my desk cleared of the rubble-laden midden that had grown there while I had no time to do anything except type. Kathy the clerk typist sits across from me and all the typing that Lt. Col. Prince hands me I explain to her and she types it and I assemble the stuff. I'm going to teach her the whole ritual, all the little aspects of my job and then we'll be able to take afternoons off maybe once each week without the desk becoming piled high with stuff that no one can do.

As Romeo Mittnecker says: The bugs I find in my food can't even stand it; they's all crawling out, instead of in.

I might go to the USO for ice cream tonight as I'm very hungry for same. "Little Old Lady from Pasadena" is on the radio now, Jan and Dean, bad Beach Boys is all it is.

This morning we had another formation at which we were told that there was nothing to be said. What a waste of time.

Lt. Col. Prince gave me a bunch of huge pictures today that were taken up north or in the delta or somewhere and I plan to use them to write a story or at least a few poems, as the stark white of the tree trunks and the green and golds of the foliage are captured and held in crushing intensity.

9:45 p.m.

I went to the Tan Son Nhut USO and all they had was cold American cheese sandwiches of which I had one which sticks in my stomach.

Earlier today I found an old item from the *New York Times* saying that Premier Ky had "taken steps" to prevent journalists from being impeded in their pursuit of truth (beaten by police). I wonder how many cattle prods and bamboo points were used in these steps. I'm certain Ky did nothing untoward personally. Like Pontius Pilate, he went home with clean hands to his stewardess, their infant, and his five half-breeds.

"Honey, I'm home."

"Did you have a good day at the office, my dear?" Mai chirps from the kitchen.

"I took steps to prevent foreign journalists from being impeded in their duties."

"Good for you, Darling. Would you like a Napoleon Brandy?"

"Yes, please." She delivers it to him.

"Oh, Darling, you've gotten a spot on your favorite lavender scarf. Must be red wine from lunch."

"Must be."

And so the war goes. My Darling comforts the Hitler of Southeast Asia with "Darlings" and brandy. And I fight my war with no handmaiden. Life is cruel.

I must shower and to bed.

6 April 1967, Thursday, 6:15 a.m.

Today is clean sheet day and I've already obtained the things.

I have on my right an aerosol can of spray made in Neodesha, Kansas: Insecticide, aerosol, synergized pyrethrins Type II, net weight 12 oz, stock number 6840-82307849, contract no. DSA 4-079403-PC409 for use against mosquitoes, flies, and other small flying insects. And the stuff doesn't do near the job that one small lizard does. One can't enter the room one uses the stuff in for a night and a day without feeling afflicted by poison gas, but the only ill affect lizards have on a room is a little lizard shit on the desks, and a little lizard shit never hurt anyone. After all, it's organically pure.

Another thing that is nice about having that WAC working on the bottom floor here is now that Maj. Tief is sitting over here in this office he'll take all of his work to her to do and stand by her desk and explain it to her, all for an excuse to look down her blouse which he never did with me, of course. So that removes him from the scene safely.

I'm off to break my fast.

10:15 a.m.

For the first time in days I have a chance to write on Army time. Most of my work is caught up. All I need is a hundred file folders and I can start revamping my file system for a USARPAC inspection that is due at the end of the month. Also a quarterly report is due, but SP4 John Stone is doing it for me as he is knowledgeable with statistics and I claim (accurately) not to be.

1:45 p.m.

Col. Ebby just came up behind me with some work for me to do and I ran my wheeled chair over his spit polished boot toe, so I guess I'll go for now.

I expect an alert tonight.

Lt. Col. Prince just went home ill with a bad cold and he'll be home for a couple days (home is the BOQ). Work has been steady all day, but with two clerks to take care of it there is plenty of time to type letters home, drink Coke, and take one's laundry over to the gooks so that they can lose it. Which is the way it should be. I'd planned to see the movie tonight with Peter O'Toole and Audry Hepburn. But I'd been told it was not so good, but then that doesn't mean that it isn't, so I might go see it anyhow.

It looks like I'll be on Task Force next week and

won't get a chance to go downtown then either. Because that restricts me to the compound.

9:00 p.m.

I just returned from "How to Steal a Million" with Hepburn and O'Toole. Not as good as that thing with Michael Caine and Shirley MacLain about stealing some old thing.

I just burned a bigger-than-hell hole in the screen with a candle that I'm typing by as the electricity is off.

I was just called a maligated beetle dick, which was a driver's attempt to call me an addlepated beetle head.

7 April 1967, Friday, 6:30 a.m.

It's 6:30 and all's well. Time for me to shuffle off to break my fast with soggy bread and grape jam, fried eggs and predictably limp hot cakes with fuzzy tomato juice, lumpy like lymph fluid, warm and unrefreshing as yesterday's Pepto-Bismol.

12:00 p.m.

The Kinks are singing "Sunny Afternoon." He's got a big fat mama—lucky him.

I'm listening to a Vietnamese station that plays American rock and roll. Give me two good reasons why I ought to stay. Lazing on a sunny afternoon, in the summer time. The Kinks are very popular here with the cowboys, RVN hoodlums who buy records.

Today is one of those do-nothing days and I hope it lasts because I'm in one of my do-nothing moods. Kathy has gone with her fellow WAC to Nha Trang on an unofficial R&R of two days as a reward for being a WAC. I've been here seven months and they haven't done the same for me. Ah well, I'd rather have it that way than be a WAC and reap the many rewards.

The rain we had the other day hasn't been repeated and the dry hot season is still very much with us. Today I learn whether I'm to be trapped in the compound next week on Task Force and I'm betting that I will be.

Ah well, there is nothing to do in Saigon except steambaths, dinner, movies and all that. There are movies here, of course.

2:40 p.m.

I found out the list of Task Force people and I'm not on it. Hooray, hooray!! Postponed, reprieved, and held off for another time, another period of seven days—next week.

3:07 p.m.

I just went over to the Mobile PX Canteen and bought a terrible tasting milk shake that was most like warm skim milk. Terrible.

6:01 p.m.

Tonight I must ready my room for inspection for Major Kolosky in the morning and also I have head count and must get up at 4:00 for that. It's bound to seem a long day even getting off work at noon for I must work on head count in the morning from 4:45 to 7:15. Mighty big pain in the neck. But I get all day Sunday off with no possible interruption foreseeable.

I'm about to go into a fit thinking about the cold beer I have in the refrigerator upstairs. It beckons to me with a cold acidy, frothy finger, beeeeer heeeeeeeere.

I'm going to sit and read at my desk and then clean my room and drink beer and then shower.

10:10 p.m.

I've spent all evening cleaning the room. We'll still flunk due to the years of accumulated grime and sludge clinging to everything, but that's life. Tomorrow up at 4:00. I'm drinking a can of Carling Black Label. Now to the shower and then to bed.

8 April 1967, Saturday, 8:10 a.m.

I survived my morning as headcount without more than minor mishap, as they say. Namely, my daily relieval cycle was sorely interrupted. Also the CQ runner came around at 3:30 to awaken me and I didn't have to be over at the mess hall until 4:45 and it's only a three-minute walk. I fell asleep several times but just made up for lost counted heads by clicking the clicker a few times.

I have to be back in the mess hall at 10:45 so this will be a shorter-than-hell day, office-wise, but that's a hardship they'll have to endure.

Another investigation is underway so that Kathy will start next week to get a terrific workout as a draft typist as I fully intend to never type another draft longer than one page if there is ANY way it can be avoided, and it usually can be.

11:00 p.m.

I've done head count, showered and been to the library where I read *The Reporter, New Republic, Downbeat,* and *Sports Illustrated.* Then I returned to my little room and bullshitted for awhile and then TV: Bogart and John Derek in "Knock On Any Door."

Tomorrow I might go downtown with old Ed and look around, most likely the zoo, and drink a few Cokes. I'll be on Task Force next week so I might as well go whilst it's a possibility.

10 April 1967, Monday, 6:30 a.m.

My alarm didn't ring this morning so I'm running behind schedule. Last night I watched Ed Sullivan 'til 11:00 and the Mamas and Papas were on and sang "Monday, Monday" and a couple other hits. It was an old show, I'm sure.

Yesterday I went down to the zoo with Ed and Alphonso and Rosy, the two drivers. I didn't spend a cent all afternoon. An old man played the guitar and sang a low-throated blues-like number while operating a kind of thunk thunk block-like thing with his left foot. His wife operated a kind of one-string instrument that she plucked. It sat on the ground and was attached lengthwise to a resonator, the end of the string or wire tied to a little wooden fish-like carving. When they finished they wrapped up their instruments and, slinging them over their left shoulders, put their right hands on each other's shoulders: first, little boy, second, old man with a rag over his head, and third, old lady with a rag over her head, and like three ducks in a line they walked off across the zoo grounds. While they were singing, the old man had a tin canister in front of him for the money, and vendors of balloons, little squeaky animals, and orange drink came round to take advantage of the crowd watching. Ed and I are thinking of taking his camera and taking movies of the whole thing and also taping it on a battery recorder. The more I think about it, the more I'm sure that I'll do it. Ed is crazy enough to do anything no matter how much trouble it might precipitate.

Old Major Kolosky, the great white hunter and owl eater extraordinaire, just arrived at work.

7:55 p.m.

Tonight is an alert and I might not have much time to write before they call us to fall out and crawl through the grass.

Today I worked my ass off and am behind even with a clerk-typist helping me and I got chewed out by the new sergeant major four separate times for the shoddy work coming up from down here. He keeps saying: I don't know who's responsible for this but it's got to stop. I'm responsible even though I didn't do the typing, any of it. My typing is perfect and he could never find any fault with my work. But Kathy is a WAC and just learning the job besides, so what does the prick expect. Screw him. The draftees always do the best work. Like Miller, George. He made SP5 last week, I learned today, and will be going with his colonel on some top secret mission up north. He's a boy who seizes opportunity by the balls and makes it to the top. I've always wanted to, but just don't have the motivation necessary. I'm basically a worm. From now on that sergeant major will see nothing but perfect work from down here. I hate worthless bastards like that to get anything on me.

Reading about Ben Hogan's performance in the Masters assures me that a 54-year-old man is capable of fine performances. I'm thirty years younger, so should have at least an iota of perfection in me somewhere. I wish it would come out.

"Combat" just came on. Write more later.

9:00 p.m.

Task Force just went out and "Combat" just finished but I stayed here as CQ to protect the building. I hope that there are no reverberations from my staying here, but I don't think there will be. And if there are, I'll talk my way out of it.

Old Dead Head Ed has been coming up with some new ones lately. I think I'll write a poem called "Skin Flute" which is one of his favorites. "Playing the Old Skin Flute." When he gets back to the States, he said, he's going to order an apple juice and tonic, on the rocks. That's what we were drinking the other evening and it wasn't bad.

Why did the sheep fall down the outhouse in that story Ed told me? He was taking a shit and hole was too big for him and he slipped right through. Could happen to anybody.

Last night I watched "Dick Van Dyke" and the first of the two parts where Jerry Van Dyke was on and he kept saying nobody knows how I feel. Except that he says that in the second part, and this was the first part.

Today for the first time in a year I was told to button my pocket, by Sergeant Major Smith, an ex-supply sergeant who should be retired. He knows nothing about administration. Nothing at all. And his assistant,

Sergeant Montandon, is a kiss-ass. Old Master Sergeant Sparks, who was Sergeant Major Mills' right hand man, has been pushed into the background and had his authority usurped. And he's the man who should be running the place.

Tomorrow is a command formation and I'm sure it will be another "no comment" session. Col. Graham is right out of "Catch 22" and as loony as a lacquered lizard. Absolutely nuts. But he's not typical. He's just in command, so he looks typical.

Time to quit and have a snack and watch some more TV and maybe even clean my rifle. Probably not, but I'm on the deficiency list if I don't at least brush off the cruddies.

11 April 1967, Tuesday, 5:55 a.m.

In about five minutes I have to leave for that formation. Right now I'm listening to country music, John D. Loudermilk and "The Wife," which is a funny song and a precursor to Roger Miller, also a great "Waitin' for the Train" by Jimmy Rogers, the old one, written, not sung, but still a very fine song and sounding more like blues when not sung by Jimmy himself.

I've got a big day ahead of me. If I'm not too busy moving water coolers and having little lessons on things I already know, I might finish the report that was due at the latest yesterday. Maybe.

7:00 p.m.

I am now, and for sure, sitting here with less than five months, or as they say four months and days. Sounds short, but doesn't feel all that short. Particularly when dealing with the sergeant major upstairs. Every error that he detects he thinks is a victory for him, crumb of an NCO that he is.

Lt. Col. Blue just called me to say that the report that we'd been working on and that was overdue went out today and made it all the way so I won't see that damn thing again and it removes a load from my mind.

Lt. Col. Prince handed the thing to me yesterday and said: Alright, do it. Which meant to write a couple pages interpreting the statistics and explaining a projected future for complaints, justified and unjustified. It's just a bunch of bullshit and doesn't mean anything but it is submitted to a general, which is about as big a deal as there is in the Army. I'm not impressed with myself, not really, but Prince is a responsible fellow, and he feels that I can do his work and do it right. I just hope that the work tapers off the next few days so that I'll have time for all these organizational things and not just be filled up to the roof with mail, classified, errands, etc., that Charlie B. will do when he returns in one week. It'll be a great relief to me to not have to unlock the safe every morning. Even though I taught Stone to do the job, he's not living in the building so he's not available the way I am to do the dirt.

I talked my way out of any trouble about keeping my weapon out all last night and most of today. I'd better not do it again, however. That they wouldn't stand for. They are dumb but not that dumb. I'll have to find some other chink in their defense.

The sergeant major just came down and told me I had to stay here this evening because the sergeant is coming in to go on emergency leave and I have to assist him. Goody goody, and I'd hoped to go to the movie tonight. Forget it until tomorrow at least.

Col. Ebby told me today that I had till Monday to redo my files so that's another thing hanging over my head.

12 April 1967, Wednesday, 6:40 a.m.

I went to the USO last evening and gorged myself on French fries, cheeseburgers and chocolate ice cream so that when I returned to the hooch all I could do was fall into bed and sleep. I kept waking up all night though because I wasn't tired enough or something. I kept having to pour alcohol on tiny little bug bites which are completely gone now. I looked at them in the light last night and they were real enough then.

I've already eaten breakfast and they had, typically: cider (not apple juice), fried eggs, pancakes which I ignored, cinnamon rolls, heavy on the roll, forget the cinnamon, soggy toast, butter and peach preserves (I think). Boy oh boy, I didn't get fed like that as a civilian.

I guess I'll go open the safe and then back down to finish this entry.

Well, that's done. One big burden removed.

My view is that the gutsy Vietnamese must all be up north or in the woods or somewhere, because the only ones I see here are debilitated, Frenchified turncoats who are products of French educations, and who seem to have not one trace of pride in things Vietnamese. Maybe they think a display of that sort of feeling a bad thing, but I doubt if they think at all about it. Premier Ky of course is a northerner. Madame Ky, I don't know. I'll have to do further research.

As a rule I think Nationalism a bad thing, but some

pride in one's heritage would be nice. Whenever I ask any questions about their food, clothing or customs, they don't know, they say. I ask them what they are eating and they don't know. I guess they have such little pride in their lives that they are afraid I'm out to ridicule them, so they just shut up and don't know. It annoys me something fierce. They strike me as a weak, derivative bunch of ass kissers. Of course I see only the worst kind, those who work for the Americans. I guess this has been a tirade, but when I read stories about the North Vietnamese, their industry, stamina, pride etc., it makes me wish that a few of them could be found to take the American side of things here. But that would be a contradiction in sense.

8:15 p.m.

Today I won a battle with the sergeant major and the NCOs upstairs. It gained me no points with them, but they can go to hell in a typewriter cover for all I care. They tried to take away my Adler typewriter and give me a new typewriter that I didn't want. I said, what's wrong with the one I've got. Nothing, they said, but this one is NEW and we want you to use a new one. Why? Because this one is NEW. This ridiculous cult of the new. I told them I wouldn't go for it if they had no better reason, as I was satisfied and happy with the one I had and didn't want to go through the trauma of learning a new method and touch. They dropped it there and I thought I'd heard the last of it, but mistaken, I. A couple hours later the sergeant major called me and told me to bring my typewriter upstairs so it could be exchanged for a new one. I said no I couldn't quite do that. Why don't they give it to Carver who has a broken typewriter instead of to me, happy and content. He said that may be true but still I had to give it up. Guess what? I gleefully pulled Lt. Col. Prince and Col. Ebby into the thing and they couldn't figure out why I had to trade at all. So I didn't and won't unless it means that the section loses a new typewriter if I don't trade, but even then — when the time comes I'll fight it like hell. And try to keep the thing, offer to buy it or something. It's the best I've ever used.

I went to the PX today with Lt. Col. Prince. I bought the new *Jazz* magazine which has an interview with B.B. King. I've not yet read it. Later I will though.

Also I've been running a battle with the sergeant major who's determined to catch me in error on suspense dates. He's tried to pin me on six cases so far, and he's lost all six rounds, and humiliatingly so. Today he had the Chief of Staff's office on my neck and we had days and days left on both cases noted. The sergeant major is supposed to be an ally, not an aid to the enemy, but this one has no intra-office loyalty whatsoever. He's a pig and a glory hound. Sergeant Major Mills, for all of the pain he caused me, was always as straight as he could be even when mad, which wasn't often, though sometimes it seemed so.

Did I mention that at the zoo on Sunday I watched a group of boys swimming under a bridge and a large dead rat floated through their midst, which bothered them enough to move aside but not to leave the water. A bloody and messy rat it was, too.

I'd like to do an Agee-sensitive novel about Vietnam. But I'm more likely to do a Snow type novel than an Agee type, as I'm not the poet that Agee was.

I was over in G-2 (Security) today and they have anti-American propaganda displayed for many yards down the hall. In the midst of this is a large banner proclaiming: Support Our Boys in Vietnam: Come to the Rally in [XXXXX] Park on Sunday, sponsored by the Ku Klux Klan, Hell's Angels, and John Birch Society. Crayoned on the thing by the security officer is "With friends like these, who needs enemies?" This war is being fought by many officers who have wit, and I love reading the many sleazy posters and mailouts that are against our policies in Vietnam. Very interesting. They don't have any good propagandists or artists working for them by the look of the crude devices and printing.

13 April 1967, Thursday, 10:45 a.m.

Carver got a pair of jungle boots for me today and a sharp pair they are too.

Dead Head Ed went before the board for promotion today for SP5. He answered all the questions with "I don't know, man" in a drawl, he said. He didn't know where the president was, or what the life saving steps were, or the effective range of the M-14, or anything.

Neither do I. And I ain't about to learn. It would take about thirty minutes of priming. And I'd muff it all anyhow.

About the WAC with whom I'm working. She can type and follow directions, and is a good clerk, but more interesting is the moral and physical description of Kathy, as of course we don't call her WAC but Kathy which is her first name. She's strawberry blonde with darkish roots, although I haven't applied the test of tests of course. Nice looking, no dish or she wouldn't be a WAC, but no dog either. Fairly normal, no nymphomania evidenced in her behavior. Just a normal (mostly) girl. And besides, she's engaged. That's the clincher.

6:45 p.m.

Things are quiet and I plan to spend the evening reading *Playboy* and polishing my new jungle boots. Fun.

14 April 1967, Friday, 11:55 a.m.

I've got the filing system in good shape, everything logged, filed, and typed. Tomorrow I spend the morning in some kind of class, which is supposed to be a monthly or even weekly requirement, but which I've attended only once since I got here.

8:10 p.m.

Nothing much happened today except I'm on Task Force and can't go to the USO tonight with everyone else for a milk shake.

I have an appointment for tomorrow with a Miss Lily, a DAC (Department of the Army Civilian) who wishes for me to interpret my quarterly report statistics for her. When she called me on the phone she talked so fast that I could hardly even grunt assent without interruption from her. I've not yet started the report for the month of March which is due tomorrow, but I figure I'll have all day, as training was canceled, and I hope I've figured right.

15 April 1967, Saturday, 6:40 a.m.

This morning I'm going to devote my time to doing the monthly report; no time for foolishness.

5:55 p.m.

I've been working steadily all day, and now to write this. For sure, Master Sergeant Montandon will come down here and ask why I'm not working instead of doing such unnecessary things, but I won't let it bother me, I'll just whip out my knife and cut off his balls and stick them in his yellow hole of a mouth. How about that?

Work is over and I'm off to the laundry and dinner and then back to write more before Task Force.

7:25 p.m.

I ate and came back and watched "Lost in Space" and most of "M Squad" which wasn't well acted or suspenseful so I turned it off.

Kathy is a pretty good worker. She's a pretty girl, if one likes them plumpish and buxom. I do, of course, but her personality is not what I'd call great. She's a good girl to do my typing and run my errands and she sits right in front of me so I'm pleased she isn't ugly as that would ruin my lunch, and eventually I'd have to turn my desk around and probably strain my back and end up in the hospital and all that sort of tragic stuff.

8:40 p.m.

No formation in the morning so I'll sleep in until 6:15. I just looked at some slides that Ed took. One of them is of two blind musicians, husband and wife, led by a small boy, right hand on the right shoulder of the one in front.

It's raining like a bitch right now and I expect the tree frogs to return any day now as the rainy season is about to begin.

16 April 1967, Sunday, 12:30 p.m.

It's been a busy morning, as Master Sergeant Montandon (Ed calls him Master Sergeant Montagnard) didn't show up today so I've been doing all of the administrative work, besides trying to get my work done, and have failed at doing either effectively. I'll give him a small piece of my mind tomorrow. (I can't afford a large piece as I need most of it myself.) Charlie showed up today. He left a week early so he wouldn't have to pay his own way back which would have cost him $500, which is quite a bit of money even for a nice trip like that.

I haven't yet had lunch and it looks like I'm not soon to.

Col. Ebby told me to go to lunch and he'd hold down the shop so I did and I'm now back and it's a bad lunch it was, too. They ran out of turkey so I got a fatty piece of ham and some imitation mashed potatoes and orange juice.

4:20 p.m.

Col. Ebby got some fudge, black walnut, and it was delicious, the nine or ten pieces I had. Also he got peanuts. He's very nice about sharing his loot with us.

I've got to burn the garbage tonight, which should be

no big deal as I'm the only one turning out garbage today and I've been very conservative in my output. Oh yes, José is in the other building turning out garbage too. In vast crumpled quantities. I've got to do some Army typing now.

5:15 p.m.

That thing I was supposed to type had an immediate priority on it for a general and I asked Lt. Col. Prince if I could leave it for tomorrow for Kathy because it was so late in the day, warm, etc., and he said sure. I've got plenty of work to do tomorrow in the order of filing, logging, etc. Kathy and I never seem to sit staring vacantly around the room as ever since she was moved down here we've had work most all of the time with only occasional breaks and slow periods. If I'd had to handle it by myself, nervous breakdown immediately. I've also decided not to burn the trash.

I hope there is no alert tonight. That would make this weekend even more unpleasant. Time to lock up the building.

9:30 p.m.

This place is a madhouse and Charlie went upstairs to get away from the noise which was splitting his head open he said after twenty days of hearing nothing louder than the noise of two quiet bodies together in bed. As his grandfather was already buried when he arrived home he spent the time with his wife alone most all of the time when he wasn't eating, food.

I think I'll shower and to bed and maybe write more

tomorrow morning. Paul Revere and his Raiders are raiding my sensibilities with their tuneless mechanics. They make Mitch Ryder and his Detroit Wheels sound like GREAT music by comparison.

17 April 1967, Monday, 7:15 p.m.

Today the electricity was off and Kathy had to use that new manual that they tried to foist off on me and she said the touch was very heavy and the letter she typed was so fouled up she had to retype it on her electric later. So I really hope I don't have to learn how to type on another machine.

I have Task Force at 7:55, and afterwards I'm swimming bound.

Later

Went to Task Force and then swimming. The water was warm and we messed around for awhile with a volleyball and then I got out and watched the movie (outdoor) which was just a few feet away. I don't know the title of the movie, but it was taken from the book *The Beardless Warriors* by Richard Matheson that I read when I first got here. There are a bunch of young actors in it that I've not seen before and it seemed quite good, what I watched of it.

18 April 1967, Tuesday, 6:45 a.m.

Only ten more days 'til Muhammad Ali reports for induction into the US Army. They are crazy to bother him and I know he'll be more trouble than he's worth for sure. Time for me to go to formation.

6:45 a.m.

They (1st Sergeant) kept us in formation for twenty minutes because my squad leader stayed in the sack. Army B.S. Sergeant Ruttencutter came dragging up fifteen minutes late. We got dismissed while he stood for a chewing out. I have fond feelings for Ruttencutter for he was present when first I glimpsed My Darling. But seeing him also reminds me of my weakness in immersing myself in Army B.S. to the exclusion of pursuing Mai, even though I have a half-formed plan.

8:05 p.m.

Today was another one of those mad mad work work days in which there was no breathing space. I did, of course, go to the PX because the colonels promised I could. Lt. Col. Prince had a car assigned to him today for his trip out to the stockade. When he returned he kept the car for ME, a lowly clerk, so that I would be able to go buy stuff. If you think I'm grateful you're right.

Today I broached to Lt. Col. Prince the idea of Kathy and me trading afternoons off so that we'd have more time off and he said the idea was fine and we could start as soon as Kathy knows the job a little better. She has an aversion to proofreading, which causes some trouble.

It's expected that tonight there could be an alert, but I don't believe it as it rained today and the cadre wouldn't want to get wet.

While at the PX I bought a huge load of groceries for a party that we clerks plan to have this weekend, hotdogs, stuff to make spaghetti, pickles, and all that stuff. As I said last night when we were riding in an air-conditioned sedan over to the compound pool to swim (only two blocks away), this is a hell of a way to fight a war, but we have to make do.

19 April 1967, Wednesday, 6:00 a.m.

I have twenty minutes until formation in which I was going to work on the files but can't because somebody is sleeping by them and would be awakened if I were to turn the light on. So I'll sit here at my desk and curse the darkness instead of turning on the light. The flying ants are back and nasty buggers they are too. They've been gone for several months. And I wish they'd return from whence they came.

Time to toddle to Task Force.

4:15 p.m.

I think there will be a Task Force alert tonight. I've Saturday afternoon and all day Sunday off, I hope.

6:20 p.m.

I got a letter today from Lorraine Jacobs and she got my address from Micky Phillips. Who are they? Lorraine has an offer of cookies or whatever I want. I think it's a Commie plot. Really! The way the thing works: She sends me cookies; I write her a letter thanking her for her kindness; she writes me a sympathetic letter about the war and wants my opinions on it; she then quotes my unflattering opinions in some little pamphlet or handout using my name, or if there are none but patriotic quotes she'll twist them around. A very good propaganda device. I'm going to bite on it to see what will happen. I'll sound like a combination of Patrick Henry and John F.

Kennedy with a little Ike thrown in for corn value. See what comes of it. It will be a laugh anyhow. And I'll throw away her cookies in case they are poisoned. That's happened over here too. Do I sound like a Bircher? The fact is these things have happened. Just as surely as military dependents are getting obscene night telephone calls calling them wives of murderers and adding obscenities as punctuation.

7:30 p.m.

Just a few minutes and off to formation. Just had a call that a letter I've been working on for two days didn't pass the general's scrutiny and must be done over again. Woe, woe.

Most NCOs are in the Army because on the outside they would have menial jobs in which they'd have no one to rule. They'd be employed alright. They are most of them steady types, just stupid, unimaginative. Ray Mills, the old sergeant major, was one in a million. An executive type with leadership ability yet still having compassion. The present sergeant major is an ex-supply sergeant, and they suck, as the bard says.

The Vietnamese. They have been spoiled by the colonialism. Why don't they have a leader like Jomo Kenyatta in Kenya who threw the white imperialists out, established a good stable government with much white money and made it a good country for white and black to live in. Stokely Carmichael is to be admired, and I do. There are a few black boys like that in military stockades around the world and when they get out . . . . The world will feel the shock of their bitterness.

8:10 p.m.

No Task Force tonight (alert). And probably not on Thursday night either, and then I'll be off the thing.

Col. Ebby said today that when Kathy makes SP5 which will be just a few days, I'm still the one who runs the show. And she's the assistant. Co-worker, actually, because I want her to know the job from top to bottom. She will too. She has lifted the old burden from my shoulders. Though Prince just adds more of his work on me. Administrative stuff, like today I did about half of his questionnaire and the statistics. That's the fun part. Typing has never been my forté.

"Skin Flute" comes off like an Ed Sanders poem. Ed (Dead Head) does that stuff by the yard all the time. He's capable of long lyric extemporaneous poem playlets like "The Skin Flute," or "Sippin Vagine Wine," or "Runnin' into the Wind to Make the Beanie Spin" and other psychedelic treats. His father is big in drama and lit. and that stuff in California. Ed has let his English background rub off more on him than he'll admit to. Another of his favorite skits is: "NCO want Banana. And Co-Co-Nut?" That's rather unflattering to NCOs and is usually given loudly just within their earshot.

This country is beautiful and I hate to hear the NCOs, as I did when a bunch of them rode with me to the PX yesterday, deride this country and its people with the ultimate derision: "They ain't no good pussy here at all. Now in Korea them girls could hump hump hump. Mothafa, I tell ya." NCOs are the bottom of the pot scrapings.

20 April 1967, Thursday, 10:45 p.m.

I've been on alert since 5:00 p.m. and have had no time to prepare for tomorrow's USARPAC inspection, which I guess I'll just have to endure the way I am, unprepared.

Today all day was a madcap day.

I've showered tonight and now I'm going to make my bed and crawl into it for a good night's sleep.

21 April 1967, Friday, 6:45 a.m.

I just opened up the office and am now going to breakfast. The USARPAC inspection is today. WOWEE.

I heard some scuttlebutt the other night from a driver whose brother is a Marine, so it must be true. General Walt sends Ky tabasco by the case. A new domestic scenario unfolds in my head.

"Honey, I'm Home."

"Did you have a good day at the war?"

"Yes, very nice."

"You ready for fried rice?"

"Aren't I always ready?" They sit down to dinner.

"Please pass the Tabasco. How is our stock holding up?"

"Fine, Honey. We still have at least a dozen cases."

"Good." He annoints his fried rice with Tabasco and chows down.

An annoying fantasy, but close to the mark I'm sure. With six kids in the house, there will be no sexual cavorting on the threshold. They'd scare the fawns, anyhow.

22 April 1967, Saturday, 6;15 a.m.

To the cries of "Get up and get your re-up chow, bacon fried to a crisp, oatmeal, well-done, — re-up re-up re-up," cried in a teeny little birdy voice by Dead Head Ed, I'm greeting what is supposed to be a half day for me. I've got this afternoon off and all day tomorrow.

Yesterday was the inspection and of course I don't know how we did but I assume that I did okay. No reason to assume otherwise.

Last night at the outdoor theater they showed "Pillow Talk." I've always wanted to see that movie over again for the scene in the little night spot where Hudson asks Day to go to Connecticut with him to stay in a friend's house, immediately after Tony Randall told him to bugger off. Then a negro singer, who sang earlier a song called "Hey, Hey, Roly Poly," breaks into the first few words of a swinging rhythm and blues number that starts "You lied, but you'll be sorry. . . ."

Today is the party: hot dogs, beer, etc., etc. What I'd really like is to buy some watermelon, mush melon, papaya and some of the other local fruit, oh yes bananas, as they are delicious and cheap and much better than Chiquita, although smaller.

23 April 1967, Sunday, 6:35 p.m.

My day and a half are drawing to a close and I haven't done anything much. Dead Head couldn't get off today so we didn't do any collecting of folk material in the streets downtown.

10:25 p.m.

Tomorrow, as are most Mondays, is destined to be a confusing day and filled with work work work. So I guess I'll go to bed now even though I slept most of the morning. Disappointment making a man out of me, and such unpromising clay I am too.

24 April 1967, Monday, 6:20 a.m.

That was a short night. It is now 6:20 and I'm tired. Old Dead Head Ed kept us up late last night with his latest religio-philosophical theory, that God is a bug and is alive in his crotch. Now I ask you, is that sound logical reasoning as they teach it in school or do you think that it smacks of crackpotism?

I'm going to have to start working a little early this morning in an attempt to get my desk and my cases straightened out after my co-worker had the thing to herself all weekend.

It's 6:30 and I've opened up the upstairs and the charred remains of the coffee pot are sitting up there, inviting comment from the Neanderthalers (NCOs). I've got the GIs from all the ice I drank up yesterday in Bierley's Orange Drinks. (Oh there's no carbonation, no carbonation in Bier . . .)

11:35 a.m.

Today is a very slow day, the slowest day that I've got recorded in my little mind for a Monday. Maybe (I hope not) it will pick up later in the day.

9:30 p.m.

Today Lt. Col. Prince told me he'd instructed the sergeant major to put me in for SP5 so I guess I'll start boning up for the board. If I have to go up before the damn thing I might as well try to acquit myself as well as possible. I want SP5 more badly than I'd imagined I would. The money is some consideration, but really it is the status that I want. I was the dud in steno school, and now I have the drive to not be a dud.

25 April 1967, Tuesday, 6:35 a.m.

The strains of Eric Burdon's "House of the Rising Sun" are piercing the darkness. For the past month I truly have hypnotized myself with Army monotony. I glanced back over my diary entries and could not believe the redundancy — but that is the way it is.

1:00 p.m.

There will be an alert tonight that I might have trouble avoiding.

Lt. Col. Prince is going to the PX this afternoon and Col. Ebby is in class until 5:00, so it looks as though I'll have world enough and time to fritter.

It's raining like hell right now and has been doing same for the last few days in preparation for the wet monsoon. As a result of the increased precipitation the water pressure is terrific, like a fire hose, which is pleasant after the trickle of the last few months. It makes a roar as it falls, drowns out the phones. A rush by the drivers to close their car doors. The tree frogs will be returning soon, I'll bet. Today I came on a bit of

Army jargon that kills me. It's better than "puking with power." "The relatively administrative situation is the thing." The only thing that gives it meaning is the knowledge that there are two possible kinds of situations, tactical and administrative. Without that knowledge wouldn't one think that a word had been left out? Relatively is an adverb modifying an adjective as Lt. Col. Prince pointed out, so why does it seem strange to me.

Today I have to fill out a form giving the weight of my baggage which I'll wish to have shipped (trucked) to Long Binh on the planned move in July, August, or September, or whenever. I'm not worried about ever seeing the place, but I will do up all of Saigon that I wish to in the event that I won't get to stay here in the Saigon-Cholon area for all the of the time I'm in Vietnam. Also I have another BIG LOOSE END I MUST TIE UP!

Kathy? Her engagement doesn't really mean that much to her, but she's an unliberated Catholic and from a fatherless (I gather) home and has all of the hangups typical of that environment. She's a cute girl, but as I spend most of my day correcting her work (just because she's new, not because she'll never learn the job) she's not very taken with me. A teacher I've never been. This girl is so young and uneducated. WACs don't spend much of their time in the library and Kathy has those sickening aspirations that don't even allow her to enjoy rock and roll without attendant guilt for remaining a teenager past nineteen.

I watched a special on TV last night from 10:00 to 11:00 which was entitled "The Beatles at Shea Stadium." They sang all of their standards that I'm very familiar with and one other — "My Baby's in Black" — a fine song. They also had shots of King Curtis and a girl with his band who sang "Sugar Pie Honey," that great Four Tops hit.

Today we were told that we have a parade on Thursday and Command formation on Saturday. Big deal, indeed. Kathy will be gone all day today, recovering from the effects of a night as CQ, and Lt. Col. Prince will be gone on an investigation and Col. Ebby and Maj. Tief and I will have the ship to ourselves. I wish Kathy were here today as Maj. Tief will have boucoup typing to be done which he prefers to give her so he can stand behind her and instruct her on how to do it, not that that isn't an innocent activity for a man his age and physical condition.

26 April 1967, Wednesday, 5:15 p.m.

Col. Ebby is upstairs in a conference that will probably result in much typing having to be done and I'm working until 6:00 or maybe 6:30. The day has been a very slow and easy one.

I've been listening to the Vietnamese stations all afternoon as there is just a ball game on AFRTS and I hate the things. RVN radio has been wild native stuff all day until now when the Animals" 'Rising Sun" came on which I hope is a good portent of the rest of the day. Col. Ebby just came down from upstairs so this may not be much longer. But I'll keep plugging away until dragged from the keyboard.

Here come at least two big projects: a TWX to type for Col. Ebby and a huge rough draft for Maj. Tief that he's been poking away on all day to drag in at the last moment for me to type. It will probably wait until tomorrow if I can possibly procrastinate until then. I'm going to try. He's hanging on my desk right now with the thing in his hand making last minute changes with a dull pencil and probably reading this over my shoulder.

6:30 p.m.

I was just seeing boogie men, as the stuff for Maj. Tief doesn't have to be typed until Friday and Col. Ebby's TWX took about three minutes to type. No sweat, as they say.

Maj. Kolosky and I had another confrontation today. This time a solely nonverbal one. Col. McCartney was expecting a draft from upstairs. I pick up the distribution from upstairs. The clerks from upstairs claimed that I'd gotten it. McCartney asked me if I'd seen it and I said no. He completely accepted that and went upstairs to find out where it was. Maj. Kolosky came downstairs and looked around at the places it might have gotten sidetracked and didn't find it. As he passed by my desk on the way upstairs he started to say something to me, like ask me where the thing was. He thought better of it and went upstairs. When he got up there and was asked if he'd found it or whether I had it, he said no. I didn't accuse him; I didn't feel up to arguing with him about it unless I KNEW I was right. Poor little fellow. And I didn't have the thing either, and it turned up in his baileywick. Ha ha.

The Kingsmen just sang "Louie Louie." Shades of the past.

Dead Head Ed went out today to do field work. He took a tape recorder and his movie camera and a little field guide that I wrote up for him to follow while filming a street singer or similar phenomenon. I hope he doesn't lose the thing, but if he does it doesn't really matter. A million years from now nobody but me will remember that he lost it.

> *A bucket of balls and a yard of dick*
> *And you call me boy.*
>
> — *Folk Saying*

27 April 1967, Thursday, 6:07 a.m.

Last night I went to the USO in Tan Son Nhut and had a cheeseburger and French fries. And ice cream, of course. Old Dead Head Ed is one of these Pete Seeger-Danny Kaye types with children, and he came back from the zoo with a tape full of children's songs. Mostly of five-, six-, or seven-year-olds singing what sounded like adult songs in adult voices and of great length and very serious. He joked around with the kids and got their curiosity aroused about the tape recorder. One of his gambits is his big nose, which by RVN standards is truly huge. They love his mugging and climbing trees and jumping in the air and all that kind of stuff. He's just the kind of co-field worker I can use. He works this weekend on Sunday though, so we won't be able to go together. I'm going by myself or with Charlie or somebody. I've got to get started on it.

I'm listening to the sickening little My Lan show. "Baby I need your lovin ..." Johnny Rivers. She plays good music interlarded with sentimental tripe about patriotism and how her little heart goes out to American boys far from their loves and how she wishes there was something she could do for us.

Are you smoking dried bananas or whole fresh? Dead

Head Ed just walked in in a bath towel and a glass with ice in it in his one hand and a can of Miller's High Life in the other. Ugh. Beer this time of the day? That's Ed.

7:00 p.m.

I just marched in a prade (it's hard to eat a prade.) It wasn't a fun prade but we did good our CO told us. I don't really have much to say tonight.

Pay call will be this Sunday morning with a muster formation prior to it so that means even though I have the day off I don't get to sleep in. Last Sunday I was awakened at 6:00 by the sergeant major who wanted to get in the building. The previous week on Sunday I worked, so that makes at least three weeks without sleeping past 6:00 a.m. I tell you this is a hell of a war.

I was chewed out today by Col. Anderson and Maj. Kolosky for my "disreputable fatigues" which had several undarned holes in them and no evidence of a press now or ever. Jungle fatigues besides. Ah well . . . I care? I'm trying to cultivate that attitude. Western Union dit dit dit dddddd . . . . That song is terrible. Tonight I plan to gorge myself on ice cream and again go to bed early as I did last night (9:30).

28 April 1967, Friday, 6:15 a.m.

After writing last night I went over to the library, after eating some ice cream, and read the latest *Esquire,* which had no cartoons in it anywhere. What do they think they are doing anyhow?

I'm listening to the My Lan show again — Bobby Darin, "Judy, Don't Be Moody." I don't remember that song from the past. It doesn't sound like a present hit either.

I hope to get this afternoon off, but it isn't likely as Maj. Tief and Lt. Col. Prince will both be returning today with investigations to be typed up. I've got a big mosquito bite on my arm for the first time in weeks which reminds me I'm delinquent in taking my malaria pill.

With the strains of Nancy Sinatra, "You been messin where you shouldn't a been messin . . . ," I'll go off to the mess hall.

7:50 p.m.

I'm sitting here listening to the final strains of Del Shannon's "Runaway" on Swinging 60s.

I had the afternoon off and spent the time reading a novel called *Homecoming Game* by Howard Nemerov.

Today I ruined my glasses, scraped the right lens beyond visibility, got a haircut and had a big battle with Kathy who pulled rank on me about some work I asked her to do. We aren't speaking yet. She told me not to lecture her on her mistakes and I told her that she had a lecture coming. I'll never make a teacher. I mean I'll never be a teacher, I've already made one many times.

The new glasses that I've got on (I got them in basic) are fine optically, but they have a different lens area and my field of vision is different. The headache I've had all day is not going to be helped by the malaria pill I just took, but I just read a scare article on malaria so I'll just suffer through it.

Matt Dillon just came on.

29 April 1967, Saturday, 6:20 a.m.

I feel bad this morning from that malaria pill and these new glasses. I didn't sleep well last night either. I'm not really suffering, I just don't feel my usual robust self.

Joe is supposed to be opening up this morning and he's one of these people who thinks it's more sensible to sleep three more minutes and be behind all day than it is to get up and get things done. I don't know where I picked up the Protestant Ethic (probably my father) but it looks like I'm stuck with it. As I washed my hair twice in a short space of time due to the hair cut yesterday, I can't make it do anything but fuzz up. And I'll get comments today from Maj. Kolosky or somebody that I need a haircut although there are people here who have their hair three times as long as mine but who put grease on it and thus fool people into thinking their hair is short.

5:45 p.m.

This was a day like all days have been lately, long and filled with work. I'm on duty for another hour and 45 minutes and sometime this weekend I'm to transcribe a few hours of taped interviews for Maj. Tief. Tomorrow morning is pay formation at 6:15 and that will take three hours, very probably. I will go to the zoo tomorrow and try to catch a street singer though. I'd like to get there at noon and stay for eight hours at least.

I'd like to trade Kathy in for a male clerk typist with brains. That girl refuses to think. She's like the secretaries that my father has had and described to me. They type

what is printed on the page. Today she typed a long,
long thing that had a very noticeable change of person
in it. She didn't catch it so it had to be typed over and
she blamed me for seeing it and calling it to the attention
of the colonels instead of letting it slip by, a crummy
piece of work.

I can't understand someone who'd type something
that looked wrong rather than asking about it and saving
the trouble of typing it over. Ah well, I'm very intolerant
of error, but that's the way I am. She sends out stuff with
the wrong number of enclosures, no enclosure, wrong
enclosures, all because she doesn't think about the job,
just finishing it as fast as possible.

The headache that I've had for two days is almost
gone.

I just had to run upstairs to answer a phone call from
Col. Yerkle who wished to speak to Col. P. What a dum
dum. The work day has been over for an hour. I can't
believe it.

Recently we got a complaint from a fellow who claims
that the Army is denying him freedom of religion and he
should be freed to civilian life where he can practice it.
The religion? Mithraism. That really killed the colonels. I
think it's pretty funny.

I don't know when I'm going to do that tape work for
Maj. Tief, but tonight I don't feel like it and tomorrow I'll
be in that goddamned formation, pay line, etc.

30 April 1967, Sunday, 9:45 p.m.

I got paid. I spent all day downtown and recorded
two different blues singers and got their songs partially
translated by some bar girls.

Dead Head Ed is sitting here making up perversions such as a nose fuck, in which the girl has one big nostril and the thrill is in penetrating deep but not deep enough to penetrate the brain and cause death. That's an interesting sci-fi theme. While downtown we ate dinner, crawled through bar after bar, I'm sick from orange pop and Coke, and got a steam bath and massage.

Petula Clark is now on Ed Sullivan's show singing "Bright Elusive Butterfly of Love."

Old Westy has a million medals and he will be a presidential candidate against one of the Kennedys one of these years. Mark my words.

I'm supposed to make coffee for tomorrow, but the pot has burned out for the thousandth time because they refuse to get a new one and just repair the old one. Today it burned a big hole in the sideboard and started a little fire and it's sitting upstairs right now upside down.

1 May 1967, Monday, 7:10 p.m.

It's a Turn Down Day, I'm being told on the radio by some ghost station that's not supposed to be on. It was one of those days, Monday, filled with work, and tons of it still to be done. But Kathy is penitent from her outburst of last week and is snatching work from my desk so that I have little to be done, except a million little errands and the three investigations I'm doing.

Old Maj. Tief had me doing all sorts of stuff for him today. He means so well and I don't like him at all. It's just stupid of me, I guess, because he praises my work continually, but still . . .

Wink has been THE drink in the club for days, and I

revel in it.

I have CQ runner on the 8th, I think. I don't know for sure, but that thing surely comes up often. Ah well, we are now going to take the entire day off next day, so fine. And the hell with NCOs. Charlie had to carry coffee in a carafe all day today. What a ball.

10:00 p.m.

My shits are gone and I'm normal and healthy again. In fine fettle.

One of the reasons Kathy is in such a good mood lately and willing to do hard work with some degree of accuracy is that she's being fervently courted by Joe and some AP. And the attention makes a different girl out of her. Which is good. Love does that to the sourest individual.

2 May 1967, Tuesday, 6:15 p.m.

One thing I forgot about the day (Sunday) that Charlie and I spent downtown was that when we returned, all the compound dogs snarled and bit at us because we smelled like gooks. These dogs never snap at soldiers. I guess the steam bath killed our American odor and the rubdown with scent and the gook food, etc., gave us a foreign smell.

8:35 p.m.

Today was a good day, even though it started early. I got old Maj. Tief's thing done and done right and out of the office and he went into paradoxisms of thanks. I had to respell almost every word in the thing, as he's a worse speller than I am.

I have CQ runner the 8th which is a Monday, I'm almost certain.

Long Binh isn't too secure where the dump is, but it's a big place and they always hit the dump, and I doubt if they'd waste ammo on the compound USARV'd be in, just as here they knock the shit out of the airfield but never touch USARV compound only a third of a mile away, just a five-minute walk. They could, of course, but we're ready for them, thanks to all that training and alert crap one of which we're having on Thursday night. It's rumored.

3 May 1967, Wednesday, 6:15 a.m.

I just returned from formation where we learned that the latest harassment in the company is no more mama-sans to clean up, polish shoes, wash clothes, etc. He said we can do that stuff ourselves. This piece of piaster reduction cuts in two directions: no p. being paid to mama-sans and less time to leave the compound to spend p. Of course the last piece of harassment (no booze in the hooch) worked in the other direction, but their whole purpose is to make it as unpleasant for us to live here as possible. Of course this doesn't affect those of us who live here in the USOM 24, but in fact we're just now going to get a mama-san, after doing without one these many weeks. Irony.

The reason I say that they make these changes just to make it harder for us is because of the way in which he (the first sergeant) made the announcement. In his hoarse grating voice, empty of any intelligence or wit he said: "Now listen up 'cause I have an announcement that none of you are going to like." His voice filled with gloating.

Ah what a way to start the day, filled with sour bile from a crud like him (he is). And it doesn't even affect me.

It looks like we'll be in here until (if ever) we move. To Long Binh.

9:30 p.m.

All the boys are hot tonight. It's raining like a SOB and everybody is busy recording the effects of the storm. Ed just went out the door with his camera and a tripod. They've been taking all sorts of effect shots.

I accompanied Col. Ebby up to the stockade today at Long Binh and hit several PXs plus saw the layout of where we (USARV) will be moving and the compound is on top of a huge bluff surrounded by a complex of protection that extends for miles. The buildings are huge, office type structures.

Both Col. Ebby and I got quite car sick and I'm still feeling the effects of it. I had chicken noodle soup and Spam sandwich for dinner.

4 May 1967, Thursday, 6:20 a.m.

I just returned from formation, got clean sheets and a sick slip.

Last night I listened to Radio Malaysia which gave me a very different slant on the news, especially on Cassius Clay, victim of racial oppression rather than a victim of his own ego and bad companions. Anyhow, Radio Malaysia had one quote that I couldn't forget:

"South Vietnam has called plans for an Asian Common Market premature." In all seriousness, that's what they said. Asian Common Market; a good plan for sometime, but there would be some little trouble here with the thing.

I'm going on sick call this morning to find out what's wrong with my eyeballs and to try to get some new glasses and sun glasses.

The first sergeant in formation this morning said that he had thought again about removing the mama-sans, but that he was instituting a new inspection policy. Schmuck. Our mama-san is doing a fine job, my jungle boots even shine and I have them on.

8:55 p.m.

Today was a hectic day for me. I spent the morning as usual in the office. But this afternoon I went to 17th Field Hospital to get my glasses checked. I got out there after about three hours on buses. That was okay. But then they checked my glasses and told me that my right lens was wrong and that it must be changed immediately to alleviate my headache. So I was given an address at 4:15 and off I went to get a gook in a cab who could get me there before 5:00 p.m. I didn't make it; I'll relieve the tension right now. Along the way I saw all of Saigon, stuff I never knew was. A child that looked caucasian as any playing in the street in front of the bars with the girls. Very Vietnamese in dress and movement, and white. I saw a girl, twenty or so, in the usual Vietnamese dress but without the western addition of a bra which is all they wear between their skin and their blouse. She had no protruding breasts or the usual padding in lieu, but the sight of her dark nipples beneath the white of the Vietnamese top carried me back to the old times and made me think what an impact these slight girls must have been on Frenchmen. They aren't really successful at aping the western woman with that padding as they carry themselves very peculiarly, as if shipping a large load. My thoughts then dwelled on My Unreachable Darling.

I came back and told my sad story to Col. Ebby, Lt. Col. Prince and Maj. Tief and they said that tomorrow I will get the things ground and they would see to it. They started commenting on my clothes again, and said that if I don't get some new fatigues tomorrow when I request some from supply they will accompany me over there and shall get new ones. That I have looked ragged I admit, and I'd like to look better to fit my "position."

5 May 1967, Friday, 6:15 a.m.

I've just returned from formation and a talk with my supply man. He told me that if I wanted new fatigues I'd have to show them to him and if he thought they weren't wearable he'd take them and in one week to two months later, I'd most likely get some new fatigues. That's too long and I don't think that Col. Ebby or anyone else will be happy. It's funny how much out of touch with the plight of the enlisted men a full bird colonel is. Well, these two will be back in touch after I tell them the situation. Maybe I can get some fatigues soonest. As Col. Ebby says: Get done soonest! I told him that wasn't English but was gobbledygook and he said do you know what it means?

4:25 p.m.

I'm on Task Force beginning this week.

I got a new lens ground today for my glasses and it makes everything look funny, but the headache has disappeared so I'm satisfied. Everything looks strange anyhow, it's just a question of degree.

Kathy has the afternoon off so I have plenty of time on my hands. Not having to redo her work or explain everything to her. I don't get to fire the M16 tomorrow as I'd hoped I would. I'm not scheduled as of yet to work on Sunday, but I have Task Force anyhow, so what?

Maj. Kolosky told a fairly amusing story today. When he was a lieutenant commanding a company of 230 in airborne training, there was an inspection by a general prior to a jump. Dog tags were to be checked. At the last moment he discovered that one individual did not have dog tags, so Maj. Kolosky took off his and gave them to the fellow to wear so he'd have some to hang out if they all were told to put out their tags, expecting of course that he, the lieutenant, would not have his checked. Well, he was both right and horribly wrong. The general was accompanied through the ranks by Maj. Kolosky and the general picked out that one set of tags out of the 230 to read. He read them, looked at Maj. Kolosky quizzically and said "See me afterwards about this, lieutenant." It's a story with a heavy moral, namely the omniscience of inspectors and their psychic qualities at checking only one thing, the one error or mess that exists. It's fun if you're the inspector. We chuckle about things like that all the time.

7 May 1967, Sunday, 6:30 a.m.

The crickets are making such a racket that it's almost impossible to hear my radio. The goddamn things. It's funny that new lens I got yesterday relieved my headache completely, but I can't see very well. I'm beginning to wonder which I want, clear vision and a headache or blurred vision and no headache. It seems a funny choice, but for the Army it's sensible enough I guess. I was told the right lens I now have is more powerful, but if that's so why do I have to get closer to things to see them? Of course I didn't take the three-week airmail course in glasses-fitting that is most likely the prerequisite for an Army job as an optometrist, so I really don't know about such things.

5:45 p.m.

I just had a shouting match with Rosey, one of the drivers, which left me trembling and barely able to type. I was sitting here trying to type this letter and a crowd of people were standing around my desk raising a bedlam. I asked them fairly politely to leave several times. Finally I shouted "Stop your fucking racket," which pretty much called a halt to the proceedings. Rosenburger, a driver, was very offended at my language around women (he means WACs) and told me that if I ever talked like that again around women he'd beat me to a bloody pulp of which feat he is quite capable, having a huge pile of muscle, having been a blacksmith as a civilian. I told him he goddamned well could go ahead and do it, as he was a worthless hulk of muscle, etc. He left giving me one more chance to reform. Nice of him.

8:05 p.m.

I missed formation although I got there in time to be counted present.

8 May 1967, Monday, 6:05 a.m.

Last night the Lovin' Spoonful was on the Ed Sullivan Show and were good, sounding somewhat different to me than on record.

Tonight at 6:00 I begin my short night as CQ runner, and tomorrow I'll take the entire day off. Others have been doing so without reprisal. Hi, this is My Lan, the little creep just came on.

12:00 noon

Tonight I have CQ runner.

4:30 p.m.

I've got only 30 minutes left to work and I'll be off work until Wednesday morning at 7:30.

It's been so hot lately that I'm not even sleeping under an Army blanket but a sheet, and with a fan blowing yet.

6:00 p.m.

I'm in on CQ right now and this typewriter is a bitch and I don't know if I'm going to be able to type very much on this bitch, bitch, bitch. I feel as if my fingers were coated with lead or cotton candy or something. Well, dear reader (I've been reading *Tom Jones*) I left you where I was going to get the mail in a rainstorm.

Well, in the course of this small adventure I got into a verbal battle with the lieutenant colonel over in the inspection division. I was kidding with one of the sergeants and the lieutenant colonel jumped me for disrespect. I will get even with him. Lately my temper has been short, but I'm short, too, and don't really care if I leave this Army a SP5 or a private E1. I'm not going to eat shit for any goal.

9 May 1967, 6:30 a.m.

I just had a run-in with the first sergeant about my duties and I was threatened with extra duty. He has 62 days left before ETS and he'll be standing in the old breadline.

8:20 p.m.

I learned at Task Force tonight that I'll be getting up at 3:00 a.m. for an alert that will last until 7:00 in the morning. This they said will exempt me from duty until 12:00, which is ironical as I've not been at work since 5:00 Monday. What, another half day? This Army bullshit is self-defeating, it could really make it hard for one to do one's job, if one were that important. I fancy myself important.

I don't feel nauseous from my glasses, I just have an odd viewpoint of everything, not blurred exactly, but just skewed. Somehow. I've not taken a malaria pill lately. I must do that.

10 May 1967, Wednesday, 2:10 p.m.

I'm back in the saddle again as the bard would say. The first time since 5:00 p.m. on Monday that I've worked at my desk. Everyone is resentful of my long absence, but it's no fault of my own. This morning the CQ pounded at my window at 3:00 a.m. and dug me out of the sack to go on an alert which lasted until 6:30 this morning; therefore, I was in the sack all morning, a fact resented by some who thought I should be a man of iron and work in spite of the fact that I'd been up half the night. Of course, in my place they'd have done the same.

Out on alert I spent two hours alone sitting on a dirt clod watching and being deafened by jets landing at Tan Son Nhut Airport. And watching the gook guards smoke cigarettes in the security of their nearby bunkers. And trying to stay awake, of course, was a primary feat. I spent most of the time thinking about how short I am, which is not totally an illusion as there are many longer than I who think and talk of nothing else.

I'm very thirsty and think I'll trump up some excuse to walk over to the command building and get a milk shake (a version thereof, anyhow).

4:00 p.m.

I went over and bought a shake and stopped by and talked to José G. and he informed me that I was on the delinquent list in the company for a dirty rifle. Pretty funny. Last night I dragged the thing through mud and muck, turned it in this morning at 6:30 and by noon am on a delinquent list. Ah well. Col. Ebby told me that that was the last time I would be on two duties on consecutive nights as he thought I was being used illy. Is that how "ill-ly" is spelled or is that not a word?

Whilst I was walking over to the shake place, it rained, so that ends the suspense on that subject. I've not that to look forward to.

This evening I'll be working late but I hope to read a couple of hours tonight. Kathy is most likely going on an R&R to Bangkok this next week. WACs are treated more than partially over here.

6:35 p.m.

I've just eaten and am now marking time until Swinging 60s comes on at 7:05 when jubilation will prevail. One more Task Force formation after tonight.

The easy-listening music they play from now 'til Swinging 60s is very annoyingly bland and puky. The drivers are all making asses of themselves and Dead Head Ed just finished doing a skit of a marriage that he was best man at last year. He also told me that he plans to take up drama and announcing when next he enters college as this is a whole new area for him to fail in, something he's not yet tried. He claims to have tried and failed at everything else.

I'm working tonight as Kathy worked the two other nights. Just Maj. Tief is on duty downstairs while I'm typing this. I can feel his ominous presence behind me as I type this, misspelling most of the words with vowels.

People are convinced that Ky will run for president, R.W. Apple, Jr. reports in today's *Times*. So it must be true.

Swinging 60s just came booming on. To the annoyance of all. "The Happening" by the Supremes, a very happy swinging tune.

11 May 1967, Thursday, morning

I have a command formation in which to march this morning. In full gear. Today is clean linen day, which means I get different linen with similar laterite stains all over it. And it'll be damp too.

7:00 p.m.

Good-for-nothing Kathy says "It won't kill you to do it, so don't throw it on my desk." Schmuck that she is. Both Col. Ebby and Lt. Col. Prince took me aside today and asked me if I was satisfied with her work as they weren't and would she work out okay. They said that she keeps asking for extra favors and R&R, all that good stuff. Col. Ebby asked me today if it was alright with me if she went on a three-day R&R to Bangkok. He literally left it up to me, because he didn't think that she was quite deserving of the thing yet, and I don't either. But she is a WAC and all. I wouldn't usually be so bitter but today I felt quite sick all day and she sat and read *Candy* and absolutely refused to do anything except for what she did that I had to do over again. No sympathy from her there. Col. Ebby asked me if I wanted a three-day in-country R&R this month and I said no, but right after payday I will and he said just say the word and off I would go. Also I asked him if there would be a heavy day tomorrow and he said why, would you like the afternoon off and I said no, but Kathy would and he looked disgusted. Because he knows that I have to work both Saturday and Sunday whereas Kathy has that time off. I said well of course I was gone from work more than a day and a half. He said sure, but that was duty and compensatory time, not time that was for myself.

I didn't even get a lunch hour today, as Kathy went when I was supposed to and I was too stubborn to go later. I was so mad at the bitch that I just burned thinking about her sitting there writing notes to Joe, who is gone this week, and reading *Candy* and another book the rest of the time.

I've got that goddamn Alert formation tonight too.

12 May 1967, Friday, 6:15 a.m.

I'm listening to the My Lan show, just finished opening up the upstairs and will be going to breakfast in a couple of minutes. I feel much better today, just weak and not near as whiney as last night. I hope to get things in better shape today, filed and folded and organized, so nothing will be hard to find. And I won't curse every time I'm asked to pull a case for examination. I feel as though I'm about to fall apart, even so.

6:30 p.m.

Maj. Tief just read that J. Edgar Hoover quote about oral genital contact interfering with interstate commerce and almost fell out of his chair laughing. That is a very funny quote if indeed it's a quote. Whatever it is, it's good.

More talk about our move. Long Binh is just a few miles from Saigon — 20? 15? — not but an hour's drive at the most. We are moving because they want to get us out of Saigon and the metropolitan area where we are vulnerable to attack in crowds, etc., and to a place that is safe, sealed off, where they can control all of our moves. We'll never be able to leave the compound on pass or otherwise. Trapped. That's why I hope we move up there as late as possible. Of course the chance that up there there would be no board for SP5 is a point (a small one) in its favor. The big minus is proximity or lack of same to My Darling.

It's dark as a bitch today for the rainy season is here and it raineth much right now. Both Prince and Tief bought blacker-than-hell sunglasses today which they are wearing and they claim to be having psychedelic experiences of their very own.

I'm just now getting used to my glasses. They are doozers. I don't know if I should have gotten used to them, but I forced myself. Everything looks almost right now, twisted up a little on the edges, but right. Maj. Tief asked me if the glasses had relieved the headaches I had for a while and I said yes but I can't see anything and he was very disgusted with me.

13 May 1967, Saturday, 6:15 a.m.

I just got back from the company formation and the latest pearl of wisdom there is: You gotta get rid of them slopehead foot lockers now and I mean now this morning and get Army foot lockers so every swinging dick looks the same and there ain't all them raggedy-ass slopehead foot lockers, is there any questions and there better not be any?

He's such a nice fellow. I never did mention that the command formation this week consisted of a harangue against my section and about how they hated to get things crammed down their throats from above and we should go to them first with a problem. Then they coerce and blackmail the guy into forgetting about whatever he griped about.

I feel great this morning, and I had a bowl of ice cream and some canned Beef-a-Roni and orange juice for dinner last night. This morning at 5:00 they had a blues show on AFRTS. Last week it was Ray Charles. This morning they played all the oldies but goodies, blues stuff. Otis Redding, Jimmy Reed, Buddy Holly — a thing about walking a girl to school that I didn't remember. My Lan is simpering about the boys who are here liberating the world from communist conspiracies, etc. It's time for me to go to breakfast.

6:15 p.m.

I'm sitting here waiting for 7:30 at which time I'm no longer on duty as CQ. I worked all day today, and steadily.

R.W. Apple, Jr. reports Ky has announced his candidacy for president. At last.

My eyes are fine now, although at first in the morning the glasses appear to me rather weird. But I'm used to them. Things look weird to me anyhow, so it makes no real difference.

14 May 1967, Sunday, 6:40 a.m.

I have to work with Sergeant Major Montagnard and once he gets here, forget getting anything done. He's already in a panic about the safe being opened today and cautioned me to be sure to have it undone by 7:00. He's a one-man panic. I've got tons of work to do today and the bet is he won't let me get near it.

3:00 p.m.

I've been able to work all day without interruption from upstairs and have everything in good order now, until tomorrow when the whole thing starts over again. Kathy made a comment last night to Ed that she'd like to switch with him so she could work upstairs. That will be what I'll be trying to maneuver this week.

I'm going to take a three-day R&R to Nha Trang week after next if I can get permission, which shouldn't be difficult. That is truly something to look forward to and I shall have to get my shot record up to date, get my khakis altered and have SP4 patches sewn on them, etc. I'll not have to pay for a room most likely and if I do, it's only a couple of dollars.

My eyes are fine, no nausea or such syndrome. I guess I just got so accustomed to a weak lens that a strong one is strange to me. No headaches since I got the thing so it must be right. I can read for hours with no difficulty and see further than before, but things just look weird to me.

15 May 1967, Monday, 6:20 a.m.

I'm listening to My Lan who is more nauseating this morning than usual. Last night I went up to the club and had a spam and egg sandwich with onions. Then to the library and I read the *Scientific American,* which had an article on negro class mobility and social structure as a product of slavery.

Next weekend I have Saturday afternoon off, all day Sunday and no task force or other interruptions.

8:30 p.m.

We had an alert tonight and the word is that we'll have to go out at 4:00 in the morning, and if so I'm not going unless there is NO way to avoid it.

I'm all pissed off at Kathy, because whenever I have an afternoon or day off (I had this afternoon off) she allows everything to get all screwed up and it takes me the next day to straighten things out.

But tomorrow we'll (Charlie and I) nail the princess and show her that she's not exempt from all of life's little laws just because she's a blond WAC. We've warned her a dozen times to lock up FOUO documents and she never does, so tonight Charlie checked her desk and she had two FOUO documents in an unlocked drawer. That's very serious, but the big thing is that when we dug deeper we found a confidential document unlocked, just a-setting there. For that we could get our asses hung, the administrative officer could get reduced a grade, etc. That's real serious business.

So tomorrow morning when Maj. Kolosky comes in we will hang her ass right up as high as it will go. Pride goeth before the fall. And all that. That is just what will happen. We are being small, tattletales, etc., maybe so. But Charlie is the EM custodian of confidential material and if that had been discovered by the CID, which could well have happened, his ass would have been grass, grade reduction, etc. We've warned her and warned her, and all she does is mock us and ridicule us. Well, we will show her. Naaah Na Na Naaaaah. "Papa's Got a Brand New Bag" is now on by James Brown.

This afternoon I sat in the library after I got a haircut and bought some mint-flavored soap and read the latest magazines.

16 May 1967, Tuesday, 7:10 a.m.

I just returned from an alert that began at 4:30. A good opportunity to study the croaking patterns of the local puddle frog. They croak together, not as individuals. They all quit at once — a few tentative croaks and they all start again. Chorus, no soloists. The ones close to me sounded like strangling roosters.

7:00 p.m.

In Saturday's paper we learn again of Ky's seeking the presidency. This time from Dalat, South Vietnam, where "lettuce, artichokes, tomatoes, and strawberries are grown." So what? Scrutinizing these articles in vain for references to Madame Ky has diluted my respect (based on hearsay, not study) for the quality of the Great *New York Times*.

17 May 1967, Wednesday, 6:05 a.m.

My Lan is simpering away in the background on 612 kiwocyklers.

Yesterday our office worked a full day's schedule with no allowances made for our being up half the night, while other sections, most of them, didn't start work until noon. We got very wet on the alert, soaked to the skin, and the first thing most of us did when we returned was to change into clean dry fatigues. One fellow in our office refused to, however, as he felt that if the Army got him wet they could get him dry. By the end of the day he was having chills and a sore throat. I've always been a great one for doing things out of spite but I think that's going much too far.

I must go and eat my soggy toast. That reminds me, last night in the club I filled out the slip for what I wanted, handed it to the girl and paid and then said, hey I want that back 'cause I didn't write my name on it, and she said yes you did, and pointed at the bottom line where it said: TOAST. I said my name is not toast, that's what I want my cheese burger on. Deluxe. I can't believe it. Of course I don't know the Vietnamese for toast, but I don't work in the club either. Kind of funny!

18 May 1967, Thursday, 6:05 a.m.

Lt. Col. Prince had a talk with Kathy and she turned over a new leaf, at least temporarily until she goes on her R&R tomorrow to Taiwan for four days and returns. That FOUO thing caused an office shakedown of everyone's desks. Mine was locked and I was gone so they didn't get to look at mine. The other WAC was found with some FOUO in her desk, but she was the only one. She did bad.

Well, it's time to go to breakfast.

9:05 p.m.

"The Fugitive" is on and it's 9:00, but I'm going to write some. I spent most of the day playing a word game with Lt. Col. Prince who, being short, likes to be pampered in this way. He's being replaced or substituted for by Lt. Col. Rollins who is the fellow I had a serious run-in with on getting the mail wet and a subsequent imagined impertinence to an NCO, which I don't remember if I wrote down or not. But Lt. Col. Rollins has a reputation for sternness and unrelenting work, and no fondness for kidding. Today Col. Ebby asked me what I knew of him and I told him of the one unfortunate encounter I'd had with him. He understood the situation and said that he was the best man available to be his assistant and that he, Col. Ebby, would be very much in control of the division and that nothing would happen which would make it harder for me to work here as he would see to it. I'll give Lt. Col. Rollins every chance to treat me fairly, but he has quite a job, following Lt. Col. Prince.

At lunch today I sat by chance with three sergeants who had been up-country and they spoke in great detail of pictures taken with polaroid cameras of individuals in US uniforms holding up VC heads by the hair of the head, etc. And other atrocities. This would be gleefully received by the anti-war folks at home. Indeed it should be.

Lt. Col. Prince leaves on 7 June. Lately he's been sitting at his desk, feet up, dark black sunglasses on upside-down, reading magazines and generally cutting up. An attitude like that is contagious and I'm getting that short-timer attitude. Our replacements should begin arriving any week now as this is about when we arrived to replace Whit and his crew.

In the field recently, seven fellows were filing complaints about the mess hall and being interviewed in the mess hall. One of them was speaking his complaint, namely that bird shit fell into the food from the rafters when at that precise moment a bird shit on the table from above. The officer saw that definite action was taken on that complaint. No hearsay evidence there. Something concrete!

19 May 1967, Friday, 6:35 a.m.

I've just now opened the upstairs and I ate breakfast early today for a change, so I've naught to do now until 7:30 when work starts, although I'm sure work won't amount to much. The rain has kept most pedestrian customers unit-bound which is where I like them. Yesterday it rained very fiercely all morning, catching me raincoatless betwixt here and breakfast.

This morning I was the only individual in the line who had a raincoat on. Those raincoats are designed to keep all the moisture from the outside from penetrating to one's skin, but also they are so effective as sealers that one gets as wet from one's own sweat. A new raincoat has been designed and will be issued in the month of July sometime.

3:45 p.m.

It's been a busy day, I beat Lt. Col. Prince in his word game in six moves and then he followed it up with not getting one of mine for about twenty moves. I learned that I'll have to spend my Saturday off firing at the firing range on the M16. Puke. It's now raining and I'm to get the mail tonight.

The rain is so powerful that it's drifting in particles through the screen and over the typewriter. I hope there is no alert tonight. I'd get wet and that would displease me. Seventy degrees in Seattle, that's two-Army-blanket weather for sure.

6:00 p.m.

I hope I get a chance at a candy bar, a Dr. Pepper, and ice cream tonight, but I won't. There is an alert tonight which I don't plan to make or take part in and I mean it this time. There is no reason for me to go out there. I'm not a valuable member of this fighting force.

20 May 1967, Saturday, around 7:00 a.m.

No alert last night to go out on and sit in the bushes. Just a standby, which is the best kind.

I must get off work today at least by 10:45 as I have to leave for the firing range at 11:45 and one must eat and attend to the other bodily needs. Mustn't one? Kathy is gone on her R&R which she managed to extend to six days, which will have her gone until next Friday, which is the next day she reports for work. Col. Ebby was upset to learn at the length of the thing as he'd okayed only three days and she got it doubled, but she's a manipulator, she is.

I just hope I get my little three-day R&R next weekend, the 26th, 27th, 28th. But it wouldn't surprise me if it fell through, though I'll get it if I have to wait a couple of weeks. Col. Ebby is convinced I'll get the R&R when I want it so maybe he'll be right.

Monday is when Lt. Col. Rollins is scheduled to begin his term in this section, under Col. Ebby and Lt. Col. Prince. Everybody who works with him now says he's totally lacking in a sense of humor. After that run-in I had with him on getting the mail damp, I'll be prepared for the worst.

10:45 p.m.

Tonight when I came in somebody had rigged up a water trap on the door, so if I hadn't spent so much time fumbling to get the door open I'd have been soaked. But the way it was I set the thing off and didn't get more than damp.

This afternoon I went to the rifle range and managed to successfully escape firing the weapon or being involved in any details. It was worth the trouble of doing this just to have the trip out there which was up and down a dozen funny little narrow blacktop laterite roads which were just wide enough for us to honk other traffic off the road and proceed full throttle to our destination with all the folk on this country lane waving and smiling and running to avoid death under our wheels. Narrowly.

I stood in the front of the back of the truck with branches whipping in my face and beetles and wasps collecting in my hair.

Today Major Tief returned from his I&I — Intercourse and Imbibation — with a lighter that had the Korean Nurses Corps Crest on one side and on the other it had the terse phrase in commemoration of this man's birthday: Fuck Ho Chi Minh. Which is a patriotic sentiment.

21 May 1967, Sunday, 5:45 a.m.

It's 5:45 a.m. and I woke up of my own accord even though I don't work today and I'm still tired, but at 5:00 I automatically looked at my watch.

6:10 p.m.

Yesterday on that trip to the range and back again, I saw dozens of fragmented images that I would have liked to have kept but most of them I've forgotten. An ARVN troop riding a stripped-down bicycle with red rubber tires, stopping it by jamming his black tennis shoe between front wheel and the frame. An ARVN soldier whipping seven little boys for selling soda on the range, making them all lie down and whipping their bottoms with a long branch. Stalking up and down, first pedaling his bicycle furiously to catch them, they scattering all over the field, hiding under cars, trucks, bushes. The front roof of a shed we were under to stay out of the rain. The underside of it geometric and perfect in its million angles, from which millions of little bugs and lizards peered at us, sitting in the dust and naming the parts of the M16.

"Premier Nguyen Cao Ky announced tonight a cash bonus for all government employees and servicemen," Jonathan Randal reports on 18 May. Sounds to me like Ky wants to buy votes with government money.

I'm thinking of taking my long out-of-country R&R in Hong Kong as that place has been so interestingly in the news lately.

Well, I guess I'll go get something to drink at the club or maybe cadge some champagne from Charlie who is drinking the stuff today.

22 May 1967, Monday, early morning

The harassment that Clay is getting for his wish for an exempt draft status is a fine contrast to the treatment that other southerner got, I mean Joe Willie Namath. That prima donna who is every bit as painful a personality as Clay, except he's white and has a physical deferment which is even more ridiculous for a professional athlete than the mental one Clay had or the religious one he wishes. Ah, it's a fine difference. I wish I had the sensibilities to understand the situation.

Today's going to be a big day. Monday is always unbearable due to all the work built up over the weekend, but today I'm going to have to put up with Lt. Col. Rollins who will be sitting in from now on, I'm told.

12:15 p.m.

Kathy isn't here and I've not got much work to do. It looks like an easy day, even though old Lt. Col. Rollins is here. Speak of the devil, I just spent ten minutes explaining my suspense system to him, which he seems to have easily understood.

Nha Trang is one of the most beautiful beach resorts in the world, I'm told, and I plan to sun, swim and take pictures of all the usual things that are found on a beach. Fun, I think. Buddha's birthday is soon so they expect some little disturbances, but that is nothing to worry about.

3:20 p.m.

This afternoon rock & roll is being played on AFRTS, much to my surprise. A break in the tradition of schottishes and polkas. Jimmy Mac, when are you coming back? A song, not a cryptic comment on a Christ figure.

23 May 1967, Tuesday, morning

It's raining this morning so I'll get wet walking to breakfast but if I skip breakfast I'll starve to death, and that's no real alternative.

I've got my new jungle fatigues on and do I look sharp? No, not really. My Lan is playing Jimmy Rodgers singing "Oh Oh Well, I'm Fallin' in Love Again." A different version than the one that was popular when I was a young thing.

I'm still planning to go on that three-day R&R to Nha Trang, it's officially a TDY, temporary duty, but they allow us to just screw around. It's all very below the board. Anyhow, I'm assigned headcount for the 26th and the sergeant major said therefore I must stay here and forget about TDY as company duty takes precedence over anything like that. I think I can use a substitute, and Dead Head Ed volunteered his services. The sergeant major will check today to see if it's alright with the CO. I discussed it with Col. Ebby and I have a feeling that he'll see that I do go on this three-day thing even if the company is displeased. They needn't know a thing about it, but the sergeant major is one of those lifers who loves to go by the book.

Don't count the days; make the days count.
— *Folk Saying*

8:35 p.m.

I'm listening to Swinging 60s right now and it's swinging for sure with James and Bobby Purify, Shake it Baby.

Today Col. Ebby told the sergeant major that I would have a weekend off starting Friday unless there was a true catastrophe, which won't happen.

Tomorrow I'm going to call old David C. and make sure he's got plenty of time to drive me around when I get to Nha Trang and that he's got no previous engagements or has time to break them if he's got some.

2,511th birthday of Buddha today, no shit. But 23 incidents anyhow. Some people don't have no reverence.

24 May 1967, Wednesday, morning

I just opened up and before that ate breakfast, sour pineapple juice.

Last night I watched "The Smothers Brothers Show." The Buffalo Springfield was the guest group. Bette Davis was there. The Smothers Brothers sang a Rod McKuen song. their skits were very funny and it was a good show. Next week they have Paul Revere and his Raiders.

> *The rain goin to come down, rhubarb goin to grow.*
> — *Dead Head Ed*

10:00 p.m.

I spent the day working my ass off and the evening reading a Luke Short novel. Tomorrow I plan to badger the sergeant major into scheduling a flight for me for Thursday for Nha Trang and getting piasters and all. I meant to call Dave C. today, but didn't have time to even think about it, I was so harried.

25 May 1967, Thursday, 1967, 6:10 a.m.

A new day is unfolding its withered wings and attempting to leave the twig. That reminds me: I saw the first of the tree frogs yesterday. A tiny yellow brown frog with delicate markings in brown that matched side for side. He hung on a small leaf, pointed toward the stem of the leaf, drops of moisture around him, insects clustered throughout the bush, but no sign of interest there.

Overheard in the chow line: Yeah, he's what you call a Southern Moderate. He'd like to see all of Them hung by their heels 'til dead.

Dead Head Ed is supposed to open up this morning and he's still in bed (petty jealousies, small thoughts). But Joe is in bed too. Officially they were AWOL from a formation, but their buddies will cover for them (that's me and old Charlie). Eventually we'll get so pissed off that we'll stop covering for them, but they are the lucky kind and will never be punished. If I were to miss a formation just once, I'm sure I'd die on the scaffold, and of course it's this fear and compulsion that drives me to BE THERE ON TIME. The God time.

12:45 p.m.

I called Dave C. today and he said they were ready to pick me up at the airport when I come in and that they'd have time to drive me around and even a cot for me to sleep on if I didn't want to stay at the Nautique Hotel, which I think I'll do at least one night. That's where all the entertainers stay when in Nha Trang appearing in the service clubs, also it's directly across the street from the beach, which would be my reason for staying there.

7:45 p.m.

All arrangements are made for me to leave tomorrow for Nha Trang and a wild weekend . . . hopefully just restful and fun in the sun, eating bananas, etc.

NHA TRANG
26 May 1967, Friday, 9:30 p.m.

I'm in Nha Trang. I had a nice flight up here sand-wiched in between a CWO and a 300-pound negro sergeant. We sat along the sides of the plane on a canvas affair and rested against an elastic red web thing that cushioned the takeoff. The plane was a 123-C, whatever that is. Through the windows I could see the fantastically colored and patterned fields, river, jungles, the scene was beautiful and enjoyable. This is one beautiful country, and Nha Trang is different from what I'd seen before.

The plane dropped in almost straight down and hit the hot air. The blue ocean and the white coarse-sanded beaches with hills green and bumpy all round. Traywick picked me up at the office, an old friend of mine who arrived in country just ten days after I did. He thinks he's getting short, and frankly I feel that way too.

Old Dave C. looks good and very sunned and tanned from beaching all of his free time. I'm staying in the office which is a big hotel with very nice accommoda-tions, located right in the bar area of town and just a short distance from the beach. Which is where I'm going tomorrow.

When I first got here today, I ate lunch and then sacked out for the rest of the afternoon. This evening Dave C., Traywick and I ate dinner at Frigate, an old French restaurant.

Some of the NCO's are fixing to go out and get a piece of pudd. But I'm going to sit tight at my typewriter, no sacrifice, as I'd give more for a cold Coke than anything else this place has to offer. This town is different from Saigon. After we ate (lobster, Cantonese rice, Chinese noodle soup, French fries, Coke, Spanish red wine, lime and papaya, etc.), we walked back to the hotel which is quite a ways.

All of the little shops were open, the electricity was off, but some shops were lit up with candles, some with kerosene lanterns, some with fancy Army generators, some with a couple dozen old truck batteries all fastened together, and some were just dark as hell with everybody sitting on the stoop.

I insisted on crawling through every record shop we passed and we passed a few. The Beatles, Stones, Animals, The Phantoms, Gerry and the Pacemakers, all of them were available on 45-RPM EP's for 200 p. each, which is excessive, I think.

Tomorrow on that beach I'm going to eat bananas and coconuts and pineapples from the gook ladies and try to avoid sunstroke, successfully, I'm certain. I hope to get a jeep ride along the beach and see what I can see. I'm told that there are topless bathers along some of the beaches here and anthropologically that would be quite interesting to me.

I'm kind of dusty and even dirty from the trip and from walking around so that shower will be very appreciated tonight, as it usually is. The mosquitoes are kind of pestering me, and I'm not used to the little buggers, as there don't seem to be any of them in USARV compounds anymore.

This vacation is restful even if I'm in another office, for things are more easygoing here and everyone is friendly and there is less of a breach between the officers and the men for they all live here together and cook with each other and eat with each other and even drink with each other, which isn't usual. A lizard just made it across the wall.

28 May 1967, Sunday, 9:05 p.m.

I'm home again at the old USARV compound, signed in and back at my desk as usual.

The morning of the 27th I stayed in bed reading and at noon, Traywick and I went to the beach. It was an overcast day, warm but no direct sunlight and I was assured that I couldn't get a burn so I didn't even bother to use suntan lotion. Well, guess what? I got the piss burned out of me. I went to bed last night at 8:00, moaning and feeling sorry for myself. I spent the afternoon of the 27th riding around Nha Trang with Traywick and Dave C. taking pictures of the natives and the scenery. We'd cruise along the back alleys, Dave would slow the jeep down to almost stopped, and I'd say "Smile, Gook," the gook would smile and off we'd go. While on the beach that early afternoon, I ate bananas and other strange tropical fruits as planned. There were no flies or sand fleas and the beach was clean and the water warm. I played in the surf on a water air mattress and didn't get bit by a poisonous snake or anything.

This morning after moaning and groaning and not sleeping all night, I read *The Saddest Summer of Samuel S.* and left for home on the flight.

The flight home was terrible, bumpy, stormy, and it had to land at Binh Hoa due to the bad weather, and that took extra hours and I had to walk about four miles to the USARV compound and I'm almost dizzy with exhaustion and my typing is even worse than usual.

I'll write more tomorrow after Task Force Formation.

Right now I can't get this fucking machine to do anything except jam up on me.

29 May 1967, Monday, morning

I'm just like a bear with a sore paw this morning and this typewriter isn't typing any better today than it was last night.

This morning I made Task Force formation with all my gear on and that sunburn wasn't improved by the straps biting into my shoulders. Ah, Whimper, Whine, Whine.

The My Lan show is on and it enrages me more than usual so I know I'd better watch my temper today or I'll mouth myself into trouble. My Lan just said I'm going to play to a song "entirtered" "I Dig You Baby," by Jerry Butler. Worthless bitch, why can't she speak English like me? Huh? She must be retarded. Not really, she's not retarded, she's just Vietnamese, which amounts to the same thing. A little racism there.

Lt. Col. Rollins just came in and it's 6:30!!!! Do you believe. I'm going to take off to breakfast before he's got something for me to do.

7:00 p.m.

I've been sitting here at my desk for the past 35 minutes belching my cheeseburger deluxe on toast.

Tomorrow is a vacation day, some military thing, I don't know for sure just what, but whatever it is it's alright by me. I plan to spend the day reading in the library or maybe I'll go downtown with Charlie and take a poke around.

It's shit or get off the pot time. We've got the word on our move to Long Binh and it's soon. We're told by the office that we will indeed move on July 6th, ready or not. Not, says I. I've decided to go ahead and to contact My Darling by dealing with the dressmaker she goes to in Saigon. Enough said for now.

One half hour I have before I must be on Alert Force. The Mystics: Hush-a-bye. That old rhythm and blues nonsense. Now that I've had lots of opportunity to listen to the stuff I find that I like it very well (good). Corny, terrible lyrics, but usually it has great style.

10:00 p.m.

I've just come back from the library where they had a bunch of new books that I checked out four of. Tonight I learned that there will be no Task Force Formation tomorrow, so I can sleep in.

Tonight old Dead Head Ed was drinking and in fine verbal form. He told me one very long narrative about when he was a small child and he stayed after school every night to kill flies, not because he had to but because he wanted to, so he could attain the goal of killing 72 in one half hour. Also, he told a story about when he was seven and used a swastika on his art work as a shorthand for his initials and the punishment he got from his teacher for being a neo-Nazi.

Ed is now talking about going to that Big Formation in the Sky when we die.

As I enter the month of my birth
I hold the horn in hand
And blow for better times. — *The Bard*

30 May 1967, Tuesday, 6:50 p.m.

I had intentions of doing all sorts of things today and accomplishing something great, but I didn't even think great thoughts. Quite the contrary. All I did was stay in the sack and from 7:30 this morning read here and there in the books I checked out yesterday from the library. Oh yes, I did deposit my laundry with the gooks and did eat and did read magazines at the library for a couple of hours.

I sacked out painfully but enjoyably in my bunk, blanket peeled back. Top sheet hanging to the wall, but body clad in cutoff cords and t-shirt to protect my butt from the coarseness of the sheet, I, with sheet littered with the four books and two magazines, listened for once to the Armed Forces propaganda on the radio and discovered that I do have a political awareness, at least one conscious of lies implicit in the media . . . "Where free society no longer exists; Where dictatorship has replaced freedom." These two phrases referring to Vietnam, North I guess, stuck in my head and made me wonder, are these accepted by those who listen. So people really think that freedom, "democracy," is the original natural state, corrupted by evil forces, to be reachieved by a US-controlled total war?? It puzzles me why they think of this country in that light. It's never had a freedom nor a democracy.

31 May 1967, Wednesday, 6:25 p.m.

I have to do the garbage-burning tonight, but other-wise have plenty of time and energy. Today was a bugger and tomorrow promises to be the same, but I'm not tired even though my sunburn still keeps me awake much of the night. I've got to get the garbage burnt, more later.

6:50 p.m.

No body to take me to burn the trash, so I'll type until one comes.

A driver just arrived, so I'm going with the trash.

Later—

Lt. Col. Prince received the Legion of Merit today at a ceremony and his however was read which was largely written by me. He is a young enough lieutenant colonel to make general and he's got the savvy and the cool to make it along with being the most competent administrator I've ever worked under. For delegation of work and for doing what he does best himself. With speed and great dispatch. I'm listening to Swinging 60s and Maj. Kolosky just walked by and said: Good good, in a joint smoker's accent, to the tune "Do the Bird Which Does Fly Along."

I'm hungry and thirsty so I'll in a few minutes go to the club.

Oh, yes, while at the range I also saw an RVN NCO knock an RVN basic trainee alongside the head with a rifle butt, which if it happened in this Army would be just cause for the NCO to never work for the Army again except in the Stockade.

I'm back. Just ate a sandwich and drank 7-Ups. My back is covered with water blisters from the burn. They'll all break tonight. I got paid today.

Lt. Col. Prince said he chewed out the people upstairs

today for my not being up before the board for SP5 this month, and he guaranteed that June would be the month that I'd make it. My big chance. I'm glad he won't be here to watch me fail.

1 June 1967, Thursday, 6:30 a.m.

I just sat down to type an entry and Lt. Col. Rollins walked in. Lt. Col. Prince never arrived this early by an hour. I can't believe how penned in I feel when I have to hide in my room as early as 6:30 to avoid responsibility and adult conversation. I've made Task Force Formation, eaten breakfast (I'm burping grapefruit sections now), gotten clean sheets, and now I'll hide in my room reading.

9:50 p.m.

I'm covered with peeling skin and I itch worse than I ever have and this itch extends to an irritation of person, a vileness that one can only imagine in its depth, and yet how close it is to humor and how easily I can step from this state to a rage or complete good humor. I'm afraid that this atmosphere is for the first. Small thirsty insects are crawling in the hair of my legs and I have a specific itch in the left small of my back that is BAD and Chris Noel is dj-ing a show on the radio and I hate her worse than My Lan.

Both WACs are here with their boyfriends and are using the recesses in which to copulate, presumably with their mates. Another thing lately, I've been scratching myself and ripping my flesh every time I stand up or sit down so I'm a mass of superating sores and half-healed bumps. And soft scabs. Annoying!

2 June 1967, Friday, 6:30 p.m.

Tomorrow morning Lt. Col. Prince leaves and I'll never see him again. We have a new bird colonel at the top too. I'm getting to be a real oldtimer. I've been here parts of ten months.

I'm recovering from my sunburn, I only itch slightly now, but for a while every time I leaned on anything my blisters broke and salt water wetted my shirt.

I have to clean my rifle tomorrow or I'll get the what-for and won't have a chance at SP5, as the company uses that as the judge of worthiness, morally. Also a haircut is in order as I'm getting too bushy for this weather. My hair *is* long.

9:20 p.m.

Old Kathy has lately been sitting at her desk every day, with a huge paperback copy of *Hawaii* resting on her typewriter, swollen the size of a year of *New York Times* issues loosely bound, because it was left out in the rain. Today, after these days of blank-faced accept-ance of every literal word, she let out a cackle of what for her is laughter. I had to ask her what moved her. What it was that moved her to such hysteria was the description of the practice of couvade. The idea of a man having labor pains struck her as science fiction. What a shallow, dull, ill-educated girl.

My legs itch fiercely due to the sunburn.

I have tomorrow afternoon off, but work Sunday, so if I'm to take action on my plan concerning Madame Ky, My Darling, I should start it tomorrow or the next day.

3 June 1967, Saturday, 6:45 a.m.

I've eaten, opened up the upstairs, and made formation, in reverse order. "Little Bit You, Little Bit Me" is on now. That could be a better song with a concept as advanced as that if they treated it more fully. Col. Ebby will be gone this morning, out with Lt. Col. Prince, helping him get gone.

7:00 p.m.

I feel great this evening. I marched for practice most of my afternoon off and then slept until 5:30. At that time I went upstairs and Ed, Charlie, and I made banana splits. Charlie bought a gallon of chocolate ice cream at the PX today and I bought a half gallon of ice cream (vanilla) and nuts, chocolate syrup, strawberry syrup, and bananas, long, green-skinned, ripe, beautiful, blemishless bananas. We ate huge splits for dinner.

I spent most of the morning at the PX, where Lt. Col. Rollins gave me permission to go. I work tomorrow with him.

An era has ended. This morning Lt. Col. Prince came into the office and said goodbye and left. He shook hands with everyone in the office and then came up to the door where I sit, as I was last. He just stood there and I stood up and we just stood and grinned at each other. I said, "It's been fun working with you, sir." And he said, "Yes, indeed it's been fun, fun . . ." and we shook hands, his baby face sunburned and his eyes bloodshot, his blond hair sparse on his head. Out the door he went.

I tuned in a short wave station that's in English as the AFRTS is so terrible.

My sunburn is no longer painful, but it's so ugly and raw, blistered and ruptured-looking that people wince and shy away at the sight.

The U.S. imperialistic rule of South Korea is being criticized on the radio right now, which must be communist. I wonder what it is? I'll know soon enough, when they announce it. We just got a phone call that there is a confidential immediate message. That means somebody has to go over and pick it up. Ed went. What a stupidity, this late at night.

4 June 1967, Sunday, 6:45 a.m.

I've just opened up the upstairs, now I'm off to breakfast.

Patriotism is the last refuge of a scoundrel.
                                      — *Sergeant Golden Boy*

5:00 p.m.

I just came back from dumping the garbage in the incinerator and am now disemburdened and ready to write. I've done NOTHING all day except sit at my desk and be on duty. Nothing productive. My work is all caught up.

Tomorrow the papers go in for my SP5, so, ugh, I expect I'll be humiliating myself before a board before too long. And if Charlie or John S. make it and I don't, well, the sky will fall in I guess. That's all.

I still have pink patches of flaking skin on my back, and it itches and I scratch it and get my nails all glotted up with shed sweaty skin.

I just learned that up at Long Binh we have all kinds of interesting details: burning all of our own shit, K.P., barracks cleaning, etc. It sounds like something to be avoided.

A drunk NCO just slammed his hand in the car door and is bleeding like a stuck hog. We just shoved the old guy into a taxi and got rid of him. He was whimpering and whining. Compassion, where are you?

5 June 1967, Monday, 6:30 a.m.

Old Lt. Col. Rollins is already here, but I think he's just writing a letter. Last night Charlie had a champagne and whiskey party to celebrate his first wedding anniversary. I had some whiskey and we left the pink champagne to him as he doesn't drink anything other than wine. We spilled a glass of booze on the floor and it removed a huge patch of paint. We'll probably get a lecture today on how we're abusing our privilege of living here. This has ruined me for the prospects of barracks life. A private room with adjoining bath. There won't even be plumbing up at Long Binh. Nothing to flush, probably no electricity half the time. And we'll form details to burn our own waste by pouring fuel oil over it, and clerical work besides. Goody. Maybe we'll be chopping weeds and building stuff too. I'm glad I'll have less than two months there and part of the time will be that R&R I've not yet taken.

Keep ye eye skinned for hippogriffs.
— Sergeant Golden Boy

12:30 p.m.

This morning Col. Ebby asked me who all the blood stains in front of the office belonged to. They are huge and ugly. I said those are just from an NCO. And he got so mad. I had to back down and say just from a drunken NCO. It still didn't sit well with him and he was grumpy (for him) all morning. This is the day my recommendation for SP5 is to go in, too. Somebody came in here last night and stole two of our radios. Not one of mine, though, as I had mine hid. I'm lucky as I usually leave it out.

Charlie B. was saluted by a sergeant major today as he walked along with a pipe in his mouth. He looks very military and strak and his sleeves were rolled up past the SP4 stripes.

Col. Ebby just returned from lunch so I'll have some work to do in short order I imagine.

Col. Graham leaves this afternoon so we have a parade in which I must march. Goody. That's another thing about Kathy. She loves marching in parades. It seems to me that in high school she much have been left out of the IN group and everything else, that thing where the girls wear boots and march, drill team or whatever, for she loves organized things, especially parades. Last night Charlie had that Champagne and corn chip party and excluded the WACs. This morning they griped to the sergeant major about the large mark we left on the floor where the paint was removed, to get even with us in their small way. So Charlie, master of intrigue, fixed it so this building is off limits for the WACs except during strict duty hours. They'll froth when they are informed. We excluded two such comely wenches because they are such selfish, unintelligent, unfeminine things that they have nothing to offer.

Col. Ebby just snapped at me again when I asked him a stupid question so he must still harbor resentment at me.

5:00 p.m.

That parade that I ruined my Saturday-afternoon-off practicing for was canceled today. I guess the practice won't hurt. I'm not really that philosophical in my acceptance of it.

Kathy won't be here tomorrow as she's assigned Duty NCO in her company. The place will probably slide into the sea.

Lt. Col. Rollins just left for the PX on foot, the little PX in the other end of the compound. Hell, I like him much better than I like Tief. In fact, he is quite a pleasant fellow in his way. No Prince, of course, but then he's still a new boy. Maybe later he'll turn into a Coldass. But I'll be gone by the time that happens, I hope. I remember when I first got here and Whit was as short as I am right now and he went around saying, "Short!!!" in a squeaky voice of disbelief. His replacement, Charlie, was here about three long months before he left. But our replacements aren't going to be here until we're as short as two or even one week, the sergeant major said. Of course Charlie and I will refuse to teach them anything if they do that to us and just work hard up to the last minute, hoarding the work, then leave, dumping a mystery of huge raveled balls of yarn with a million loose ends visible and the replacement having no idea which one to pull to get the end string. Poor fellow, it'll take him a bit of time to catch on to the state of affairs, but with our competent NCO's I'm sure he'll have it all figured out in maybe six months.

My radio is off right now as Col. Ebby and I had a short round about my being able to hear him. So I compromised by turning off the radio, putting away my movie magazine, and sitting with my arms crossed and looking at the surface of my desk.

I'm due to leave here in 25 minutes but by the look of things someone might try to pile the work up and detain me, so I go now to return later this evening.

8:25 p.m.

I left the joy of bugging those drivers watching "Combat" by predicting every action of Rick Jason as he went through his paces, and also as a bonus translating the German. As I'd seen the thing before, I was annoying them very much. Which wasn't nice, which was one of the reasons I left off. I was just in the library where I dropped the *National Observer* and returned here to see "Combat."

6 June 1967, Tuesday, 6:45 a.m.

I'm sure it'll be a big day for me as Kathy won't be here. The last week hasn't shown us much work, so today is bound to be the day that everything breaks. I hope that that is an overly pessimistic view, but oft times things do work out that way.

Last night we were jolted out of sleep at 3:00 by an NCO who wanted to sleep here. He stood and pounded on the screen by my head. One thing, and only one, about Long Binh is that there won't be this resident slave aspect to our work. One hell of a tropical storm just came on. It's one of those solid outbursts where the water falls heavy and wet with no sprinkling aspect about it at all. Just a solid soaker.

2:15 p.m.

The more I hear about Long Binh the gladder I am that I'm not just now arriving in Vietnam but instead am preparing to leave.

Col. Ebby and Lt. Col. Rollins are gone for most of the afternoon and I hope they don't bring tons of work back with them. I've got my confidential files to get in shape for an inspection tomorrow, but I could care what they say. What are they going to do to me if they don't like them? Not a thing.

R.W. Apple, Jr. reported the other day, "Ky still censors the Saigon press." My suspicions confirmed. Rarely if ever do I read anything interesting, let alone controversial about the Kys in the Saigon English language papers. Not that the US press does much better. I have little sense of Ky the man. So he's dapper, young, has a mustache, likes cockfighting, married a stewardess. What do we really learn from the press about him? We learn from Mr. Apple that Ky "has installed young air force officers in the censor's office . . ." Better there than flying expensive American planes.

7 June 1967, Wednesday, 6:20 a.m.

Today is the big file inspection and I've not yet started to prepare for the thing. I should type a few new labels and try to organize my confidential stuff instead of having it thrown in a drawer of the safe, but I doubt if the inspectors care anyhow. I'll find out later.

It was a bad drumstick, Motherfuck.
                              — *Sergeant Golden Boy*

8:00 p.m.

Today I did nothing all day except read a book by John Creasey. I was so bored. The files inspection was routine and I passed with no trouble. Two minor deficiencies amounting to nothing.

Tomorrow both Ebby and Rollins will be gone most of the day, leaving only Major Tief to harass us with his trivialities.

My sunburn is now in the stage of cusped lichens, flesh discolored and peeling off to the scrape of my nails, leaving pink new skin.

I open up tomorrow. Big deal, eh? I got something of a haircut today although nobody would notice it. Still long, and I'm crawling with little hairs. I think I'll go sack out and read, right after I shower, that is.

8 June 1967, Thursday, 6:08 a.m.

I just made the formation, but poor old Ed, who claims he was there on time by his watch, missed it and is AWOL. On the record this time.

Last night Ed did some of his orifice routines and I wrote three of them down. This is the worst of his material. I don't believe that I've written any of this stuff before, but it's a bit too early in the morning to remember.

His worst routine is about finding a girl with one

large nostril so he can fuck her right in her nose and end with an orgasm strong and his prick buried in her brain. Another one related to that one is his quest for a girl with a glass eye so there's one more place to fuck. That's his quest, one more place to fuck. Some people want louder music and madder wine, not Ed. The last of his bits that I'll bother to mention is the one about greasing the girls arm pits with cock cheese and toe jam and fucking them one at a time. That's enough in that vein. It even makes me kind of sick, although the literary quality is beyond doubt.

Every advantage is more of an advantage than a regular advantage, that's what I always say . . .
— Sergeant Golden Boy

10:25 p.m.

Today I had a flap with Major Kolosky concerning shorthand and the fact that if I have a shorthand MOS, I should be able to take the shit. I convinced him finally that I could have the MOS and not know the stuff, so I don't think I'll be bothered again. I hope not. The whole thing was started by that mental cripple Major Tief who returned today from an investigation and had boucoup shit for us to do.

I didn't do any of it, I just sat and read and so did Kathy. I made a couple of phone calls for him, but that was it. Col. Ebby warned me to not let Major Tief get hold of any of our cases as he always screws everything up, so I sat on the stuff and made sure he didn't get to it.

9 June 1967, Friday, 6:30 a.m.

Today promises to be a dilly of a day, with much bullshit and bother. I was just told to put on a happy face. I've got a monthly report to do and the buggers in the units haven't even sent in the info yet. Woe, woe is me.

> *Don't take any wooden knuckles.*
> — *Sergeant Golden Boy*

10 June 1967, Saturday, 6:30 a.m.

Last night was an alert and we of Building 24 opted out and did not take part.

This week I've worked three days that Kathy hasn't been here at all: Sunday, Tuesday and Saturday. I'm getting tired and hope that I can do the same for her next week, but I doubt if I will. This week has involved almost no work, which has been part of the fatiguing thing about it. The work has just piled up and I think they both plan on making a big day of it and doing it all today. Joy. I also have my monthly report to do and Maj. Tief has a million little pieces of busy work as usual.

Yesterday Maj. Tief asked me why I was in such a bad mood as he hated to see the troops feeling low. That pissed me off so I gave him a speech on the gap between appearance and reality, etc. Which he didn't comment on.

This morning there was a change of command ceremony in the company. Old Dead Head Ed showed up with two rifles under his arm and this ceremony wasn't one that involved rifles. He was standing behind

me in the formation trying to conceal two rifles and I
was giggling as it's rather funny to see a guy trying to
hide two rifles. The first sergeant walked up to me and
put his nose to my nametag on my shirt and said
Anything funny? I said No sir, and he walked off not
noticing Ed with his two rifles. Old Ed always comes
through things like that with no difficulty. What's that
old saying: Fools and volcanoes are friends.

I've done less work this week than any since I've
been here. Tomorrow Charlie and I plan to go to Saigon.
I hope to start my wrapping up of my one big Asian
loose end.

10:45 p.m.

Today I spent the morning at the PX and at Chase
Manhattan Bank, and the afternoon in the library reading
and the evening downtown getting a steam bath and
massage. I also put into motion my plan for connection
with My Darling before I'm banished to Long Binh. I
work tomorrow and have to open up, etc. I'll be working
with Lt. Col. Rollins who is as lazy as I am so the chances
are I'll have plenty of chances to read and loaf.

Today at the PX I bought cigars for everybody in the
office (the accepted custom) so at this point I'm broke
and don't even have any money to buy more SP5 stripes.

11 June 1967, Sunday, 6:30 a.m.

I just opened up the upstairs and now will go to
breakfast. Eating doesn't take so long any more as I now
stand in the NCO line which is much shorter. Privileges,
privileges.

8:45 p.m.

This is going to be the most difficult entry I've ever written, because the transformer blew out behind the office and a breeze is blowing and my candle keeps going out. Tough, eh. It's really a torment and I could have written earlier this evening but just put it off sitting in the library reading.

The only natural light is some heat lightning outside, and I'd not like to be walking guard tonight.

Dead Head Ed has continued to set precedents over here. His latest was to walk into Finance with 175 pennies and demand military scrip for them. They didn't know what to do as no one had tried that before. Ed was at the head of a long line of fellows wanting to get piasters for MPC and get out and make the local scene, and they were quite restless while the clerk took his time making up his mind and consulting the authorities in charge who didn't know what to do either.

Tomorrow Kathy and I will have one of the hardest days of typing ever. There are about twenty draft letters to be typed and lots of other stuff due to come in. UGH UGH UGH! I'm not going to kill myself though, really.

The radio just said Spencer Tracy died. An era has ended.

12 June 1967, Monday, 6:30 a.m.

The lights are still off and even though it's light outside, it's dark as hell in the building and I have to use a light.

Just the thought of all the work that's to be done today makes me quail. And quake, even.

How would you feel if the ordinary quit?
                              — Sergeant Golden Boy

6:45 p.m.

Today I got another haircut. Usually a haircut here is
a brisk, brusque clip around the ears, a shave of the
neck, and an out-held hand for the tip which isn't forthcoming, about a 45-second thing from beginning to end.
Today I thought I was in fantasy land. The barber gave
me a HAIRCUT. Every hair was attended to. My head
was massaged, rubbed with nutrient oils, sprinkled with
sweet water, and he all but kissed my pate. The thought
of the tip he would expect was causing me to tremble
with palsy. He prepared my neck for the shave with the
straight razor and as he held the sharpened razor that
he'd stropped for about ten minutes, as he held the
razor parallel to my eyebrow to trim my sideburn, he
leaned over me and whispered, "You buy me Winston,
two packs." With the razor sitting so, with one swipe he
could have cut my entire face off, ear lobe to ear lobe. I
answered yes indeed. Then he continued the treatment,
ending with a series of flourishes more rococo than
those he began with. I expected him to roll out a red
carpet for me to walk over to the cashier on, but just as
he was about to pull off the white cloth covering me, he
slipped his hand under the thing and handed me a wad
of paper money. Suddenly I'd been launched into CRIME.
THE BLACK MARKET. Scared and shaking, I paid my bill
and walked over to the PX to get his Winstons, unrolling
the MPC on the way. Gooks are not allowed MPC, by the
way, and all barbers are gooks, of course. I don't know
why the "of course," but anyhow they are. The PX had

no Winstons, so I crawled back to the barber shop and dropped the MPC in his hand and almost ran with relief at my reprieve from crime, and if you think it's a melo-dramatic story, it was that way, I tell it the way it is!

A pair of CID men just waltzed in for an after duty security check. UGH, but I'm going to keep typing until the last dog is hung, or whatever.

Like ravening wolves, the CID men just went through the building and the desks downstairs, moving out the door ominously. WOW. They are gone, gone, gone.

> *Black berries are green when they are red . . .*
> — *Sergeant Golden Boy*

13 June 1967, Tuesday, 6:25 a.m.

Last night the lights went off again.

5:15 p.m.

It's raining with force, frantic and pitched high one moment, and threaded off to a dribble the next. It's been another one of those days. Full and with old Major Tief requiring a million petty things to be done, all of them annoying and complicated.

I took a malaria pill yesterday, so I'm not in good shape bowel-wise. I hate those damn orange things.

8:05 p.m.

These girls: The WACs hardly qualify. Sweetness and femininity they lack totally, having much more of the fabled shrikishness that the American woman is supposed to have, and which I've only rarely encountered. WACs have a very low opinion of males, sort of a Blondie opinion of Dagwood, so it's obvious why I'd not get along with that group, as I have a very large opinion of myself and an ego that likes frequent reinforcement, which is not forthcoming from these selfish creatures. Now all of the latter can be found in the bar girls, skillfully, wittily, seductively, and totally false with a desire to bilk and milk the victim, so they aren't desirable either. There are no casual female acquaintances here. The only chance for a real relationship with a woman is to take a mistress from the Vietnamese females, and Graham Greene has for all time shown the flaws in that. And besides, all I'd like is a girl with whom to occasionally talk books, current scene, like that. I wonder how Madame Ky is in that area? Maybe I'll find out. If my plan works. My plan involving the dressmakers. They are making a dress for me. Not for me to wear, but for another. And guess in whose size?

My desk looks like a pop art exhibit, as there are arranged symmetrically a multitude of brilliant pop cans, along the edge.

10:05 p.m.

Tomorrow morning we all have to stand in line for our TB sensitivity test. What a waste of good time.

14 June 1967, Tuesday, 7:00 p.m.

I was at the PX most of the morning, but this afternoon Kathy was off and I spent the time reading. I let the work go and will throw it into Kathy's basket tomorrow for her to do. And then take the afternoon off, I hope.

Ky has been proclaiming on billboards that "the Nguyen Cao Ky Government is the Government of the Poor." What does that mean? He isn't poor, never has been. Maybe, like the Kennedys, he fears poverty, so has sympathy for the poor.

I checked out a book today by Susan Sheehan called *Ten Vietnamese,* which looks like it is something that may say truth (what's that) about the people of RVN.

Dead Head Ed is on a new kick. He's recorded about fifteen minutes of machine gun fire from "Combat" on TV, and he and the drivers have a formalized thing they go through, a routinized battle thing with their arms as machine guns and then old Ed says "I have to go pee-pee." The real and the ideal.

15 June 1967, Wednesday, 6:10 a.m.

I'm listening to the radio now, and the reports are of the dangerous summer that the US is having: rioting, racial violence, etc. It's less hot here in Saigon, riotwise.

Last night before bed I had a baloney sandwich and strawberry ice cream, and I had nightmares all night. I'm very hungry this morning.

That Vietnamese book I mentioned earlier has a picture of a sad-faced Vietnamese woman, face worn and grooved by age. Why do the media prefer this view of the Vietnamese people? One of the most outstanding things about the people is their kidding around, jokes, affection for their children and smiles. Teasing and grinning, they are to be seen on their cycles, bikes, in their shops, etc. Sure you can see sad Vietnamese here and there, but there are many more smiles in the street than in the US.

Yesterday I had my TB sensitivity test and also brought my shot record up to date by getting my typhoid shot. Now I'm told that I must make a shot formation today at 1:15 which cuts into my lunch hour by 45 minutes, but I go anyhow even though I need no shots. That's life.

I talked to General Ploger's secretary yesterday, a Department of the Army civilian. Anyhow, she said that she typed a report yesterday on recreational facilities at Long Binh, and so far there is nothing but a snack bar. A library won't be in for months and neither will be anything else.

There are more instances of the abridgement
of freedom of the people by gradual and silent
encroachment of those in power than by violent
and sudden usurpations.

— James Madison

16 June 1967, Friday, 6:15 a.m.

I'm listening to the My Lan show, the song: Peaches and Herb singing, "Close Your Eyes, Take a Deep Breath." What a fine song!

I had yesterday afternoon off, except for having a formation for shots. I had to put up with being marched over to the dispensary, standing in line, taking off my shirt, just to be told that I didn't need any shots, a fact I already was in possession of. But my name was on the roster so I had to go through with it. Only four months and six more days of this Army bullshit.

I spent the afternoon reading in the library, after I dropped off a huge bundle of dirty clothes at the laundry.

While I was gone yesterday Lt. Col. Rollins and Col. Ebby decided to completely revamp our filing and logging system. They think I'm going to resist the change fiercely because they know that I think change for the sake of change is worthless, and I see no advantage to their system at all, it being the system that I used for the first couple months of this job and which I discarded as unworkable. But I'm going to comply 100% with their nonsense, no back talk, the hell with them and their change. It means about twice as much work for me and I'll be able to do that much less typing. I'd rather do the logging anyhow.

This morning I'll have to force myself to do my monthly report, like it or not.

7:15 p.m.

An editorial in today's paper: "Unfortunately, Premier Ky's soldiers have not even shown the determination needed to defend their own people in the pacification program." Fine, let's go home then. The editorial then seems to recommend bringing in the Israelis. I must have read it wrong, but it's not a bad idea.

> *Everything I do gives them the jaws.*
> *Especially when I do nothing.*
> — *Sergeant Golden Boy*

17 June 1967, Saturday, 6:05 a.m.

This morning I open up the upstairs. Had a Task Force Formation earlier, have training at 7:30, and have to have my TB sensitivity thing looked at so they know it's negative. What a bunch of bullshit.

I have training all morning: just a movie, lecture on

VD, etc., and the rest of the weekend off except for Task Force 5, which won't take any amount of time.

I'm told that I go before the SP5 board on 23 June, so I guess I'll have to start girding my loins for that as I want to pass very badly, as all of my friends are up for it at the same time, and it's certain they'll pass and I'd be disturbed if they got the thing and I didn't.

I must eat breakfast and then go to the TB thing.

10:00 p.m.

No work today, just a bunch of stuff. After the training today, some marching to and fro that reminded me of the Stateside Army and made me hope that I'll never see any of it again, I ate and then stayed in the library until 12:30.

Our section had a party tonight. It wasn't much, just some hamburgers and Dr. Pepper and a bit of Coke. I talked to Col. Ebby and Major Tief for awhile and cut out to listen to the Folk Music Show on the radio at 7:10 and then the Grand Ole Opry.

18 June 1967, Sunday, 9:30 p.m.

I didn't do a thing today.

There is a rumor that all those in the company up for SP5 this month who have more than four months in grade won't have to go before the board, but will be judged on their paper record, and mine is very good indeed. I hope this is true. Of the eleven men put in for SP5 in the company this month, only three can be picked to go before the board, and it's obvious that I'd not be one of them, as I have less time in grade than almost anybody who's ever put in. I hope to God I get the thing as it would make Long Binh much easier, having that rank. I'd be in a supervisory capacity rather than peon, whenever possible, that is. Also the money would be immense in comparison.

Ky is haunting the streets of Saigon's Chinatown, kissing babies and eating fried wonton. "He was accompanied by his wife, Tuyet Mai, a former airline stewardess, who wore a white silk ao-dai, the traditional Vietnamese dress." No new information about Tuyet Mai there, but I didn't expect any. I know as much as I need to know and more. The reporter, Bernard Weinraub, tells us that Ky is "slim, dapper" and that he's drinking Coca Cola. That's a first — scotch, iced tea, and now Coca Cola, that all-American icon. It's about time.

Old Dead Head got drunk last night and ruined another pair of pants. Every time he gets drunk he ruins another pair. We finally figured out how he ruined those last night. He cut across a yard and got hung up in a barbed wire fence and just struggled with it until he slipped through. Another thing about old Ed. He sleeps with his eyes open and he looks dead as he is a very shallow breather. A weird sight: eyes bloodshot and his body rigid, and he on his back. Good old Ed.

19 June 1967, Monday, 10:00 p.m.

R.W. Apple, Jr., reports on Ky's campaign. An accompanying picture shows the dapper, mustached Ky in a baseball cap and lavender scarf.

I'm paralyzed lately, thinking about that damn SP5 thing that might be coming up. The way I used to be during finals.

I have a lot of dull work to do, but it just gets that way for me after a while. If I got SP5 it would be a spark to keep me jumping for a while, but I KNOW I won't make it whatever their criteria, as I'm not suited for the Army and know none of the little things that would fool them into thinking I belong. They know better.

20 June 1967, Tuesday, 6:40 a.m.

The rain is not letting up a bit. It varies in force and intensity but it isn't going to quit soon and I'm very hungry.

9:20 p.m.

Today was a long old day and I'm going to try to get to bed tonight a little earlier than usual and to sleep.

Ed is yelling in the background. I expect him to break into his Orange Jews routine pretty soon. That's the drink with which he washes down Arabs. Either Orange Jews, Grape Jews, or Pineapple Jews — they are half Hawaiian.

21 June 1967, Wednesday, 5:55 a.m.

Here I am back at the old typewriter. I had a headache which kept me awake much of the night, but it's gone now.

Time to go to breakfast.

22 June 1967, Thursday, 6:15 a.m.

When I get up to Long Binh there will be all sorts of new things on which to comment and gripe.

Those sandbag details will take up much of my time,
I'm told. My Lan is on right now and talking about "All
freedom-loving people everywhere."

Yesterday I sat at my desk and read most of the day.
I read one entire book: *The Whole Man* by John Brunner
and most of a John Creasy book which I'll finish this
morning most likely.

Rollins and Tief will both be gone today on investigations, which will be a pleasant thing, and I hope to get
the afternoon off and sleep and read and do other
exciting things.

It's just a chip off the old pig . . .
— *Sergeant Golden Boy*

23 June 1967, Friday, 5:50 a.m.

I believe that I'll get the afternoon off today and also
the whole day of Sunday off. I believe that Wacky Kathy
and Wacky Gwen will be working. That is what they are
called with disdain, I believe it is called.

Old Dead Head Ed is going up to Nha Trang for a
three-day TDY (R&R) today so things will be very quiet
here until he returns with his sunburn and his empty
pockets.

Time for me to go eat breakfast.

24 June 1967, Saturday, 6:30 a.m.

Lately all I've felt like doing is hiding myself between
the pages of an escape novel.

Last night was an alert in which I didn't participate,
but I think the days of volunteer participation are about

over as the CO is going to start watching things more closely. Up at Long Binh there will be no office in which to live and hide, so I'll be party to all that Army crap, but only for three months and two weeks, I think. Which I should be able to stand.

Lt. Col. Rollins is already at work and it's still almost the middle of the night.

11:00 p.m.

It's rather late at night by my standards, but I have the day to sleep tomorrow if I wish, and I have no money with which to go downtown, so I'll probably read and sleep the day away. I read my fifth Ed McBain novel in two days tonight, just finishing it, and I have yet another that I'll read in the morning after I get up and open the safe and eat breakfast prior to sleeping until mail time at 11:00.

I rather feel in a period of transition, betwixt and between this Long Binh move thing and the possibility of somehow making SP5. Trivialities really, compared to my one big concern, but something to think about when I'm not reading Ed McBain.

Off to bed and Ed McBain for a while anyhow.

25 June 1967, Sunday, 6:40 a.m.

I dreamed last night of Ky's yard filled with dead Bambis and six crying children consoled by a smooth faceless Asian woman. Dreams. I wonder what it means? Dreams are weird. The fawns weren't just hacked to pieces, but carefully eviscerated, ritually, as by a Voodoo practitioner. Not a good omen.

It's chilly today and overcast which reminds me of Seattle. And I have a slight sore throat which is a result of sleeping with just a sheet as a covering. It'll soon disappear though. I almost slept through the alarm this morning and thus would not have wakened Charlie so he could go to the EM Club and perform a Sunday morning detail of counting slot machine slugs. If they deny him the right to attend church this morning, he'll raise hell. Also it's not fair for them to take the only day he has off all week for something like that. He opposes gambling and never ever would gamble, but has to spend his Sunday morning counting slugs. That's the Army.

6:00 p.m.

The electricity is off and it's still slightly light or I would wait until later to write this entry as I feel rather ill from the hash patties I just ate for dinner. Today wasn't much of a day off, but I did get some sleep and read a very good procedural novel by Ed McBain called *10 Plus One* about a sniper and an orgy. His books are engrossing and I wish I'd not read the five that I dug up, but had a couple left to read tonight.

Dead Head Ed came back from his three-day R&R to Nha Trang today. He's very bitter about it as he lost (had stolen) his watch and wallet at the beach where we advised him not to take them, but that's Ed. He never listens. Also, he and Stone spent most of their three days sitting in airports as they kept getting bumped from flights. I just put the typewriter on my desk where I can see the copy, but the machine is thus away up in the air.

Lt. Col. Rollins is working out fine. He has his quirks

but he's basically fair-minded and has a sense of humor, warped, of course. He's getting short and leaves the Army the same month I do. Col. Ebby is still number one and everyone in the building likes him. He is firm and when he makes a decision or a statement he stands firm and never backs down or avoids issues. He's none of the ass kisser.

Old José just came in and said that Long Binh has no shower facilities, no laundry, no nothing, no club, no PX, etc., etc. It's going to make the time go by faster, I hope.

26 June 1967, Monday, 5:45 a.m.

Another dream of dead animals. This time fighting cocks. Their heads were still flopping and pecking around their enclosure while their bodies lay limp on the block near the bloody ax.

Dreams do motivate. Thoughts do convert to action if fueled from the subconscious by fears of sex and death.

I've got about seven minutes before I must leave to get to the big formation.

Last night Robert Mitchum was on the local TV station live in an interview on his impressions of Vietnam. He said that he thought Saigon was cleaner than it was a year ago. That's hard to believe.

Also last night there was a flap about Charlie finding the safe unlocked. Kathy had the clerical duty yesterday upstairs so of course everything will be screwed up. Leaving the safe unlocked is a big deal. A SECURITY violation and all that. She should be drummed out of the corps for that.

Also last night I went to the library and found an Ed

McBain novel, *Ax,* that had been misfiled, so I spent the evening reading it. A gory novel about an ax murder.

> *Nobody knows better than the professional*
> *soldier that war is about the bloody silliest*
> *pastime ever thought up by humanity.*
> — *Nicholas Blake (quoted by Sergeant Golden Boy)*

27 June 1967, Tuesday, 6:30 a.m.

I was extremely tired last night and went to bed before 8:00 and was asleep almost immediately. I woke up at 5:00 so I got a very good bunch of sleep. It was needed, as yesterday I felt exhausted for some reason. Not much work yesterday, but what there was tired me out.

Major Tief is gone on an investigation that he left on days ago. I dread to see him return with his illiterate notes and his unreasonable demands. He's a crumb. Well, it's not much more than a week until the big move to Long Binh and the rumors burgeon and increase. I wonder how many of them will be true?

> *Unleash Chiang Kai Shek* — *Reisner's Graffiti*

8:45 p.m.

M finally got here and I read most of it the other day. About the company that comes to Vietnam. It was displayed in the new current book section in the library. It's a good book, with some of the best writing on Vietnamese-US things that most omit, although it departs from the universal experience sometimes. For instance, it describes the stewardesses of the flight over as nasty, etc., whereas ours were quite sweet and spent much time with us and gave us all the milk, juice, good snacks, etc., that we wanted. They had a bad bunch unfortunately, but most aren't like that, I'm sure.

28 June 1967, Wednesday, 5:50 a.m.

It's time to go to formation almost.

8:40 p.m.

This is one of those days in which I didn't do nothing all day, no work or nothing. Just sat at my desk and read.

Ky is still censoring the Saigon press and plastering Saigon with posters. No news to anyone who lives in or near Saigon.

The flying ants are really creeping tonight all over my sweaty bare torso.

29 June 1967, Thursday, 6:05 a.m.

I just went to formation and it came to naught, for there were so few there. I hope the next couple weeks get so screwed up that formation is omitted.

Dave C. got back from his R&R and had a nice time in Penang, which he said is very clean and modern but still picturesque. They have ice cream and all the modern stuff. He said it was a rather quiet place and sleepy. I think Hong Kong is the place I'd like to go.

Only two more working days until Monday, as I work Sunday this week. I think I'll have Saturday afternoon off and hope to get downtown and have a farewell dinner and steambath massage which I'll not have a chance for again in Saigon.

Time to go eat breakfast.

5:15 p.m.

Major Tief got back from his investigation and will be rushed over to confer with the general. And then he'll have a million things for everybody to do. I hope I leave the office before he gets back from the conference.

Lt. Col. Rollins wants me to make a call for him so I'll write more later.

30 June 1967, Friday, 5:35 a.m.

I have a formation at 6:15 for whatever they have them for, and then pay later. I was up until 11:00 last night watching "The Song Makers" so I'm quite tired although it will pass. Burt Bacharach was interviewed and supposedly filmed whilst his genius was working. Made me sick to my stomach.

No hole is the wrong hole. — Dead Head Ed

8:30 p.m.

I've made SP5, also Charlie has made it, that makes two of those four from our section who were up for it this time. We made it over the two others as they were clerk-typists and Charlie and I have the higher MOS of steno, neither of us knowing the thing, of course.

I was sitting at my typewriter and the sergeant major called Charlie and me up to the colonel's office. Col. Ebby was there with Col. Murphy, the new headman, and there we got the thing. We are both so excited about it that you couldn't believe it, and we're both shorter than four months with not a reason in the world for caring, but . . . And how much I wanted to make it.

The rest of the day I spent sparring with Major Tief who almost begged me to be good and not bug him, but he brings out all that's small and nasty in me.

Another very important thing about this stripe is the thing about not having to do shit-burning details, etc., at Long Binh but instead, being in charge of them. You smell the smoke just the same. But not from your own hands. Also on KP, guard duty and all that kind of stuff.

Also today I got a card from General Cole congratulating me on my birthday, which I think is sweet and I'll send him one on his birthday, I think. He thanked me for my "Contribution to 'Win in Vietnam'." Ha!

It's raining vigorously outside now, and blowing in through the window.

When Ed was congratulating Charlie and me on our SP5 he did a lawnmower imitation that would have been a hit on any TV variety show.

I wasn't naked when Col. Murphy pinned my striped on, but when he said "I expect to see new and finer achievements from you two fellows in the future . . ." I responded with a "Yeah, for about six days . . ." before I thought. Ah well, it's too much trouble for him to remove the damn things.

1 July 1967, Saturday, 6:40 a.m.

I overslept and just made formation. Now I must hurry to make breakfast. I woke up still a SP5, which surprised me not a little.

8:30 p.m.

R.W. Apple, Jr. reports that Ky bags out of the presidential race and agrees to run as vice-president, with Nguyen Van Thieu in the top position. The pictures with the article have Ky on top, though. On the same page with the R.W. Apple story on Ky is a tiny little story in which Ky makes it clear he does not consider the *New York Times* reporters his friends — they've not supported him or the war. I think he's right and if I were R.W. Apple, Jr., Bernard Weinraub, Jonathan Randal, et al., I'd step lightly when out anywhere near a "patrol," whatever a patrol is. How can they put out of their minds what befell Bernard Fall? We are in a war zone, don't forget. My guess is that Ky does not soon forget a slight. Every time the *New York Times* reminds the reader of Ky's slip of the lip concerning his respect for Hitler, he must get a mental image of an exploding journalist. I know I would.

2 July 1967, Sunday, 4:20 p.m.

It's been a leisurely day, as I've typed very little and done little else either. I've purchased all of my SP5 stripes and have them ready to be sewn on tomorrow, so I'll be all straight before the move to Long Binh. Out there it would have taken weeks to get those things sewn on due to the screwed up arrangement of everything. But I'll have at least ten clean pairs of fatigues when I go out there and could last a long time with them.

Kathy won't be at work tomorrow as she is CQ for her company today and then the 4th is on Tuesday and I don't know who works that day, but I hope it's a holiday, as I need some time to pack and ready myself for this move to Long Binh.

It just started raining. It always seems to at this time of day when one is about to take the long walk to the mess hall. War is Hell!

9:00 p.m.

The electricity has been off. I'm hungry and am off to the Club to return a little later to write more.

9:20 p.m.

The sandwich was very good. White bread, ham and mayonnaise and catsup. I was so hungry that my mouth tingled to the catsup and watered at the white fat around the edge of the ham. I'm still hungry, but breakfast isn't far away.

3 July 1967, Monday, 6:30 a.m.

I've eaten breakfast and now have only to shine my belt buckle front and back and I'll have my loins girded for a new day. I hope today is a light day but Monday rarely is. I don't feel like marathon typing today.

11:50 a.m.

It's been a very busy morning. First I had to go over to the laundry and leave eight shirts there for them to sew my new stripes on. The rest of the morning I ran errands for Major Tief. He's easier for me to put up with now that I'm a SP5, but not much. He's a crumb and a loser. Yesterday he praised me for about one half hour for the assistance I gave him with his investigation, and all I did was punch some holes for him in his exhibits and type a one-page list of exhibits. He had Kathy do the same thing the day before and she got the list wrong, names misspelled, numbers left out, etc., and he displayed the thing to the colonel and he got ridiculed for it. Also Kathy punched holes in the paper so that the holes hung off the edges of the paper which didn't suit him. She makes me look good by comparison so she's worth the trouble.

It's an easy day, work-wise, that I like. The work I'll get I'll try to save until the morrow when Kathy returns.

2:20 p.m.

It is still raining here, but not enough to be an inconvenience. Up at Long Binh it will not only be an inconvenience, but a torture. No grass or trees to soak it up. The place has been totally defoliated. It all runs right off into spill trenches, or stands in large puddles on the red laterite soil, and turns the dust to red clay.

7:50 p.m.

I really didn't have to do a thing the rest of the day except read and talk to Col. Ebby (still a number one fellow in my book). Tomorrow is the 4th of July and the Spoonful is singing "Better Make Up Your Mind," which is good advice. I'm trying to decide whether or not to pick up "my" dress or to just quietly go off to Long Binh and forget about My Darling. It's a long shot anyway. My feeling at the moment is twofold: (1) I've started something and may as well play it out and (2) What harm can it do, to me or anybody?

Larry C. got back from R&R today and is suing for a divorce. Typical. Reminds me of my own past mistakes.

Today I went to Sergeant Golden Boy and threw myself on his mercy. I've walked past him a dozen times a day ever since I arrived. He'd become a fixture rather than a person. I told him I needed $200. He asked me why I needed the money. I told him to have a dress made for Madame Ky. He told me that he thought he'd heard them all and that that one was a new one on him. He then dug out two hundred-dollar bills from somewhere in his swimming trunks and said that should do it. "We're not going anywhere. Pay me back $300 when you get it and we'll be even." He then went back to his sunbathing.

I didn't tell him that I'd torn a picture of a Paris original out of a newsmagazine and that Madame Ky's dressmaker had agreed to copy it for me in Madame Ky's size. I didn't think that information was any of his business.

I have tomorrow off and I'm going to go downtown for the last time.

I'm getting hungry so I think that I'll go get a sandwich and write more tonight or tomorrow morning early.

9:45 p.m.

It's a wacky evening. Ed is supervising another weird sound effects tape, something he is very fond of. This one consists of a series of sounds that he has gotten from a three-string guitar, some very Oriental sounds, with a series of exclamations of "GRENADE" with a variety of sounds following the shout. It doesn't sound too funny, but imagine the sound of a scared-to-death "Grenade" followed by a small paper bag popping. Unexpected and even a little perverted. Do that a few times so the audience expects it and then when the cry is given there is a pause and a big rubbery sprongggg like a big rubber band. It's funny, it really is. You have to be there!

4 July 1967, Tuesday

Today I will throw myself on Her mercy. She will be, if God is in his heaven and I heard right, visiting her dressmaker today at 3:00. I have set an appointment there for 3:30 for which I shall be early. My relationship, semi-carefully nurtured with the proprietor, will allow me access. Also my white American face. I have fully come to terms with her mutilation, forgiven her. To blame her, a victim of racial prejudice, was beastly of me. Surely my offer to take her away from this war-torn country, this rotting emerald of the East, will not fall on deaf ears.

She can set up a boutique in America and be mine, and all this will soon fall to the communists anyhow—and welcome to it. And I'm certainly no Com-Symp. But the writing is on the wall to be read.

I'm off to meet my destiny.

5 July 1967, Wednesday

Yesterday all my plans went awry. Hooligans (more likely VC) made an attempt on My Darling's life. I intervened—reflexes nurtured on John Wayne and Audie Murphy films causing me to valiantly soak up a bullet intended for the perfect body of my Jungle Princess, or maybe for her bodyguard. I suppose it could have been fired by accident, but anyhow I caught it. In the scuffle I somehow managed to get out my switch-blade and stick the miscreant (in a non-vital spot) with it.

I am a hero, a hero unsung and unrecognized because not a word of this momentous event will ever appear in print, especially in the censored Saigon papers. Rewarded with not even a kiss from Her petulant lips. Browbeaten and threatened into silence by The Authorities, both RVN and US. Some little solace for me though. My suspicions concerning who's running the country are confirmed. Why else try to assassinate her?

Tomorrow it's air-evac for me to Japan and mandated amnesia.

All is not well in Saigon, but the world thinks a war is being won against communism. The first lady of the land is unsafe in her own streets, but the truth will be unknown until the lid blows off or the balloon goes up. When that happens, I'll be home watching it all on television, and the *nuoc mam* stink of this wretched little country will be as intangible a memory as the sweet French scent of Her, whose spoiled-brat, only-child perfection I protected with my stalwart American body. She gave me a dream with which to occupy myself.

I'm not one much for reflection or introspection, but events this momentous have caused me to look back over these months in RVN as recorded in my simple diary entries. I wonder how I could have done the things I've done and for the reasons I've given, how I became fixated on Madame Ky, buying a switch blade, pestering her telephonically. Did I really pin romantic doggerel to her door or imagine it? I know I had a red silky dress made in her size — and then what? Force her at knife point to put it on? That wouldn't have been fun for either of us. Inveigled her into leaving her beloved Vietnam and migrating to the US.? Unlikely for a xenophobic Vietnamese. She might go to France, but it was near insane of me to imagine her opening a boutique in America. She's as likely to go to the Black Hills with me to prospect for gold.

I surmise I'm just a poor loony boy who filled a great void with a fixation. Easier to love a stranger than one whom one knows. Cling to cherished illusions. No mildewed towels. The girl I love she's so far away, the girl I hate I see her every day. Man was meant to be an eremitic monk in the wilderness with ravens for friends, not to be married with dead albatrosses around his neck. Or even with a sweet princess to rescue from some tower or another. It all goes sour in the end. I've got to learn that and act accordingly. Or I'll be condemned to repeat my mistakes for all eternity. At least it will seem like an eternity. This was my chance to turn over a new leaf, and I'm not sure, did I muff it or not? I made contact with her and maybe saved her life. I certainly did her no harm. Who knows? Maybe against all odds and common sense she and I will meet again in God's Country. And I'll feel ho-hum and no adrenalin rush at all. And she'll be nuts for me. Anything is possible in this freaky world. But not likely. Maybe some inarticulate peasant loved Marie Antoinette from afar. His love did her no good either.

Goodbye, War Zone. Goodbye, Gooks! I'm sure they'll be glad to see my back and the backs of all my American brothers. Someday soon they'll have their wish. An all-gook Vietnam. They'll be sorry! Soon enough I'll be able to join the dissidents in the streets and see the war from a different angle.